# SUPPRESSED

## SINS OF OUR ANCESTORS BOOK TWO

### BRIDGET E. BAKER

*For Job.*
*You were one of my first readers and your feedback helped keep me going. I'm so proud of how you've kept going, no matter how hard things get.*

# CHAPTER 1

More than a decade ago, I hid in a closet while a madman murdered my father. My dad's twin sister and her husband swooped in soon after and relocated me along with their two children to my dad's secluded cabin to mourn.

Unbeknownst to six-year-old me, the move also ensured my biological mother couldn't find me. In the weeks that followed, a deadly virus transmitted through simple touch spread across the world like wildfire. Less than a million people in North America survived. My family only escaped infection because my aunt took us all into hiding.

In a way, my dad's kidnapping of me from my mother saved us all.

Of course, before I give him too much credit, I have to factor in the fact that good old Dad engineered the virus that wiped out most everyone. It's a travesty that he didn't tell me before he died that he injected me with what amounts to a vaccination for the virus the night before his murder.

We only know about the vaccination in my blood because of the journal in my hands. A journal I stole from the leader of the world's largest and most secure political and economic group. Unfortunately they're also fanatical religious zealots. Right after I stole this journal, I shot the leader with the Tercera virus, which he totally deserved. I found the dart I used on David Solomon in his own desk drawer, for heaven's sake.

I wish I'd known what was in my blood a decade ago, when I could've used that information to save some of the billions who died. Or last month, when I could have saved my long time crush, and best friend, Wesley. Or last week when my aunt contracted Tercera from raiding Marked kids. If I'd even known three days ago, I wouldn't have left my cousin Rhonda to take my place with a posse of angry Marked kids.

I hope I'm not too late to save Wesley, Rhonda and Aunt Anne.

I glance back down at the leather-bound journal I retrieved from a hidden safe in my dad's old lab in Galveston. I could barely make sense of his cramped handwriting in the best of circumstances. With the bumping and jouncing from the van that's tearing down the road toward the bridge off this island, I'm struggling to put a dozen words together.

"Geez Sam," I say, "how fast are you driving?"

"Why are you so crabby?" Sam asks.

"I'm not crabby," I say.

"Well," Sam says, "After everything we risked, is there any good news or not?"

I nod. "Good news, yeah. You could say that. Maybe not the silver bullet we were hoping for, but the journal describes a cure of sorts."

My cousin Job, who's more like a brother after being

raised by the same parents for a decade, sits up straighter. "It says there's a cure? Does it say how to recreate it? Is it hard? Is that the reason for all the weird breathing and muttering?"

"I'm not muttering." I scowl at him. "I haven't had time to pore over the scientific equations, or technical notes. The bad news is, the journal doesn't mention details on the virus Dad mentioned, the one he called the hacker virus. Or at least, it doesn't in the passages of commentary. The notes I've read at the end focus on something else entirely."

I don't know how to tell them it has been inside of me all this time. It feels like it's my fault we didn't know all along, like I should've realized it somehow. It's like I've been sitting on a box full of food in the middle of a horrible famine, so I can stuff my face after everyone else has perished.

The bridge from Galveston to the mainland looms in front of us. I glance at the backseat where my mom stares out the window despondently. She's no longer crying, but her mouth is slack, and her shoulders are slumped. She's probably in pain from the beating her awful husband just gave her, but I'm worried the worst damage isn't physical. Bruises will heal, but I don't know how to even start to repair the damage I can't see or study under a microscope. David Solomon deserves to pay. I hope he suffers.

"This is it," Sam says. "But we've still gotta get past the first guard tower, and then the other two."

Josephine sits up and blinks repeatedly as though she's just woken up. "You may need my help to do that. They'll have questions that won't be easy to answer."

I hope she's able to help. I'd really hate to get gunned down now that we have my dad's last journal. Although I guess there's never really a great time for being gunned down.

Josephine taps the window with her index finger. "The guards know we were headed to the Palisade Palms with David. He notified his security team, because they keep tabs on his location at all times. They'll want to know why he isn't with us, and where he is. If we tell them he's still there, they'll be alarmed that they've lost communications."

My mom's sadistic husband rules this entire island with an iron fist.

"Tell them he's sending you out as a delegate to speak to the Marked who are gathering," Sam says.

"That will be a hard sell. I haven't left the island by car in years. When we travel, we usually go by boat. They'll want to know why David would risk my safety by sending me toward a dangerous mob of Marked children."

She sucks at improvising. "You're a queen, though. Tell them King Solomon sent you to deal with the Marked that have gathered, but his plans are top secret and you can't divulge details. You'll be negotiating on his behalf, and he's sending your daughter to learn from watching you."

She shakes her head. "David doesn't negotiate, not with Marked children, or anyone who comes to make threats."

I shiver. He doesn't negotiate because he just kills them. In fact, he's got a "Cleansing" planned, in which he intends to wipe them off the face of the earth forever. He sees the children on the hormone suppressant as a plague to be eradicated.

Sam slows the van, and turns around to face her. "Josephine, I need to know if you can handle this. You don't have to say we're negotiating. Say you're taking a message for the Marked from your husband, or that you're delivering an ultimatum, or that you're painting their fingernails. I don't care, as long as they believe you and they let us past."

She frowns. "They'll never believe I'm headed over to

paint their nails. That doesn't even make sense."

I roll my eyes. "The point is that you tell them something and you're firm about it. Anything you think will get us past. Can you do that?"

Josephine folds her arms under her chest. "Nothing will make this seem normal."

Sam growls. "Tell them you baked cookies that cure Tercera, or that you're going to teach them to read because God commands it. Tell them anything, I don't care, as long as you don't tell them we left your husband, infected with Tercera and lying in a pile of unconscious guards. Guards I knocked out. Got it?"

My mom starts shaking, and I wish I was sitting in the back seat so I could put my hand over hers. I try to make eye contact, but she drops her gaze to her lap.

She needs reassurance, but Sam barks at her instead. "Can you keep Ruby safe? That's what this comes down to. You lost her when she was a baby, and never found her, not in seventeen years. She's survived entirely without a mother. Now that she has one, will you shelter her, or are you a liability?"

Josephine stares at her hands for three full seconds before looking up. "I will keep Ruby safe."

"Good." Sam drives up to the guard tower slowly and rolls down his window. A tall, thin guard with a carefully trimmed goatee walks over to the van. He's holding a clipboard and a pencil, but the men behind him are armed. They look at us with narrowed eyes and twitchy fingers. Sam glances at the clipboard dismissively and turns his eyes back to the road. "We're headed off the island on King Solomon's direct order."

The guard looks at Sam and frowns. "I've never seen you before, and there's an army of infected infidels on that side of the bridge. Maybe you hadn't noticed them."

Sam doesn't even glance his way. "We're aware."

Goatee shakes his head. "I have very clear orders. No vehicles in or out."

"Orders change." Sam glances back at Josephine, but she stares straight ahead without saying a word.

Goatee follows Sam's gaze and this time his eyes widen, and he bows. "Queen Josephine, you're planning to leave the island?" He steps even closer, close enough that I see my own reflection in his shiny buttons.

He taps on the window, but when Josephine doesn't react, he looks her up and down. His eyes narrow, probably because he's noticed her empty eyes and disheveled appearance. The right side of her face is puffy and red, and her dress is torn.

Goatee clears his throat. "Your Majesty, would you please step out of the vehicle while I call for confirmation? I want to make sure I understand King Solomon's instructions and we're all on the same page."

He opens the side door and gestures for Josephine to step out. At the same time a shorter, squattier guard in an identical navy-blue uniform with the same row of shiny gold buttons appears on the other side, just outside of my door. He yanks the door handle and opens my side before I can think of a reason to object.

He motions for me to exit the van, but I shake my head dumbly. "We're under specific orders to leave the island and approach the Marked. You have no right to detain us." And yet unless Sam's willing to mow them down, we aren't driving past them.

"I am not trying to detain you, merely to ensure you're safety," Squatty says. "On whose orders are you leaving?"

"Are you deaf as well as short?" Sam asks, "We just told you. Queen Josephine is here, and we're all following King Solomon's direction. Right, Your Highness?"

Josephine nods, but counterintuitively exits the car as they asked. Something comes over her when she leaves the van, as though being around all these soldiers fills her with the confidence of command. Her shoulders straighten, her back stiffens and she walks straight ahead with assurance. I wish I knew why she was walking briskly past the guard tower, and the grouping of guards in navy-blue uniforms. I scramble out of the van, Dad's journal clutched in one hand, and jog to catch up to her. Sam and Job exit the van too, and fall in behind us quickly without saying a word.

Squatty and Goatee both call out for us to stop, but Josephine ignores them, so I follow her lead. Eventually they stop calling us, but I notice they've picked up the phone and are calling for direction. Not good.

We walk quickly toward the second guard tower where four other guards are standing. Their faces are full of uncertainty. I glance at a black phone on the side of the guard tower, relieved it's not ringing, and none of them have thought to pick it up.

One of the four men next to the guard tower reaches for Josephine as we pass, but a sharp glance from her and an inhalation of air, and his hand drops to his side. "Your majesty, are you sure you want to leave the island? And do you really mean to proceed on foot?"

She glances his way, eyes snapping in a way I've never seen, and he falls silent. We all follow her lead, walking past them as though they don't have any authority to detain us. Once we've gone more than a few dozen paces away, she whispers, "Never allow an inferior to believe they have any control over your actions."

We walk steadily along, but I really wish we hadn't been forced to leave the van behind. Does she mean for us to walk the entire length of the bridge? We've gone more than a mile, and there are several more to go. I want to ask, but no one else seems to be concerned. I glance back at Sam and widen my eyes, but he just shrugs. We can't very well argue with Josephine in front of so many armed men.

Thirty yards past the second guard tower, Josephine slows down. I keep walking fast initially, hoping she'll match my pace, but she doesn't. It occurs to me belatedly that she might be in pain. King Solomon beat her brutally when he thought my blood unlocked Donovan Behl's safe, confirming in his mind that I wasn't really his child. King Solomon thought he was my father, and sadly he may yet be. Donovan's safe has a blood key, so only someone of his bloodline could open it.

After reaching Galveston and discovering my mother was alive, I sort of fell apart. I didn't want to deal with any of it, so I borrowed some blood from my cousin Job, who is undeniably Donovan Behl's twin sister's son, plain and simple. I knew his blood would work, and it did.

Of course, David Solomon thought it was my blood that opened the safe, which would mean that I was Donovan Behl's daughter after all. He didn't process the news well, beating my mother brutally until I stepped in to stop him.

I touch her arm gently. "Are you okay?"

She looks up at me with eyes wide with sorrow and a quivering, swollen lip.

I repeat my question.

"You shot him," she says. "I don't understand why you shot him. He wasn't hitting me anymore."

When I stole the tranquilizer gun from his drawer, I assumed the dart would only incapacitate him. It was labeled with a capital T. "I stole that gun from a drawer in his desk. The only reason he's infected with Tercera is that he had it hidden in a drawer. King Solomon obviously used

8

it to infect other people. Otherwise, I never could have infected him to begin with."

"Either way, now he's going to die because of what you did. There's no cure."

I don't remind her that I hit him with the accelerant too, also taken from King Solomon's own desk. It was labeled only with an A. I wasn't sure at the time whether it was an antidote or an accelerant. If I'm being honest, I'm glad it was the accelerant.

Tercera kills slowly, far too slowly for the man who killed my dad and beat his wife for at least the last decade. During its normal progression, other than a minor rash on a patient's forehead, there are no other symptoms for the first year. The sores start in year two, worsening throughout the year, and organs stop working properly sometime during year three, eventually leading to total organ failure. It's a miserable way to go, but slow. Very, very slow. With the accelerant, which I'm pretty sure King Solomon developed himself, he shouldn't make it more than a week. Two at the outside limit. Our only real gauge is that he used the accelerant a decade ago to wipe out hundreds of thousands of people—the entire US government. He killed them all so he could seize control, so I'd call being hit with the accelerant himself poetic justice.

Seems like my mom, who inexplicably still loves him, might not agree with me.

"I thought it was a tranq at first, but the bigger question is, why do you think he even had that stuff? Was he infecting people with Tercera for the last ten years?"

Why isn't she wondering why he had it? Why isn't she upset at him for hiding a deadly virus and using it for. . . Actually, I have no idea what he'd use it for. Perhaps to eliminate rivals or threats? The entire situation is disgusting.

"Why would you shoot him at all?" Her voice wavers and her hands flutter up and down.

"Let's review. First of all, he undeniably shot my dad, while I watched. He hasn't said he didn't do that. In fact, his only defense is that Donovan Behl isn't my biological father, which I don't think we know one way or another."

"Don hid you from us for years."

I nod. "Which is actually really sad if I'm David Solomon's daughter. But even so, killing Donovan seems excessive."

"You can make that determination once you've lost a child," Josephine says, the steel in her voice surprising.

It's the first time I've seen any real strength in her.

"I'll give you that one, but Solomon doesn't contest that he wiped out the government, and let the world burn while he hid here in Galveston. He's basically a dictator."

"He keeps our people safe and prosperous."

"History shows that the people frequently love their dictators, but it doesn't mean their people are free. But even if we allow all of that, I watched him beat the crap out of you. He kicked you in the stomach over and over with no sign of stopping until I stopped him. You didn't even seem shocked, so I'm guessing this isn't new behavior."

"And?" She frowns.

"He deserved to die by Tercera. If I'd had a regular gun with regular bullets, I'd have used that instead."

"I deserved the beating he was giving me. I made him angry."

My jaw drops.

"Don't act self-righteous here, young lady. Wouldn't you be angry if you learned your wife had been unfaithful to you? If you believed she lied to you, you would react poorly as well."

"Mom, you were married to Donovan."

She shakes her head. "I was, but we were separated when I met David, and I was faithful to him. I swear I was. If we go back, I can explain to him." She looks down at her hands, staring blankly at her empty palms. "There's a misunderstanding somewhere in all this. It isn't true that you're Donovan's daughter. You're Solomon's child, I know it in my heart."

I draw my eyebrows together and really look at her. My mom's still shuffling along, eyes fixed on the ground beneath our feet. "If you were married to Donovan when I was conceived, I don't understand how you can be so sure I'm Solomon's daughter."

"I was married to Donovan." She sighs. "But I know you're David's daughter. I knew it then, and now that I've met you, I know it now."

"I look just like you. I look nothing like either of them."

She tsks. "It's in your eyes and your smile. Even your sense of unyielding certainty and your intelligence all speak to me. You're David's child, you must be."

I growl. "So what? Who cares whose daughter I am? Even if he thinks you lied seventeen years ago, do you really think you deserved to be shoved and kicked, Mom? No matter the reason?"

"I let him down. His anger and disappointment and frustration was justified, yes. We all must atone for the things we do that are wrong, and what I did was wrong. I should pay for that. Don't you agree?"

I grab her arm and she stops walking and turns toward me. "You didn't do anything wrong! Geez, I'm not even sure I am Donovan's daughter."

My mom yanks her arm away, her eyes wide and clamped onto my face with burning intensity. "What are you talking about?"

She needs to keep walking. Why did I say anything? I

glance behind me and notice the guards. Even with the wide space between us, I can tell they're shifting and watching us. "Nothing. Let's go."

She grabs my arm tighter than I'd have imagined possible with her waify, delicate frame. "I demand you explain yourself, young lady."

I sigh, and whisper, "I used Job's blood to open the safe, not mine. He's Donovan's nephew, so I knew his blood would work. I wasn't sure whether mine would at that point, and I wasn't ready to find out."

She shakes her head. "I watched you use your own finger."

"It was a trick, okay? I don't understand why you're fixated on this so much, because no matter whose blood I have-" I think back to my dad's words in his journal. *Her blood now carries something that is more mine than any DNA could ever be.* My dad didn't think I was his daughter, not biologically, and he didn't care. My mom's sure Solomon is my dad. I shiver. "Donovan Behl *is* my dad, okay? Not your sick, twisted husband."

My mom's face flushes red. "If you didn't use your blood to open that safe, you *are* his daughter, Solomon's flesh and blood after all. He'll forgive me, he'll forgive both of us, I'm sure he will." My mom smiles then, so wide it nearly cracks her face in two. "We must tell him right away." Her fingers dig into my arm, and her eyes take on a feverish light.

I shake her hand off my arm, barely succeeding. "He isn't going to hear it, Mom. He's dying, remember? Quickly, since I hit him with the accelerant too."

Mom turns toward the guards, and they notice she's intent on them, even from this far away.

"Stop! Mom, there's nothing for you back there."

"No." Her eyes widen in terror. Her hand shoots back

out to grip my wrist. "He mustn't die. You said there's a cure, when we were in the van headed this way. I heard you say it. What is it, and where can we find it? You have to help him, he's your father!"

I grit my teeth. "I'm not going back. I've been over this and over it. He deserves to die. He killed the only real father I ever knew."

She stops walking and raises her voice. "If we don't save him, he'll never forgive us."

I don't point out the absurdity of her statement. Sam and Job flank us now, keeping one eye on the guards and one on me. Sam doesn't say a word, but I know he's wondering how I want to play this.

I glance back toward the World Peace Now, or WPN, guard tower and notice the guards aren't confused anymore. I'm surprised to see they're moving backward, but it's purposeful. My eyes track ahead and I notice the tallest guard is heading for a large truck.

This is bad, very bad.

"Mom, we'll talk about it once we've reached the other side, I promise." I point at the mass of bodies we can barely make out just out of range of the final guard tower, near the end of the long bridge, still more than a mile away.

"Those are Marked kids, Ruby. That's why the guards didn't want us trying to leave. Why would you run into the arms of infected children when you know King Solomon's your father?"

I yank my hand free again and stomp my foot. "You aren't listening. It's like he's broken your brain, and maybe he has after all these years of beatings. That man may have donated DNA to my body, but he *shot* my real father. He's a monster, do you hear me? He's planning on killing a bunch of innocent people because they're infected with a virus that for all we know, he unleashed on the world! He isn't my dad and he never will be. My only real regret is that I hit him with Tercera back there instead of an actual bullet."

Mom's face drains of blood, and her hands shake. "You shouldn't speak that way about a man you don't even know. If only my ex hadn't gone mad, you'd have been raised by your father and me and none of this would be happening. We'd be a happy family right now." She glances down at the leather journal I'm holding, and before I can guess what she plans to do, she snatches it from my hands, spins on her heel and sprints backward toward the black truck that's now barreling our way.

I'm so shocked I don't even move for a moment, but Sam, perfect Sam, never misses a beat. He jogs past me, pursuing my mom. Only his concern for her well being keeps him from tackling her to the ground I imagine, but eventually he circles around and blocks her progress with his body. He yanks the journal away, and holds it over his head. Unfortunately, the truck full of guards has nearly reached them.

He glances toward me and then back to my mom, as if trying to decide what to do. She's obviously been brainwashed, but I don't understand why she'd run back to Solomon, now that she's nearly free. Sam tries to pull my mom back toward me and Job, but she struggles.

I call out. "It's okay, Sam. If she won't come, just leave her."

So many guns pointed in their direction. I want Sam headed toward me, not fighting with my insane mother. My heart crumples a little bit, but I'd pick Sam a million times over between him and a crazy woman I barely know. She didn't care enough about me to even track me down seventeen years ago, or any time in the years since.

My mom spins around and points at the journal clutched in Sam's strong hands, and idiot that I am, I'm surprised when I hear her yell at the approaching guards. "King Solomon's injured. He needs that book. You must get it to him. Fire freely, as long as you don't hit the book."

The guards react immediately, not even exiting the truck first. Their guns, clasped in uniformed hands, point out of the truck windows like antenna from some malevolent bug. Six shots fire in quick succession. Sam's body shakes, blooms of red sprouting on his chest. My heart races, and I feel dizzy. My body slumps forward, and only Job's hand keeps me upright.

I breathe in one jagged lungful of air and try to step toward him, my hand outstretched.

Job stops me. "Don't go. You can't help anything, not now."

Six gunshots. Sam should be lying in a heap on the ground, but he isn't. I blink back tears, shake myself free of Job and run faster than I've ever run before on my way back toward him. Even running at my fastest, Job passes me a second later. I hate this tiny body I'm stuck inside.

Sam pulls his gun out, and stumbles down the road toward Job and me. We're two hundred feet apart, then just a hundred and finally, only fifty. Usually Sam runs twice as fast as I do, but not now, not soaked in blood. He's barely stumbling toward me, and he's close enough that I can focus on his gun shot wounds. All six are in his torso, and if I had to guess, I'd say heart, lungs, stomach, liver and maybe a glancing wound over his ribs.

In my concern for Sam, I'm not watching my mom, and neither is he. She runs up behind him and snatches the journal back, just as the truck barrels up behind them. Brainwashed or not, abused or not, broken or not, I'll never forgive her for this. My mother deserves Solomon.

Motion behind Sam draws my eye. More vehicles full of armed men roll toward us behind the first, but the first stopped twenty-five feet from Sam. I need to get there faster. My lungs scream, my legs shake, but I push harder still. He's too far away.

Sam fires three rounds over his shoulder before collapsing. The three men who just exited the truck collapse like puppets with cut strings. Job stops and crouches near Sam for a moment, his hand on Sam's neck checking for a pulse for one moment, then another. Time stands still when Job stands upright and runs toward the truck. Why isn't Job dragging Sam back to us?

Job opens the door and jumps in, and then he drives the truck to where I still stand, dumbfounded. Job motions to me, and I climb inside the cab.

"Are we taking the truck back there?" I ask. "Was he too heavy for you to carry?"

Job shakes his head.

I turn back, expecting Sam to straighten back up. Maybe Job's giving him a break, distracting the guards until Sam can get the strength for one more push.

But Sam never moves. And suddenly, I realize that Job wasn't planning to do anything else for Sam. He's leaving him.

"No!" I yell. "NO!"

I leap from the truck and run toward Sam again, my eyes drawn inexorably to the blood pooling around him. He looks exactly like my dad did that day, more than a decade ago. Except the pool of red is bigger, so much bigger from the six shots instead of just the one. I can't even see the pavement anymore. His body's an island amidst a lake of red.

I've closed half the remaining distance between us when Job grabs me, but this time he doesn't try to take my hand. His arms encircle my waist and he lifts me into the air. My arms pinwheel and my legs flail as he carries me to the truck and stuffs me inside. I can't breathe, and my hands are shaking so bad that at first, I think that's why I can't open the door. I claw at the handle over and over, cursing and shouting. "It's broken. Why is this broken?"

"It's locked, Ruby. You can't get out. There's nothing we can do, and they're coming. We have to go."

I hear a gunshot then. It hits the back of our stolen truck. Job locked the door and he's putting the truck in gear.

I claw at the handle in despair, and look desperately for a lock to lift. Ignoring my efforts, Job slams on the gas, and the truck peels out, wheels screeching against concrete. I look behind us and I can barely make out Sam's shape. I watch in horror as the pool of red grows larger and larger around him, and as we drive away, his body shrinks.

I try to call for him, but my words emerge as a croak. "Not again," I try to yell. I can't fail someone I love again.

If I can't open the door, I'll stop the driver. I claw at Job's hands on the wheel. I clear my throat and force words, though they're hoarse. "Stop the truck. Stop it, please! We have to go back."

Job doesn't hit the brake or even slow down. He speaks clearly, detached, and his words sound foreign to my ears. "He had no pulse. You took anatomy Ruby, so you know I'm telling the truth. You can't survive gunshots like that, no one can. Not even Mom could help him now." He chokes up, barely getting the words out. "Sam's gone, but we still have a chance, and without that journal, what's in your brain may be Mom and Rhonda's last hope. I won't let you throw your life away and theirs in the process. Besides, there's a war going on in case you didn't notice."

I slump into the seat. Job doesn't know how right he is. My blood's the cure. I can't risk the one thing that might save all the Marked to go after Sam's corpse. That truth sinks deep into my soul, and I know what Sam would say, what he'd tell me to do, but it hurts so bad I can't breathe. Job is still talking, trying to soothe me I think, but with my heart exploding inside my chest, it's hard to hear anything else.

I look ahead at the line of people standing near the midpoint of the bridge. Hundreds upon hundreds more stand at the land near the edge of the bridge. As we draw closer, the Marks on their foreheads stand out starkly. I may be the cure for all of them, and it's earth shattering and miraculous.

Except, I don't care anymore.

I only want to save one person, and he's the one person I can't do a single thing for. I suddenly feel a little empathy for my dad, for Donovan Behl. He didn't save the world, but he saved me, and maybe in the end that was enough for him.

I bang on the door and pull on the locked handle again, but this time, I don't pull as desperately or as hard. Job won't let me out, and I can't even see Sam anymore. Josephine has Dad's journal, and I guess that means my mom doesn't care about me, because no one's following us. Dozens of trucks have reached the part of the bridge where Sam was shot, but none of them have driven any further.

I pull one last time, half-heartedly, on the handle of the door. It still won't open, and I can't get out. I'm stuck on the truck seat, fingernails bloody and broken, sobbing wordlessly. I can't let him go too. I can't.

But I don't have a choice.

# CHAPTER 2

I'm utterly unprepared to greet anyone when we reach the Marked kids. My eyes are puffy, I croak when I try to talk, and tear stains streak both my cheeks.

Job stops the truck in front of a line of kids who are all pointing guns at us. I'm sick of people pointing guns at me. I stop crying and hiccup a time or two. "What's going on?"

"I doubt they can see through the windshield, with the sun at our backs. They probably think we're from WPN."

Job unlocks the doors and opens his. He steps out with his hands up, palms forward. "We mean you no harm. We barely escaped WPN ourselves."

Not all of us escaped. I choke on a sob.

"Job!" His twin sister Rhonda rushes forward and hugs him. Even knowing I can cure him, I still feel sick at the thought that he's hugging someone who's Marked. When she lets go, I peer at her face through the front windshield of the truck.

I blink several times to make sure, but she isn't Marked. I jump from the unlocked truck, startled into action. "Why aren't you infected?"

"You left me a vial of your blood, remember?" Rhonda smiles.

My heart constricts. "How did you know that would help?" I ball my hands into fists to stop the shaking. Somehow Rhonda knows what I only just discovered in my dad's writings. How can she already know what Sam died to find out?

My breathing accelerates again and I need to hear her answer, but I don't want to hear it at the same time. I want to run away screaming, or tear off down the bridge toward Sam's body. I missed my dad's funeral, and now I won't be at Sam's, either. Will they even hold a funeral for the boyfriend of the girl who shot their king?

Before Rhonda can answer, a tall young man with dark hair steps forward and waves at me shyly. "You're a hard gal to catch."

Wesley Fairchild.

I was in love with him for three years, or at least I thought I was. What did I know about love? Seeing him today, I barely recognize the face I spent so much time dreaming about. He's still tall and just as handsome. His hair is longer, but that's not the real difference. I can't put my finger on why, but he looks closer to twenty-five years old than he does to seventeen. I'm sure the events of the past few weeks, from leaving his home, his family and me, haven't been easy on him. One thing I don't see on his familiar but different face is a Mark. And I clearly saw the telltale rash the last time I saw him.

I shake my head in disbelief. "How are you Unmarked too?" I hoped I could save Wesley, Rhonda, and Aunt Anne, but it never occurred to me they wouldn't even need my help.

"I was Marked. I saw the rash myself," he says, "after you told me it was there. I scrubbed on it and rubbed at it and it was real. After that I waited for you at the tree like we agreed. When you still didn't appear after a few days, and patrols started circling, I ran. By the time I reached the Marked encampment, I hadn't seen my own face in days. With my hair down over my forehead, none of them questioned me when I said I'd been Marked."

"But you weren't?" I look from Rhonda to Wesley and back again. "I don't understand."

"I was Marked Rubes, but your blood cured me." He lowers his voice. "Do you remember our kiss?"

I blush and then I look down at my feet, flooded with guilt for some reason. Which is stupid because I had barely talked to Sam at that point. I'd known him for years, but we didn't speak much.

Wesley steps closer, his voice barely more than a whisper. "Once we realized I *wasn't* Marked, even after living among the Marked for days and days, we knew something must've happened. How could I be immune?" Wesley steps aside and a new boy, not quite as tall as Wesley, steps toward us.

He's strikingly handsome, this new young man, with a strong jaw and beautiful green eyes. His russet hair is spiked up in a mohawk, at odds with his classic good looks. He grins at me like we aren't standing on a bridge in enemy territory, like there's still good in the world, like the person I care most about didn't just die. Of course, he knows nothing about Sam.

"Hello." His voice is far too deep for someone on the suppressant. The voice matches the intensity of his eyes, but not the coltish body. His arms and legs are too long, too gangly, and too thin for the timbre of his voice. "I'm Rafe." In fact, even from just a few words, his voice sounds familiar for some reason, but I can't figure out why. I wrack my brain for memories of a Rafe, trying to remember if maybe I knew him back at Port Gibson. Maybe he was someone's son. I glance at Wesley, but his face shares no clues.

Rafe's nearly as tall as Wesley, and he carries himself with a quiet assurance. The other Marked kids watch him, waiting for some kind of reaction. They track his movements in much the same way David Solomon's people watched him, waiting to see how he greets me, observing how he treats me. No one has said so, but I'm positive that Rafe's their leader.

"I might never have pieced it together," Wesley says, "without Rafe. My Mark appeared, and then you and I kissed. You split your lip, remember? I must've ingested your blood. Somehow, something about your blood cured me."

Job grunts. "A lot's happened since you left. Ruby sat in quarantine for days. She read her dad's journals, and discovered that her father created the virus we know as Tercera many years ago. That's why we came to Galveston. To find his research and to figure out whether he finished the cure he began."

Wesley raises his eyebrows. "I could've saved you all the trip. I tried to tell you, several times, actually."

Job cocks one eyebrow. "Are you saying her dad did something to her? That we didn't need to deal with WPN at all?"

Rafe tilts his head sideways. "Rhonda told us about Ruby's father. What did you find at his lab, or did you make it there at all?"

"We did," Job says, "but I'm not sure exactly what we found. Ruby was reading the journal, but her mom-"

"Wait, Ruby's *mom?*" Rhonda shakes her head. "Are you kidding?"

"No, we found out her mother survived the Marking,

and Mom and Dad probably guessed at least that much. Then her mom helped us off the island until she realized Ruby switched our blood for the test, and then she grabbed the journal and ran, but Sam stopped her-" Job makes a choking sound, probably not quite ready to follow that thought through. My mom screwed it all up and Sam died. Plus, we don't even have the journal anymore. Job clears his throat. "The point is, I don't know exactly what the journal said. Ruby?"

"It said that my dad. . . Well, you're right, Wesley, that I—"

"Maybe this isn't the best place to talk." Rhonda glances behind me and I turn to look.

No one's driving our direction yet, but WPN troops are milling around the second guard tower. I glance back at the truck we took and notice several bullet holes in the truck bed, and back window. I only recall hearing one. How out of it was I for that last mile?

Rafe nods. "We need to move, but tell me something simple first." His eyes lock on mine, lit by a strange light. Again, I'm reminded of someone, but this time something clicks inside my brain and I finally realize who.

Sam.

Which makes no sense at all. I shake my head. I'm tired, and scared, and desperately sad. This boy looks nothing like Sam, my Sam. Tears spring up again, and before I break down in front of them, I say, "What? Just ask me."

Rafe looks around at the other kids. They've slowly inched closer to us and I can feel them all hanging on his words. "Did you find an answer? Is there a cure?"

These kids have lived their entire lives hand-to-mouth, taking hormone suppressants that lock them inside of children's bodies they should have long since outgrown. They've been frozen in hell on earth. Sam's gone, and I feel

23

numb, and cold, and shaky. I want to collapse in a heap never to move again, but they deserve the answer. They deserve a little hope after a lifetime of despair.

"Maybe. I think we may be able to figure something out."

The cheer that goes up around me from the two dozen kids close enough to hear is almost deafening. Clusters of kids from here to the base of the mainland begin to cheer as well. I wish Sam could hear it.

For the first time, it hits me that if I'd been brave enough, if I'd insisted on telling the truth, the Marked would have taken me and not Rhonda. We'd already have known without going into Galveston that my blood healed Wesley, if not quite why. And if we didn't go to WPN, I would have no idea that my biological father might be the awful David Solomon. I could have avoided Galveston entirely, and if we did that Sam would be alive right now.

He died for nothing.

Actually, the worst part is that, like my dad, like millions of people around the world, Sam died because of me.

My heart cracks in two, and my breathing speeds up. Before blackness consumes me and I feel my body sink away, strong arms catch me. And then nothing.

## CHAPTER 3

When my eyes flutter open, the world around me overpowers my brain. I blink rapidly against the rays from the setting sun.

"I think it would help her to see it. We should wake her up." Rhonda's voice is soft, but urgent.

"I agree," Wesley says. "She should see what's at stake if she's as devastated as you say. It may help her to recognize the joy that she's bringing along with her." He knows about Sam. He must.

I choke a little and push myself up in what turns out to be the backseat of the truck we stole from WPN. I know because I can see the clawed plastic that mars the front door handles, where I tried to escape when they were locked. When I try to speak, barely a whisper emerges. It's like I swallowed jagged glass shards. Or like I screamed it raw when I lost someone, I suppose. I wince in pain when I clear my throat to try again. "Where are we going?"

Rhonda's head swivels like an owl. "You're awake, oh that's good. I'm so sorry about Sam." Her eyes well up and I know she's as broken up as I am. "It wasn't your fault, you know. It really wasn't. None of us knew about you, or about your immunity I mean. We all did what we thought we had to do so you could reach Galveston and find your father's lab."

I nod, too numb to do anything else. "I did know Wesley was looking for me."

This time it's Wesley's head that swivels. "So he finally told you?"

The car jerks left until Job reaches over and steadies the wheel. "Easy Wesley. Watch the road."

I open my mouth to ask how Wesley knows Sam didn't tell me right away, but Wesley grins.

He knows me well enough to answer before I can even ask. "I knew he didn't tell you he saw me right away, or you'd have come to find me immediately."

The truck hits another patch of bumps and I bounce in the seat like a rag doll.

"Watch the road, man. Seriously." Job scowls.

"We're almost there," Wesley says. "It's fine." He turns his attention back to the road anyway, and I ignore his implied criticism of Sam. I won't talk about any of it right now, I can't.

Instead I ask, "Where's there?"

"You heard what they said about the suppressant failing back when I pretended to be you, right?" Rhonda asks.

I nod.

"Well it's more widespread than I thought that day," she says.

"No one in Port Gibson had heard anything about it," Job says. "They should have heard right away when it happened, since we were the ones supplying it, but I hadn't heard anything about it. It's not something Mom would have kept from me."

Wesley scowls. "Rafe says they left messages at the drop

location, but I swear my dad never mentioned it either. How could none of us have known?"

Rhonda sighs. "Between six months and a year ago, it stopped working for sporadic groups of Marked kids, becoming progressively more widespread with time. Now that their bodies are actually. . . developing, well. There are uncontemplated ramifications."

"I still don't know where we're going." I glance out the window at the freeway. It looks like every stretch of land between Galveston and Port Gibson. We could be anywhere. Except I recall the number forty-five. We've got to be at least somewhat close to Galveston. I doubt I was out for very long.

"Sorry, it's so easy to get sidetracked." Wesley sighs. "When the suppressant failed, the hormones wore off. And as you can imagine, people who have loved each other for a while, well, things got complicated quickly."

Job snorts. "We're making a stop at the Marked maternity ward that they set up out here. It's close to WPN because your crazy father was sending priests to perform weddings for them, the kids whose suppressants failed. A lot of them wanted to get married. That means Solomon knew the suppressant was failing, and that was probably why he came up with his plans to exterminate them."

My jaw drops.

"Wait, her *father*?" Rhonda asks, at the same time Wesley says, "Hold on. Solomon is Ruby's what?"

I sigh. "Turns out, Donovan Behl was married to my mom, but she left him for the leader of WPN before he was leader of anything. David Solomon stole my mom from Donovan Behl. He's a horrible person, and for all I know, Josephine may be too. She let me get kidnapped, possibly because she wasn't sure who my dad even was. Dad stole me from Josephine and David Solomon as they left the hospital, which sucks I guess, but after seeing Solomon, I kind of get why. I can't even imagine being raised with him as my father." I shudder.

"It's been a long few days," Job says.

Understatement of the year.

"Ruby, can you tell us," Job asks, "what exactly the journal said? Or at least, any details you can remember?"

Right. Because I passed out last time they asked.

"It was full of equations and notes, which I'm sure we could really have used." I close my eyes. Focus on the journal, not what happened when we lost it. I breathe in and out a few times. "But once I skimmed past those, I found a passage that explained how Dad injected me with antibodies. He didn't dose me with the hacker virus he wrote about before. I know we expected to find information about that, like how he developed it, or where his samples went, but that's not what I read about. The part I read talked about how my blood contains a cure of some kind."

"It didn't list the virus as the cure?" Job sounds disappointed.

He can join the club. I have my doubts about the antibodies curing everyone else. At least, from what I know of antibodies, it's going to be problematic. "I was hoping for more about that, too."

Job turns back toward the road, as disappointed as me.

I lean forward, poking my head between Rhonda and Job. "My turn to ask a few questions. If Wesley was cured by my blood and he isn't Marked, why haven't you used his blood to cure everyone else?"

Job sighs. "That's why I was hoping you saw something about the virus. Antibodies are great at preventing infection, but they aren't a very effective cure. Occasionally they can, as they did in Wesley's case, stave off a brand new infection. Think of it like Tetanus. It's bacterial, but the idea is the same. A super shot of antibodies directly after infection might knock the virus out, but an injection once the virus has taken hold... well."

Wesley's hands grip the steering wheel so tightly his knuckles are white. "To answer your question, we tried my blood. It didn't do anything, at least not that we could see."

I lean back. "If my blood worked, yours should too. You'd have an active immunity, which should be stronger than mine, because mine's always been passive."

I think about the journal entry. My dad said he injected me with a triple dose. Mine was strong, and Tercera was designed not to set off warning bells. Instead it spreads and lays dormant. I curse under my breath. "Dad mentioned a virus in the other journals, but in what I read, he said he was exposed to Triptych, his name for Tercera, and he injected the hacker virus in himself, but not in me. He wasn't sure what type of side effects to expect and wouldn't risk it on his daughter. I imagine he thought the antibodies wouldn't be as effective for him." My stomach turns. We may not have a cure after all.

Rhonda taps the window. "For someone who doesn't speak science, can you tell me what exactly this means, like the Science 101 version?"

Job knows way more than I do, but I might be able to explain it more simply because of that. "Job can stop me if this is wrong, but essentially antibodies are little proteins that run around in our blood. They help boost our immune system. None of them respond to Tercera, because it's not perceived as a threat at first, not for a long time really. Dad created a monster virus with a huge incubation period. It lays dormant for quite some time so if it ever did get out, there would be plenty of time to treat any patients before symptoms hit. He spliced together pieces of lots of awful things, so he could create a vaccination to treat them all at once."

"He made something bad to do something good?" Wesley asks.

"Exactly," I say. "He wanted the virus to be passed by touch so he could use that same methodology to pass the vaccination by touch. He had almost finished his equal and opposite immunization when he died. I guess he'd made some of the opposite antibodies too, a sort of passive vaccination if you will, for Tercera. It was meant to work for any of the sub-viruses he used to create it as well. Essentially a vaccination for Tercera would keep you safe from Ebola, Varicella, Leprosy and on and on. You follow me so far?"

"Sort of," Rhonda says.

Close enough. "Antibodies hunt for foreign proteins or chemicals and attach to them so they can destroy them. While researching Triptych, Dad happened upon a tiny little virus that attacked other viruses. One of his friends was trying to develop it into something that would eat cancer cells. But Dad took it and fostered mutation until it attacked other foreign viruses. In that way, it was even better than an aggressive antibody, and smarter too. The night before he got murdered," I choke up a little, the image of my dad lying on the ground making my hands shake, "he was exposed to Tercera. His business partner came and they fought. I remember the shouting."

"Wait," Wesley says. "You were there?"

I close my eyes tightly. "I wish I could remember what his partner looked like." I recall that they spoke a lot on the phone. Ever since Solomon told me that his partner, or someone else came back and finished my dad off, and knowing it might be total rubbish, I've been desperate to recall what the man looked like, but I can't think of any time I actually saw him.

"Do you remember anything?" Rhonda asks.

I shake my head. "I'm sure he must have met with him, and I must've seen him. I just can't think of a single time it actually happened. Why can't I recall anything about him?"

"Not to digress," Job says, "but you said your dad was exposed to Tercera? Could that have been how it got out?"

I sigh. "No, I don't think so. According to the journal, he dosed me with antibodies after the exposure, but only after he dosed himself with the virus. His rash disappeared, and he limited any contact with me until he could verify that it worked. I guess there's no way to know much about its effectiveness since he died the next day. I doubt he infected anyone else, though. Especially since he had contact with David Solomon, who's obviously not infected, and I remember seeing him that last day. His forehead was clear."

"So that's a bust." Job swears this time.

"Dad did mention the only other live strains of the hacker virus. He said there were two, and that they were stolen by whomever stole Tercera, probably the partner I can't remember."

"Ruby's blood is the closest thing we have to a cure, then?" Rhonda asks.

I sigh. "It looks that way. And I'm worried if Wesley's blood didn't work..."

Job groans. "Yours may only work on the recently infected or to prevent infection by the currently healthy."

I slump in my seat. "Exactly."

"Well," Wesley says, "we have a recently infected baby, or we should quite soon. Her mother was in labor when we left the maternity ward to head for WPN. No time like the present to test out your theory."

Wesley pulls up in the parking lot of a hospital and cuts the engine. "We're here."

The sign out front looks surprisingly clean, its lettering recently painted. It reads: Mainland Medical Center. I do a double take when I notice there's an entire pasture full of cows next to the parking lot, which several kids seem to be shooing toward trailers.

"Cows?"

Wesley opens the door for me and whispers. "Most of the mothers die shortly after giving birth."

The cows are so the babies can survive their mothers' deaths? My eyes well up with tears. I wish I'd never even heard about this. "How exactly is seeing this firsthand going to bring me joy?"

"Follow me and I'll show you." Wesley takes my hand to guide me out, and I yank my fingers away without thinking, pulling away from him as though his touch burns me. I may be immune to Tercera, but the feeling of his fingers reminds me of the hand I can't ever touch again. My knees weaken, but I breathe in and out deeply and force myself to stand up on my own two feet.

When I glance up at Wesley, his eyes are wounded, his spine stiff. "This way."

Rhonda and Job climb out and follow us without speaking. We walk past two dozen cows, and the five kids trying their best to herd them into metal boxes on wheels. After we walk through the front door of the medical center, cries, whimpers and mews from babies accost me from all directions.

"How many newborns are there?" I ask.

Wesley shrugs. "Even before the suppressant failed, some people went off it voluntarily. It's depressing taking something that freezes your body as a child while your mind grows and ages. For some of them it became too depressing. This maternity ward has been here for a while. Most of the babies have been born in the last few weeks, but there've been babies here for years now, always accompanied by a sibling or friend who was still taking the suppressant. The friend would care for the baby after its birth."

Wesley coughs, and I realize what he's thinking. For years, moms have died shortly after having a baby, while someone else cared for their children. That explains the existence of the starving young girl who exposed Wesley. But now without anyone on the suppressant, with it failing across the board, all these babies will be left without caretakers. I think back to the years after Tercera tore through America, and kids were all left with no parents, and no guardians to help them fill their needs.

The babies and young children will all starve to death.

The horror in my eyes matches the despair in his. "Unless you can cure them, they'll all die. They're hoping you'll cure the mothers and the fathers as well as the newborns, but even if you can't because of the advanced progression of the virus, if you can at least cure the babies, it's something. Rafe's hoping if the babies aren't infected, the Unmarked might take them in."

"And you already tried your blood?" I ask.

He nods his head solemnly. "It didn't work."

I close my eyes to process what he's asking of me. If my triple strong blood can heal these babies, their parents will die with the hope that someone else might keep their children alive. I hate this virus down to the tips of my toenails.

"We need to find your mom," I tell Job. "She might know how we could supercharge my antibodies enough to heal everyone." I wish we still had that journal. I suppress the pang in my heart when I think about what else we lost.

"I agree," Job says. "Mom's our best bet."

"She's Marked." I turn toward Wesley and Rhonda. "Do either of you know where she is?"

Wesley shrugs. "I haven't seen her, but Rafe doesn't tell me everything. We can ask him tomorrow."

"We'll see him tomorrow?"

Wesley nods. "It's dark, so we'll sleep here tonight, but tomorrow the entire camp's evacuating. We can't let Solomon exterminate us, not now that we have hope. We're pulling back with as many cows as we can manage, and all the mothers and babies who are able to travel."

"You tried your blood on Rafe too?" I ask Wesley.

He nods. "Duh."

I sigh. "Just thought I'd check."

Dozens of heads turn and stare when we walk down the hall, mouths opening, some gaping like fish, all with desperate eyes, all staring at my clear forehead. I notice one familiar face. The boy has dark hair falling in his face, and an angry red scar crossing one cheek.

I smile at him. "Hey Sean."

He smiles and waves, and the whispers pick up. I hear the phrase. "Promised one," and "Ruby" and "cure" over and over. I'm going to fail all of them just like I failed my dad and Sam. If this doesn't work, their wonder and their hope will turn to hatred, anger, and disgust.

I'll deserve it, too.

"Hey," Wesley says. "Are you okay?"

Job and Rhonda turn toward me, and Wesley waves them forward. "Go and see if Libby's ready for us."

Rhonda hugs me tightly, and Job squeezes my hand, but they leave like Wesley asked.

I don't need a pep talk, so I need to head this off at the pass. "I'm fine. I'm sorry. I just-" I can't explain it to Wesley. He won't understand, because he's always thought the best of me. He won't blame me, even when things really are my fault.

"I want you to know how sorry I am about what happened to Sam today on the bridge. I know you've been friends for a long time. Losing people who are close to us is always awful. Believe me, I've become an expert on that in the last few weeks. Even more than before." He reaches for my hand again.

This time I pull my hand away intentionally and shake my head to drive it home. "Don't Wesley, please."

"Rubes," he says softly, "I'm not Marked, and even if I was, you can't be infected."

I spin around and stare at him. He needs to understand all of it, exactly what's between us now. "It's not that, Wesley. When you left I was devastated, and I felt so guilty that I was fine and you were Marked."

"I was relieved when you didn't come," he says. "Honest, I was. A little lonely, but so relieved that I hadn't doomed you. You don't need to feel guilty at all."

I shake my head. "It's not that either. Let me finish. I read my dad's journal while I was in quarantine and discovered he created Tercera. I knew I had to go for the cure, but it was in Galveston. My aunt and uncle refused to take me, and I didn't think Rhonda and Job would help either. Actually, they'd already left without me, although I didn't know that yet. I was all alone, and I had no one to help me track down my dad's lab. Until I convinced Sam to help." I hold his eyes until he understands the subtext. Sam and I set out as friends, but we became more. I'm not mourning a family friend, I'm mourning family. The only family I really had left, or maybe the only family I ever had.

"Oh." Wesley's face closes off, his eyes wounded, his mouth pressed into a firm line.

A huge lump rises in my throat and I can barely

breathe, let alone talk, but I need to say the words. Wesley has to understand. Somehow now that it comes to it, subtext isn't enough, not for Sam, not to convey what I'm feeling. Wesley means a lot to me, and he deserves to know. "Sam wasn't perfect, and it was brand new between us, but somehow on that trip, I fell in love with him."

"Wow. Well, I guess I'm really, really sorry for your loss, then." He looks at the ground and kicks at a chipped tile. His eyes flash and his fists clench. He opens his mouth to say something, but I don't want to hear it, not now.

"I can't deal with your teenage angst, okay? Not right now." I brush past him and through the door Job and Rhonda opened earlier. I know I'm not being fair to Wesley. He has feelings too, and he had no idea how things changed between me and Sam. He wasn't there to see it, or understand what happened. I know he's confused and his feelings for me haven't changed. The worst part of all of this is that Wesley's expectations are being crushed through no fault of his own.

In fact, he's probably processing the fact that Sam's gone, and thinking maybe if he's patient, I'll eventually get over Sam. I wonder whether he's thinking about how long it might take before things can go back to normal for me and him. If so, he's wrong.

Things will never go back to normal for me.

I look up from my inner turmoil and into the face of a worried mother. Mothers should be older than me, and wiser than me. They shouldn't, aside from more pronounced curves, look exactly like me. The suppressant clearly isn't a great way to live, in stasis, no progress. But it kept them alive.

This new mother, with her wavy blonde hair and delicate features, looks as much like me as Rhonda. Maybe more. That would probably mean more before I found out

Rhonda probably isn't related to me at all. When I glance down into this new momma's lap, a white-swaddled bundle wriggles. I focus on the tiny thing, one itsy-bitsy, pinkish hand waving in the air, and a button nose scrunched into an apple-sized face. A tiny wisp of strawberry blonde hair curls onto her forehead, but what really draws my attention aren't her delicate features or her beautiful curl. It's the tiny rash on the perfect baby skin.

I gasp.

"My name's Libby. Can you help my baby? Can you help Rose?" Libby's voice shakes with fear and her eyes shine with hope, but it's the desperate longing that kills me.

I shrug, trying not to get her hopes up, as if that's possible. "I'll try."

Job offers up a needle and I cross the room to where he's standing. "Oral, like Wesley?" I ask. "Or intravenous? I assume that's better."

"It should be." Job shrugs. "There are quite a few viruses that pass via the intestinal tract, so it makes sense the immunity can too, like the kids' flu vaccination, but it's still more effective when given intravenously. We're lucky you're O Negative. If you weren't a universal donor, we'd need way more equipment right now."

I try not to look at Libby and her baby while Job draws blood from the cradle of my right elbow, but I can't help it. The fingers on Rose's hand are delicate, with perfect, miniature nails at the end of each one. She whimpers, and the sound makes me want to curl my arms around her and rock her. I want to fix everything, and she's not even my baby. "Why did you name her Rose?"

Libby smiles ear to ear. "I wanted to give her an R name to honor you, but my mother's name was Lily, so I wanted to name her after a flower too. Gardens and blooms have survived the destruction of Tercera and still bring beauty and joy into the world, just like I hope my Rose will."

"Try dosing Libby too," I say when Job finishes.

Libby shakes her head so violently that the baby cries out. "No, give all of it to her. The more she gets, the better her chances, right? I'll give her my entire dose."

I frown. "Draw another syringe full. They can each have one."

Libby sets her jaw and I know she's planning to refuse.

"Believe me," I say, "This is far, far more than Wesley got, and look at him."

Wesley smiles. I can tell it's forced, but Libby probably can't.

"Alright." She slumps forward and when she looks down, I notice rings under her eyes that signal more than exhaustion. Before Job can approach her, Rhonda takes the syringe, widening her eyes meaningfully. "You haven't been inoculated yet, Job. Let me."

While Rhonda treats Libby and Rose, I walk across to find another syringe. I draw my own blood, which I'm proud I can still do. It's been years since I practiced this in Science. I hand the syringe to Job and whisper to him. "Time to dose yourself. Can't have my star scientist going down with the ship."

He glances at Rose and Libby, clearly feeling as selfish and guilty as I do, but he injects himself without arguing. "Thanks."

Baby Rose cries when she's injected, but calms quickly when Libby feeds her a bottle. I'm not sure what I expected, really. Maybe I thought the Mark would magically disappear when Rose got my blood, but of course it's a physical rash. Even if the antibodies are doing their job, the rash will take time to resolve.

After watching them for a moment, both noticeably

calmer than when we entered, I stand up.

Wesley hasn't said a word since we entered, but he puts a hand on Libby and squeezes her shoulder as we prepare to leave. Once we reach the hallway, he walks us to a room and points at the door. "This is where you and Rhonda will sleep for the night. Job will be next door. There should be bowls of soup waiting in the rooms. I asked them to leave you some of what we made for the new mothers. Please let me know if you need anything else." He inclines his head stiffly, which I've never, ever seen him do before, and then spins on his heel.

"That boy is depressed," Rhonda says. "What did you say to him?"

"That boy doesn't even understand true suffering. He'll survive," I say instinctively, and then it hits me all over again.

Wesley will survive, but Sam didn't.

My shoulders shake first, and I fly into the room and throw myself down on a bed before the curious people up and down the hall can witness my complete collapse. I'm not sure how long I cry into the pillow. However long it is, when my tears dry up, I know it wasn't nearly long enough.

The bed creaks when Rhonda sits down next to me. She reaches her arm around my shoulder. "I know it's hard right now, because I can barely breathe when I think about him, but for the first time in a long time, things really are better in the world now than when you went to sleep last night. We have a, well, sort of a cure for Tercera, once we get some help from Mom to iron out the kinks."

I know Rhonda's right. The world's brighter today, and humanity has a future again. I should be happy. Maybe if I keep repeating that over and over, I'll start to believe it myself.

# CHAPTER 4

My eyes open and I look around for Sam. I want to see his half smile, touch his hand. My foggy, early morning brain finally processes what I know, and the realization I'll never see Sam again hits like a load of rubble.

I don't even have a photo of him, much less the two of us.

It's a stupid thing to worry about, but once the thought reaches my core synapses, tears well up. I imagine his face in my mind so clearly now, but how long until it fades? How long until I can't quite recall the way his eyes aren't quite green or gold, but a mixture of the two? How long until I can't get the details right of how he stands when he's scanning the surroundings? How long until I can't remember how his hand touches the side of my face, and his eyes soften before he kisses me?

I sob into my pillow so I don't wake up Rhonda, and for the first time in my life, I want to roll back over and never get up. Except that would negate the benefit of his sacrifice, so I do get up. I put one foot in front of the other until I find myself standing a dozen doors down, peering around the corner at Libby. She's awake, and cradling her perfect little baby in the inside of her elbow.

The smooth, clear skin of Rose's forehead almost breaks through the sorrow-saturated fog that's taken residence in my brain. My blood did that, killed Tercera, saved a baby. My dad's research and his triple shot of antibodies allowed me to heal this tiny life, a child who would surely have died two days ago, but now might live to adulthood.

When I glance up at her mother's face, I almost can't breathe. Libby's Mark is fading. I try to tamp down my hope, because the shrinking of her rash may mean nothing. Libby has sores on her arms, which also look improved, but she's been off the suppressant for quite some time. If she's had a baby, she's been off for over a year, and there's no telling how far the viral progress of Tercera has gone.

Even knowing it's a long shot, even knowing that positive signs may mean nothing, my lips turn upward. I need a smile like a drowning man needs a floaty.

"I know." Libby's eyes are red-rimmed from crying, but her own mouth breaks into a contagious grin. "It's a miracle. Thank you, a million times thank you."

Her expression is different when she looks at Rose this time, and I easily recognize why. For the first time in a decade, hope has outpaced fear. She might survive to see Rose's first steps. She might hold her daughter and rock her, and sing to her, and hear her speak her first words. She might be there for Rose for more than a month or two, or three. Libby might be there to see it all, to care for her own child. She might be able to do something the world took for granted ten years ago. But today, the hope of many tomorrows is a miracle today.

And I'm part of it.

That thought pulls me through the next few hours as I dose the newborns and their mothers in turn, and then as we begin the more mundane tasks of helping the pregnant girls, the new mothers and their partners, siblings and friends pack up to flee. I personally help Wesley load two more cows into the back of our stolen truck, but there's only enough transportation for seven cows beside those two. That means we'll have to leave more than fifteen behind. Rhonda let the Marked know about WPN's plans to exterminate them, and they don't want to wait around this close to the threat.

My infection of King Solomon turned him into a ticking time bomb as well, and we can't even guess how his illness might change those plans. We're all positive we'd rather not be around to find out.

I try to ignore the worried glances from caretakers and mothers alike at the cows being left, because there's nothing we can do about it. Hopefully the nine we're taking will make enough milk for the babies whose mothers are sick or dead.

When no one's watching, I ask Wesley, "Do you know how much milk these cows make?"

He sighs. "We're taking the top producers with us, but on average two or so gallons a day. They used to feed milk cows grain Before and they made several gallons per day, but we don't have much of that to spare. They produce way less milk when they're eating mostly hay and grass."

By my count, there are fourteen babies, and forty-three pregnant girls. "How much does a baby drink?"

He frowns. "Ruby, we're taking care of this. You don't need to stress. One cow can feed eight babies, or maybe ten if we need them to. Besides, some of the moms can nurse. Especially if we cure them before..."

Before their bodily functions shut down and they die. Ugh. I thought this through already. It takes six months or so from the suppressant failure for their bodies to develop

43

to the point of sustaining a pregnancy, I assume. At least nine more months to grow a baby. At that rate, they're well into year three before the baby is born. The stress of pregnancy advances the disease course, which means these moms have months left at most, if not weeks. Looking around at the strength, or lack thereof, for each of these mothers confirms that I'm right.

One mother has bright yellow skin: jaundice. One mother has swollen ankles: heart failure. One mother looks rail thin. I can't believe she's sustained this pregnancy. I'd guess her intestines aren't processing food correctly, which means the newborn will almost certainly be low birth weight. I shake my head and try to think of something else, because Wesley's right. Worrying won't help us right now, but I really wish my aunt was here.

Rafe's talking to a mother-to-be a few feet away about the same things I was worrying about. "I know the cows take a break each year. I know that makes you nervous, and you need to trust me." He raises his voice. "We'll come back for them, okay? Make sure they have food and as much water as we can provide, and ensure the fencing is secure, but you mothers are our priority. Cows can be replaced."

Every time I turn around, Job hands me another glass of water. "Drink."

I drink whenever I'm told, and try my best not to feel like a walking blood bank. It gives me some insight into the life of these poor cows.

The worst part isn't worrying, and it's not loading cows, or even dealing with their bodily functions. The worst part is saying no. At least twenty of the forty pregnant mothers beg me for blood. I always agree, because how can I possibly say no?

Wesley, who otherwise ignores me, stands over me

like a guard at the now defunct Fort Knox. He shakes his head each time, putting a hand on theirs, or an arm around their shoulder. "I know it's hard. I know you don't want to wait," he says. "But you know we have to make a plan for all of this, and our top priority right now is research. We need to figure out what works and what doesn't so we can treat everyone as quickly and safely as possible."

After the first few, Wesley frowns when he walks back over to me, and mutters under his breath. "You shouldn't have given any blood to Libby, you really shouldn't have. Rafe's orders are there for a reason. Other than brand new births, no blood from you until we've run tests and made some kind of plan. Your blood isn't limitless, but the people clamoring for it. . . they are. You won't do anyone any good if you die of blood loss."

He's right. I know he is, but if I die at least the pain will stop.

I try not to think that way because I know I shouldn't, but it's hard. When armed guards supervise our departure, I think of Sam. Every gun reminds me of him. Things as mundane as cans of food bring to mind making tea with Sam. When Rhonda repacks her backpack, the defense rations remind me of his jokes. I'm so pathetic that I even think of Sam whenever I see Rafe turn the right way, or smile, for some inexplicable reason, and Rafe looks nothing like him.

By the time we all climb into the black WPN truck, weighed down with people, supplies, and cows, I breathe a heavy sigh of relief. Wesley drives again, but this time Rhonda sits in the back with me.

"Where exactly are we going?" I ask.

"The Marked encampment outside of Port Gibson isn't very large. We're headed for their home base near Baton

Rouge. WPN sticks to port towns like Galveston and New Orleans, so the Marked set up a little more inland."

"How long's the drive?" Job asks.

Wesley shrugs. "Depends on roads. We'll take I-10 past Lake Charles, just like we would if we were headed to Port Gibson, but then instead of branching North, we continue east. The scariest part of the trek is crossing the Atchafalaya, for me at least. So far one side of the bridge is fine, but it's a long bridge and no one maintains it." Wesley shudders. "Assuming all is well, the drive should take seven hours give or take. We've got to move slower than normal with the cows in the back."

The Marked are a lot more organized than I expected them to be.

After two hours Job takes the wheel, Rhonda moves up front, and Wesley climbs into the back with me. Rhonda and Job are chatting and laughing about the last time we had this many people in a truck, our trip up north when they had to make reports to the DecaCouncil. Job had an upset stomach, and we spent the whole trip with the windows down, stopping every twenty minutes. It's funny now, but it really stunk at the time, like literally. Listening to them bickering back and forth and reminiscing, I almost forget all the things that are wrong. I lean my head against the side window and close my eyes.

I almost forget Wesley's sitting next to me until he speaks.

"Do you feel lightheaded or tired at all?"

His voice is caring, kind, and familiar. It's just the wrong voice. I know it's not Wesley's fault Sam's gone, and it's not like Wesley can be Sam. Even so, I fake exhaustion. "Yeah, tired for some reason. I may try to take a nap."

As I say the words, I notice a big tree with a Cracker Barrel sign right in front of it. I freak out a little bit, the screams breaking free from my throat against my will. "Stop, wait, stop the truck. Pull over!"

"Umm that little fit of yours just took a year off my life," Job says. "What in the world is wrong?"

"Pull over! Just pull over!"

Job slows the truck and swerves onto the weedy, cracked edge of the road. I notice that several other trucks have stopped behind us since we're caravan-ing east to Baton Rouge. I should care that they're all being inconvenienced, but I don't. They can wait a few moments. I race down the dirt path Sam and I stopped on that first night on the road. The pile of branches he dumped out of the truck bed still lies on the edge of the clearing, but the tire tracks are almost gone, along with our footprints. I shift some of the branches and find the gas cans, the ones Sam forgot that left us stranded. He was so angry at himself, at the world. Of course, if he hadn't forgotten them, we'd have been caught by WPN and we couldn't have saved Rhonda and Job. Even Sam's missteps worked out in the end.

Except for the last one.

I point at the gas cans and Wesley and Job glance at me with identically baffled looks.

"I left these here last time I was on this road," I say. "Hopefully the lids are tight enough that the gas is fine. You should take it to the truck."

Gas is precious. Maybe they'll think that memory is the reason I made us all pull over. My throat closes off, and I can't talk any more. I stumble toward the clearing where Sam and I ate our first dinner around a campfire.

I sit on a stump near where he cooked the little rabbit on a spit. I think about the story he told me that night, about his uncle, about his parents. I almost welcome the pain, because it's a connection between us. I bend over silently while the agony claws at my heart, shredding ventricles, destroying my aorta.

When I straighten, I see the trees off in the distance, where Sam taught me to shoot. I remember that he shot around my bullet holes, transforming my erratic shots into the shape of a heart. Showing off for me, even then. I walk toward the tree slowly, remembering how he taught me to shoot, shifting my stance, his hand on my hip. He loved guns so much, and I hated them equally. If possible, I like them even less now. They took my dad, and I felt adrift for years, never quite fitting in, never quite having a family. Then I found Sam, and now guns have taken him too.

I reach out to trace the heart in the tree trunk and notice he did something else. He must've done it when he said he was picking up shell casings. He connected the gunshots with a knife, so it looks like a connect-the-dots picture. He carved something inside the heart, a sequence of letters. SR+RB. Sam carved our initials into the heart he shot. He hadn't lied. He'd loved me all along. And now because I dragged him all the way to WPN for no reason, he's gone forever.

Everyone I love the most dies.

I sink to my knees, and sob. If half the world's population wasn't relying on me to be their living blood bag, I'd never get up from this spot. Rhonda must've followed me, because she clears her throat, crouches down next to me, and pulls me against her chest.

"It's okay." She rocks me back and forth, and back and forth, again and again. "Or at least, it will be okay eventually." She smooths my hair away from my face and keeps rocking.

"It's not okay." I hiccup. "It'll never be okay. The world won't ever be right again."

"I know it feels like that," she says.

"You don't know," I say. "You don't understand."

"Then tell me," she says. "I've known Sam as long as you, and loved him too. If anyone can understand a little bit of what you feel, it's me."

I shake my head. "You have Job and your parents. My dad's gone, and now that Sam's gone, I've got no one."

Rhonda pulls back far enough to look down into my eyes. "You have me and Job, and our parents, too. I've always been more a sister than a cousin to you."

I look away. "We're probably not even related."

A sharp exhalation of breath draws my attention. Rhonda's cheeks flush bright red, as though I slapped her. "You're my family, do you hear me? You'll be my family until the day you die, and then after that too. Who knows what happens after death? For all we know, Sam's sitting right there." She points at the tree. "He could be watching you right now. So stop talking nonsense."

I appreciate her assurance, I really do, but she'll never quite get it. She and Job are like two sides of a shiny quarter. I'm like a dirty penny they found on the side of the road. I'll never be the same as them, and I'll never really have a place. Sam was my shot at making a home in this messed up world, and now that's gone with him.

But the world needs the antibodies my dad shoved into my veins, so I stand up inch-by-inch, without anyone's help. I walk back to the truck by moving one foot at a time. I climb back into my seat, forcing my limbs to move, my lungs to work, and my heart to keep beating. This isn't about me, not anymore, and that keeps me going forward. Maybe somehow I can find a way to redeem myself or redeem my Dad. If there is life after death and either Sam or my dad are watching me, I can't let them down. Not again.

# CHAPTER 5

Wesley and Job load the gasoline into the already full truck bed, shifting the cows into yet a smaller area. They moo and moan and stomp their feet, but the world doesn't pay them any more attention than it does me. No one mentions my outburst, and we pull right back out on the road.

A few miles down the road I see it, the bridge over the Atchafalaya swamp.

It spans miles and miles. I don't know quite how many, but it stretches ahead of me as far as I can see, and behind me into the horizon. My stomach flips and flops, looking at the enormous drop from the road as we drive. Cypress trees and their knees, Spanish moss, enormous cranes, bullfrogs and even alligators live riotously in the swamp below. Our truck, suspended more than thirty feet above the standing water underneath, plows ahead, and my heart rests uneasily in my throat. At one point when I glance to my left, I see where the bridge on the other side crumbled away. The rest of the drive it's had two more lanes, probably intended for the traffic going the other direction, but the concrete pilings holding it up gave way. I think about the concrete pilings underneath us now, just as old as those and subject to the same conditions below. I wonder how many alligators, snakes and other creeping things would swarm us if we plunged into the swamp.

I shudder.

Wesley must feel the same way, because we don't stop at all over the Atchafalaya. I breathe a hearty sigh of relief once we clear it, and we do stop several times to clear vegetation after we pass back onto dry land. With so many people to help, the blockages are cleared quickly. We reach the edge of Baton Rouge almost exactly seven hours after we left Texas City.

I expect to see a few thousand Marked kids in the city, a city I've never seen before. I'm wrong by a wide margin. Tens of thousands of kids work, play, rest and interact all around us as we drive past. So many more than I expected. I'm accustomed to seeing kids with rashes, kids who are likely not kids, but who resemble children nonetheless.

I'm not accustomed to seeing young adults sporting the same rash. These Marked look older, taller, and less like kids than I imagined they would. Even knowing the suppressant is failing, it's a bucket of ice-water dumped over my head. I knew a lot of people were relying on me, but I didn't have a good feel for the time pressure we'll be working under.

They're sicker than I anticipated as well. Some are up and walking around, cleaning, tending animals or gardens, visiting with each other, but many of them are lying down. It's cold, but even covered in jackets and coats, I notice some of the sores that appear in the second year. These kids are dying.

We have a lot less time than I thought.

Wesley pulls up in front of a huge building with large

windows and a spacious parking lot. He parks the truck at the front of the lot, near a sign that reads 'Baton Rouge General Medical Center'. I suppose that makes sense. Ten years ago, the kids would have started out here tending for sick loved ones, so it probably organically became their home base from there. When we climb out, cheers go up all around us. Some kids hobble over, and some run. Some eyes widen in awe, many clutch their hands in desperation, and some faces light up with joy. I try not to flinch at the raw expectation. They know who I am, or at least, they know who they want me to be.

The Promised.

I hear them whispering, talking, and even a few shouting the same phrase over and over. I've never heard of any prophecy, and I'm quite sure I'm not part of some grand plan. In fact, I don't feel like the Promised at all. That sounds far too optimistic. I'm definitely less than that. I fear I'm doomed to disappoint them all.

I close my eyes and imagine Rose's face. Hope may be gone in me forever, but I try to summon up every last bit of compassion left inside to channel as I face them. I'm worried they'll spot my fear, my pessimism, and they'll wilt. I want to be what they need. I want them to live and work and love and laugh without fear. I want to fix the mess my dad made and restore a future to all the kids looking at me with longing.

I wish I knew how to fix everything.

While I'm wishing, I really miss Aunt Anne. She'd know what to do. I'd rest easier if she were running this show. Where did she go after she was Marked? Why isn't she here with Wesley and Rafe?

Deep in thought about my aunt, I barely notice when the first Marked girl touches my jacket.

"You're really here?" she asks, her hazel eyes soft. A sore

the size of a cherry tomato weeps fluid on her exposed forearm. It's chilly enough that I hope she takes my involuntary shiver as a reaction to the cold air, and not what it really is. Revulsion.

When another hand tugs gently on my hair, I glance behind me and notice they're converging. A large hand takes mine and tugs me forward, and my heart rate spikes. Rhonda's hand goes to her gun and Wesley throws an arm out, shooing the boy who took my hand and a tall girl back a few steps. But more of them press toward us, murmuring quietly, reaching and grabbing.

"Give her some room to breathe," Wesley says, his voice firm.

"I need help now." The pale boy who grabbed me whines. "My brother can't even get out of bed. He's in bad shape."

He wipes at an oozing sore near his left eye, and I wince.

I want to help them all, but there are so many. Even if they only need a drop of my blood apiece, even if I knew my blood would actually cure them, I'd die long before they all got treatment. When I glance from face to face, I realize they know it. They're running out of time, but by the looks of things, I might be too.

Rafe's voice cracks like a whip from the roof of a truck behind us, and a cow moos beside him. "Back to your chores. I've given you a moment to celebrate and welcome our new visitor, but you will not mob her, and you will not frighten her. Back away from her right now. We have a lot of work to do, and we need to figure out how best to make our new discovery available to everyone. You trust me, you know me, and I will work night and day to make this happen for all of us, not just a select few. I haven't had a drop of her blood, nor will I until the rest of you have all been treated."

I finally pinpoint the similarity between Rafe and Sam. Rafe's face and hair are different, but I've seen the same look in Sam's eyes, the air of command. Rafe and Sam share the same set of their jaw, a uniform confidence of purpose.

When Rafe climbs down and crosses the street to where I'm standing, the Marked kids disperse like cockroaches fleeing the light. He certainly commands easily, which must be hard when you barely look thirteen years old. I wonder how old he really is.

Rhonda glances around warily and shifts from foot to foot. "Who runs security around here? You must have someone in charge of that. Kids are running around with guns all over the place."

Rafe nods. "Todd and Marco handle most of that." He pulls a black walkie talkie from his belt. "Necessito seguridad aqui pronto."

"Spanish?" I ask. "Why in Spanish?"

Rafe shrugs. "Did you understand what I said?"

I shake my head.

"That's why."

The tall man with the mahogany skin who tried to detain me before we headed for WPN jogs over to where Rafe is standing. He's never been on the suppressant, or I'll eat my gloves.

"What's wrong?" His eyes scan the surrounding areas twice before circling back around to Rafe's face.

"Our guests wanted to meet you, Todd." Rafe motions toward us. "This is Rhonda, who you've met briefly, her brother Job, and Ruby—"

"Who I nearly caught. It would have saved us all some

time, if this one," Todd tosses his head at Rhonda, "hadn't lied and tricked us." Todd pointedly returns his gaze to Rafe, which isn't necessary. We all know exactly how he feels about us. "Well, if there's nothing more you need from me."

Rhonda puts her hands on her hips. "Nothing we need?" She shakes her head. "How about a baseline level of competency? WPN was planning to eliminate the entire Marked population, and you had no idea. Your people almost swarmed Ruby just now, ready to suffocate her with their desperation, and Rafe was standing right next to her when that happened. I can only imagine what they'll do over the next few weeks as symptoms worsen and we work on developing this into something we can manage. If I've learned anything, it's that science takes time. Nothing happens overnight."

Todd's eyebrows rise. "I'm not even going to address most of that, because you have no idea what life here is like. You have no concept of what my job entails. But as to the rest, why would it take weeks to parse out her blood to all of us?"

"How could it not?" Rhonda asks. "First of all, Ruby doesn't have a cure so much as an immunity. Trying to extrapolate that into a treatment will be difficult, even if we were doing this in Unmarked territory in my mom's lab. It might be impossible even then, but here? Even if Ruby's blood was the cure you people seem to assume it is, there's only one of her, and in case you hadn't noticed, she's tiny. Blood cures do not grow on trees."

Todd's scowl deepens. "I've seen Libby. We all have. Her Mark's gone, and her baby's head is clear too. So you can say what you like, but Ruby has cured you, Libby, and pretty boy here." He points at Wesley. "The rest of us want our shot. That's not a security issue, that's the reality of our situation."

My heart sinks. I should be happy to hear that Libby's Mark is gone. I should be pleased that my blood can cure them, but based on what I know about antibodies... the improvement doesn't seem likely to last, not in the long run.

"The disappearance of the rash doesn't mean someone has been cured," Job says. "Many people conflate the two, but it's more of an indicator of symptoms than anything conclusive."

"What about this?" Todd yanks up his sleeve. "What does this mean?"

Near his elbow, there's a small sore.

"It means you've entered year two," I say. "Symptoms have begun to manifest, which means your immune system is weakening. Eventually Tercera will begin to attack your entire body, but you probably have a year or so until that happens."

Todd spits. "I'm doing better than most, little girl. You may be small, but you're the first hope we've had in a long time. You better not let us down."

I shiver.

"Why don't you have any sores, Rafe?" Rhonda asks.

Rafe frowns. "The suppressant stopped working in the far flung areas first. It only stopped here a few weeks ago."

Job's eyes meet mine and he nods.

"You said it failed," Job says. "As in, you kept taking the pills, but they stopped working like they did before. Are you sure that's what happened?"

Rafe tilts his head and folds his arms. "We took our pills, if that's what you're asking. We may look young, but we aren't stupid."

The Unmarked provide the suppressant. Our scientists developed it, and Aunt Anne spearheaded those efforts. It's not possible, what Job's thinking. She may have lied to me, but she was trying to protect me. Aunt Anne would never have allowed this, she'd never have sent out faulty suppressant.

"He didn't mean to imply anything like that," I say. "We're exhausted, is all."

Job grunts. "It seems odd the meds would stop working in certain *places* instead of for certain *people*, varying based on how long they've taken it, and how their bodies respond."

Rafe blinks rapidly. "We assumed it was the climate in each place, or something about the differences in what they ate. You think it stopped working because of something else?"

I shake my head. "We don't know what to think, but it might not be a bad idea if you provided us with whatever information you might have on the dates, locations and times the suppressant began failing. Once we've had time to review them, we can let you know."

Rafe frowns. "Your mom asked for the same thing."

Job and Rhonda both step toward Rafe, and I have a momentary feeling of vertigo, like I'm seeing double. They both ask, "My mom?" at the same time.

Twins are whack.

Rafe nods. "She and your dad found the same camp Wesley originally joined, and they sent word asking for that information. I sent it on, but I never heard back. When I sent a message asking about her, they said your dad left first since he wasn't Marked, and your mom left a few days later."

Aunt Anne refined the initial suppressant and then spearheaded the efforts to manufacture it for the Marked population. She's the reason I can't imagine that the failing suppressant had anything to do with the pills provided by the Unmarked. Aunt Anne would never allow a failure of that magnitude, and the idea she might intentionally provide a faulty product is inconceivable. But if she knew the failure couldn't have come from the Unmarked side, why would she ask for any information the Marked kids had? Wouldn't she know the pills themselves were fine?

I glance at Job, and he shakes his head by way of response. He doesn't know what it means, either. I intend to find out, but the quickest way will be to ask Aunt Anne. We'll need her help to make sense of my antibodies and figure out how we can use them to save all these people too. That should be our top priority, really.

Rafe points at Todd. "Rhonda raises some good points. You need to review plans for security around the plasma center. We're using it as a home base for this whole operation. Why don't you take Rhonda with you? Now that she's one of us, we should be making use of her expertise. Work with her, that's an order."

Todd stares at Rafe for a moment, and I wonder whether he'll argue, but eventually Todd drops his eyes and grunts. "This way." He heads back up the road the same way he came, and Rhonda glances at me.

I nod. "It's fine. Go see what you can do to make things safe for us."

She trots off behind him.

Marco, whoever he is, never showed. I think about asking Rafe why he didn't, but a throat clears behind me, and I spin around. At first I think maybe it's Marco with a tag-along. Two people walked up behind me so quietly, I had no idea they were there. A boy and a girl, with almost identical long noses, sloping brows, and weak jaws. They stand at almost an identical height, about four inches taller than me, but their facial expressions couldn't be more different. The boy's eyes are wide, eager and welcoming. When I look at his face, he waves shyly. The girl slaps his hand down and sighs in disgust, frowning at me with suspicious eyes and crossed arms.

Rafe walks from the middle of the road to the edge of it so he can stand near them. "Amir and Riyah are siblings. They run our Science division. I asked them to set up a place for you."

I smile at them and Amir smiles back. His sister doesn't spit at me. That may be as good as it gets with her. I study her face, her eyes as bitter as a green lemon, her mouth twisted into a scowl.

"Wonderful to meet you both," Job says. "I can't wait to discuss my thoughts. I'm assuming you've already heard that the 'cure' is really a triple shot of antibodies Donovan Behl injected into Ruby, here. Obviously antibodies like Ruby's dad's journal says he provided shouldn't have lasted quite as long as they have."

Job pauses for input. When they don't reply, he continues. "My initial thought was that exposure at some point boosted them, or that maybe her dad had an agent that bound to them to keep them around. But when I thought about that, I figured what happened, probably, was he stimulated the CpG oligonucleotides, which activated the protein inside B cells called the TLR9. There was some great research about that Before, and I think it was coming out of England. My mom had an article I read on it, but as a leader in his field, Donovan would've been abreast of everything like that. That would explain how she has such a strong immunity a decade later, but it might be problematic as far as a cure since passive immunity is usually short lived without a CpG stimulation, which we don't have the capacity to replicate."

Riyah opens her mouth, her brows drawn together, her hip cocked, but before she can speak, Amir cuts her off. "We don't really do a lot of research, exactly. The Marked science team mostly handles things that better our lives in the here and now. Our parents ran a dairy for a company called Horizon Organic Before. They home schooled us and loved actual books, so when Tercera hit, we had a food supply, basic knowledge of how to maintain it, and books that held some answers."

Job closes his mouth with a click. He glances from Amir to Riyah and back again. "Well, I'm glad to have your help here, anyway."

"Me too," I say. "We all want the same thing. To figure this thing out and end Tercera."

Riyah raises one eyebrow. "Sure. We're basically the same. Except, our dad didn't create it in the first place, and none of us are immune. Which means you can't die, but we all will, and soon. Thanks to your dad."

I can't swallow past the lump in my throat, so I look down at the muddy toes of my black boots. "Yeah." People here either seem to love me for no reason, or hate me for something I didn't even do.

Wesley takes my hand and his support makes me choke back a sob. What's wrong with me?

"Ruby was six when her dad's work was stolen. He was murdered for his refusal to weaponize Tercera. Neither Donovan nor Ruby had anything to do with its release. The next time you want to carve something with your sharp tongue Riyah, feel free to take it up with me. I don't appreciate you attacking her, and I won't allow it. You can be replaced, and you will be if you prove unable to work with us. Is that clear?"

Amir clucks. "My apologies. Riyah's had a hard day. Her best friend Peter was one of the first suppressant failures. He's not doing well. If you'll forgive her sharp tone, you'll find she's quite capable, and motivated to help. There's an old plasma donation center we thought might work out well for your research. When we got word from Rafe that you were coming, we started cleaning it up." Amir makes eye contact with me when I look up and then points down the road. When I nod, he steps down the path he indicated.

Wesley lets go of my hand when I start walking, but he stays next to me, almost close enough to touch. I've almost forgotten in all my grief that Wesley was my friend first. For years I thought it was all we'd ever be. Somehow, one kiss confused me and I forgot that. When he jumped in to defend me, it bridged a gap I didn't even realize was there. My exhaustion, and depression, and fear still crowd around me, but I'm a little less alone.

I've only taken a few steps when something bounds out from behind a tree and leaps into the road in front of us. I stand transfixed, afraid if I move it will flee.

I barely whisper the question for Wesley, "Is that what I think it is?"

He grins. "I don't know. Do you think it's a kangaroo with a baby joey in its pouch?"

My jaw drops. "It looks just like I imagined it would." It bounces away, pivoting mid bounce and disappearing into the trees that line the road. I can't quite help the note of wonder in my voice. "What's it doing here?"

"Baton Rouge boasted an awesome zoo Before. After the Marking someone freed the animals. Seeing kangaroos and wallabies, who have apparently thrived in the wilds of Louisiana, is awesome. Let me know if you feel the same when you hear wolves howling, or watch a tiger take down one of our cows. My least favorite critters are the gators in all the waterways, although from what I understand they're indigenous."

Job jogs up to stand on my other side. "Was that a kangaroo?"

I grin. "Yep." Pretty cool.

We walk down the main street and around a corner, and once the ambient noise dies down, I notice another set of footsteps behind us. I turn and notice that Rafe's walking a few steps back.

"Oh," I say. "I didn't realize you were coming."

Rafe arches one eyebrow. "I'm here to make sure you're safe and that you have what you need. I may not have the history with you that Wesley has, but seeing this through is sort of the main focus of my job for the foreseeable future. That and preparing for this Cleansing, I guess."

I nod and turn back to the path. The sun's setting, so if I don't pay attention, I might fall flat on my face. Three buildings down, we reach a one-story, red brick building with a sign that reads: Life Share Blood Center.

A few windows are boarded up, presumably where the glass was smashed or broken, but several are intact. When we walk inside it looks relatively clean. Someone took the time to clean the windows enough that the last rays of the sun's light streams through. I only notice two cockroaches in the corner, and I'm pretty sure they're both dead.

Rafe turns to Job. "Will this work?"

It annoys me that he's asking Job instead of me. It annoys me that I'm going to be living in a plasma center now, as though I'm literally a walking blood repository.

But most of all, it annoys me that I'm so irritated by everything instead of taking charge of things myself. I clear my throat and before Job can answer, I do. "Will it work for what? A dance party? My walk in closet? A roller skating rink?"

Rafe forces a laugh. "Job mentioned you'd need to run some tests, and of course when more babies are born, or for the very ill-"

"Oh." My hands clench into fists. "You meant will this

work for draining me of my blood until I'm nothing more than a dry husk?"

Job frowns. "Antibodies should be in the plasma, which replaces—"

I cut him off. "Every 48 hours. You may be a few years ahead of me, and I may have taken some time off, but my understanding of blood and viruses is pretty solid, Job." I spin on my heel and glare at Riyah. Her friend's dying. Well, get in line to be pissed, lady. Everyone here's dying soon. We're running out of time, and I'm expected to wave a syringe over my arm and fix all of it.

She raises one eyebrow at me.

"How much blood will it take to atone for my father's mistake, in your estimation? By my calculations, I should have about eight pounds of blood in my body. I'd say I've given less than an ounce in the past few days, all told. Will eight pints of blood be enough for you? Or will it take ten? Fifty? None of it will bring back the billions who have already died."

Wesley clears his throat. "No one requires any more of your blood tonight. I hope we all feel better tomorrow morning."

Rafe nods. "I've ordered beds to be placed in the office in the back for you and Rhonda. I assumed Job would feel better being on site, as well."

"Oh good. I've guilted you all into backing off. But see, that wasn't my goal, not really. I'm as eager as you to see what we've got to work with. It's not even dinner time yet. I imagine Job's fingers are itching to throw my plasma under a microscope."

The gleam in Job's eye answers that.

"I am too, and there's no reason to wait. There's nothing magical that dinner will fix."

I sit down by the apheresis machine. The Marked kids

may not know much about science, but there's a stocked cart next to the machine. They all want what my dad hid inside of me, and they may never have heard of gamma globulins, but they knew enough to put me in a place with plasma machines instead of a straight up blood donation center.

"Well?" I look over at Job. "Do I have to do everything myself?"

Wesley shakes his head. "You just got here. You don't have to do this right now."

I point at Riyah. "Don't I? People are sick and they're dying. There isn't any time to waste."

Job grabs a needle and opens the hermetically sealed pouch. He turns to Rafe. "Is there any power? The only light in here is coming from that window."

Amir smiles and takes a step closer. "We have generators, and I made sure one was allocated for this building. That's the kind of science we spearhead. Propane and gasoline are both hard to come by, but the Unmarked have actually provided a lot of information on that type of thing over the years. We only have one manufacturing plant for each, so we use energy very sparingly, but we do have enough fuel for this type of thing. We've already hooked the generator up outside."

Riyah walks toward the door. "I'll get it going."

Job preps my arm with nearly dry alcohol wipes and uses a rubber band to help emphasize my vein.

Wesley exhales loudly. "I'm going to find some kind of food for you to eat. This rush is ridiculous. We won't fix anything by forgetting what it means to be human." He storms out the door.

Job draws two small vials of blood while we wait for the tell-tale hum of the generator. When we hear it, he turns on the machine and punches on some buttons. "It appears to be working properly." He grabs another kit, this one with the double flexible tubing and connects it to the machine. "I'm excited to compare the blood and the plasma components. I'm hopeful the plasma will provide what we need, but it'll be good to consider each separately."

I watch as the wide-bore needle goes into the vein in the inside of my right elbow crease. A tiny pinch. I see my blood flowing out of my body and into the machine. Job presses some buttons and I realize what he's doing, calculating total blood volume. The volume to remove is usually based on weight. He turns to me. "You're what? A hundred pounds?"

I nod. "Ninety-two when I left Port Gibson."

He shakes his head. "If anything, it looks like you've lost a few pounds on this trip. Better stay on the low side." He programs it to take less than half the normal amount of plasma.

Yet again, I underperform. If Sam were here, he could give half again more than a typical person.

I think about all the people we saw on our way into the center of Baton Rouge. Even if I donate plasma twice a week for the next six months, it won't be enough. Maybe we can stimulate the healed or boosted individuals like Wesley, or Rhonda to make antibodies if Job can reverse engineer what he thinks my dad did. Even so, I can't help the despair that creeps inside and curls around the empty places inside my chest. I wonder if my dad foresaw this when he realized Tercera was stolen and injected me with the antibodies—that I'd become the mop used to clean up his mess.

Once the machine starts with the first blood pull, Job takes the vials over to the table that's been set up with a microscope and other tools. I close my eyes and try not to think about any of it. Of course, that's hard to do when the freezing cold saline starts to flow back into my arm along with my recycled red blood cells. I try to suppress the shivers that start as my body temperature drops from the infusion of room temperature saline. I learned how this process works a few years ago, but it's my first time to experience it myself.

The Unmarked don't allow donations until the age of seventeen, so even if I were back home, I might be doing the very same thing right now. The machine pulls whole red blood cells out and the centrifuge spins it around. Then the plasma's collected and the red platelets are added to saline and sent back into my arm in the flip side of the same wide-bore needle.

I breathe in and out while listening to the beeping and whirring of the blood draw. Every time I glance at Riyah, who came back in silently after turning on the generator, I have to look away. If she hates me this much, you'd think she would ask for someone else to be assigned to this position. When the door bangs open and two figures enter, too backlit to make out, I sit up quickly. I bend my arm without thinking, forgetting about the needle. I straighten it back out quickly, and fall back to the chair with a whimper.

"Are you alright?" a female voice asks. I rack my brain to place the voice.

Libby walks around to the side of my chair and I look up into her face. Her completely clear and blemish-free face. She beams at me, a tear sliding down her cheek.

"I begged Wesley to let me bring your dinner. I needed the chance to thank you from the bottom of my heart." She sets a bowl of some kind of stew on a little table next to my left arm, the one not stuck with an IV. "Thank you, thank you, thank you—" Her voice cracks at the end, and I take her hand in mine, something I'd have been too afraid to do last week.

"You're welcome."

After a few more moments of gratitude, Wesley leads Libby out.

While Job is bent over the microscope and Rafe's busy talking to Amir and Riyah, I lean over the machine and press the buttons that will double the amount of plasma it's taking. Surely I can at least give the normal amount of plasma, in spite of my size. It's not like I'm giving blood. Plasma refreshes in 48 hours. If anything has become clear to me today, it's that some of the people out there can't wait.

# CHAPTER 6

I must have dozed off, which makes sense, given how tired I was.

When I open my eyes, I'm not in the plasma center anymore. I know because it's bright, so bright I can barely see. I'm not hooked up to the IV either, but I'm cold, even colder than the saline made me. I sit up in bed, rub my arms, and breathe onto my hands. I look around, surprised to see I'm in a clean, white room, sitting up now on a small, white cot. I didn't expect the Marked to have cleared out an old office quite so effectively. I blink my eyes several times to make sure I'm seeing things right. Wasn't I supposed to be in the plasma center? The entire room is clean, bright, and white, and sunlight streams through a window high on the smooth unadorned wall.

I sit up straighter, swing my legs over the side, and slide off the cot. I'm wearing a white, sleeveless nightgown in the middle of winter. Geez, no wonder I'm freezing. The room's so empty that there's nothing else I can put on to cover myself up. In fact, other than a second cot that's empty, a small metal table that's bolted to the wall, and chairs that are bolted to the floor, I don't see anything else in the room.

"Rhonda?" I call out quietly at first, but when no one answers, I raise my voice. "Rhonda?"

No answer.

I cross the room, one shiny white tile at a time, my bare feet gobbling up the space between the white door and me. My hand looks pale when I reach for the knob. Why am I so pale? Probably because I upped the amount of plasma a little too high. Goosebumps stand out on my arms, and I remember that when your blood volume is too low, your body has trouble regulating your temperature. Maybe in two days when I can donate again, I'll keep the settings where Job says they should be.

I shake my head again to try and orient myself, and turn the knob. It does not open onto anything resembling where I was when I closed my eyes.

I am not in the plasma center, or anywhere near it.

A chill runs up my spine, and more goosebumps pebble my skin. I step into the empty hallway beyond, and look at door after closed door running ahead of me as far as I can see. "Rhonda? Job?" I call out loudly this time, as loudly as I can. My voice echoes in the hallway, but there's still no answer.

I spin around and see the same thing the other direction. My heart rate spikes. Where the hell am I?

My bare feet slap on the alternating black and white tiles as I run the length of the hall. I reach for the closest knob on the closest door, but before I even touch it, I already know. It's locked. My hands begin to shake. I pivot on my heel and sprint for the door I exited a moment before.

Also locked.

I choke back the sob that threatens to escape my throat.

I'm alone, in a bizarre building, without anyone to help. I'm cold, and volume depleted, and locked in a never-ending hallway in a white nightgown that doesn't cover enough and won't keep me warm. I cross my arms over my chest and force myself to breathe.

I will not panic. I will not collapse. I will be calm, and logical in this situation that I don't understand. I need to pick a direction and keep track of doorways, counting as I go. Even so, I can't keep my pace from escalating as I walk past doorway after doorway, checking each knob with growing panic. Locked. Locked. Locked. Always locked.

I've passed a hundred and twenty-seven doors when I finally see it fifty yards ahead of me. One black door.

I can't explain how I know, but I do. Someone is behind this door, someone who is no longer alive. A dead person waits behind that dark painted door. When I close my eyes, I can picture a casket as dark as ink, shiny, and long. My heart sinks. I don't want to see a corpse. I don't. I can't. But I walk toward the door, strangely unable to stop myself, my hand reaching for the knob involuntarily. When I finally reach it, the knob turns like I knew it would, and I leap back as if burned by fire. I slip on the slick tile and fall on my backside on the unforgiving tile. I scrabble backwards until I feel the wall behind my back, staring all the while at the door in front of me.

The ominous black door.

My hands are stiff now, arctic, ice-cubes covered by my skin. Even blowing on my fingers doesn't help. For the first time, I wonder. Maybe that door doesn't have someone dead behind it. Maybe it's for someone who's dying. Maybe that's why I'm here. Maybe that's why I'm so cold. Maybe that's why I'm all alone.

Maybe it's for me.

The ventricles in my chest ice over one by one, as the

frost reaches the middle of my body. Frozen, my heart doesn't hurt nearly as much. I force myself to stand, stiff and cold, and shuffle toward the door. I think about death.

My dad's dead, murdered by my, well, by my bio father. Probably. I could've saved him and I didn't. My biological father will be dead soon because of my actions.

Millions and millions, maybe billions, are all dead because of my cowardice. If I'd saved my dad, he could have saved them all. And then, I held the key to saving them all after my dad died, but I was too dumb to figure it out.

I couldn't save my mom, or Aunt Anne.

Sam.

I refuse to think about him. I can't. My heart will stop beating if I do, I know it. I reach for the knob, turn it and walk inside, ready to let it all go. The black door, the death door, where my casket awaits me.

I welcome it.

Except when I walk inside, there isn't a casket as dark as sin, as shiny as a mirror, as long as a bed. In fact, there's no casket at all. There's just a bed that's much nicer than the cot I woke up in. It's a single bed, sized for one person. I finally remember where I've seen beds like that. In hospitals, including the one Libby lay in just last night.

I'm so caught up in identifying the bed, that I don't immediately realize it's occupied. The one room that's open and there's an actual person lying on it. This person is covered by a sheet and a blanket, but I can see the chest rising and falling, steadily. He's sleeping. Why do I think it's a male? Because of the broad shoulders under the sheet, and the wide frame. I walk closer, one agonizing step at a time, and as I do, I make out more details. High cheekbones, golden skin, a chiseled jaw, full lips, and long, blond hair.

"Sam!" I shriek.

No casket, but not a hospital either. Lying on a bed behind a door of death. My icicle hands are so stiff I can barely move them, but I rush to Sam's side and place my frozen claw on his cheek, expecting it his skin to feel like mine, devoid of life, devoid of heat.

It doesn't. His skin is warm like the wind on a sunny day, like a seat in front of a fireplace, like a cat curled on my lap. His eyes, his beautiful, soul searching eyes open with a start and stare into mine for two full, glorious seconds. His hand lifts from the bed to cup my cheek. "Ruby, why are you so cold?" His voice is heroin for my ears. My lips are so numb that I can't make them move to respond.

Why *am* I so cold?

The more I struggle to answer, the more I can't make a peep. My field of vision narrows, from the entire room to just his bed, and then down to the curves of his face. I'm being sucked into some kind of black hole, and I can't shake away from it. I reach for Sam with my other hand, cupping his face with both shaking hands, and his eyes widen, but I can't stop it. I'm drawn inexorably down until...

I wake up to the sound of my name like the pop of a balloon, like the crack of a gun.

"Ruby!!" Job calls out hoarsely, as though he's used up his allotment of noise for the day. His brows are drawn together as though some equations he's working on don't align the way they should.

I blink my eyes repeatedly to bring the details of his face into focus.

"Why am I here?" I moan. "I'm not supposed to be here. I'm supposed to be. . ." I want to say dead, because I'm pretty sure that's why I had to leave Sam. I'm not dead. I can't stay with him, but I want to go back. I don't want to be here in the land of regret and shame and pain.

I want to scream and cry and race back to him as fast as possible. It felt so real, and wherever it was, I want to be with him again. I don't want to be alone anymore, alone in this world without Sam in it.

"Ruby," Job says, "try to focus on my voice. Can you hear me?"

I nod.

"Ruby." He snaps in front of my face and moves his hands back and forth, checking whether my eyes will track across the midline. "Did you change the settings on the apheresis machine?"

I nod, vaguely remembering. My brain feels stuffed with cotton candy. I'd love some cotton candy right now. I try licking my lips, but my tongue is so dry it hurts.

"You did change the settings? Did you make the machine take more blood?"

No cotton candy. I sigh. "There are so many people. So many who need my antibodies."

A string of curse words behind me draws my eye. I can barely make it out by the two candles lighting up the room now that the sun's gone down, but Rafe's fists are clenched, and his face is flushed red.

"What happened?" I ask. "Why am I so cold?"

"You doubled the withdrawal," Job says. "That put you into hemorrhagic shock. You should've known it would do that. You're a scientist."

I shake my head. "I only changed it to a pint, which is a normal amount. Plus, it's plasma not blood, so it's fine."

Job swallows hard. "You've lost weight Ruby, and given blood several times in the past few days. You're volume depleted, and possibly already in shock from Sam's death.

Do I need to go on?" As he speaks his voice softens, but his eyes are still flinty.

I try to swallow but my throat is full of sand. "I'm sorry, okay?"

"I'm going to get some blankets." He points at the machine and talks to Rafe. "Make sure she doesn't touch anything else." The reproof in his tone stings.

I look around as my head clears. Rafe's the only other person I can see. "Where's Amir and his sister, my number one fan?"

"They have other work to do. They left."

I hear Job in the hallway, slamming cabinet doors, and I roll my eyes. "He's acting like I tried to kill myself or something."

Rafe folds his arms and stares at me. "Did you?"

I snap at him. "Are you kidding me?"

"I don't make jokes."

"No, okay? I didn't try to kill myself. Geez."

"Riyah's not the only one who doesn't like you, but I'm trying really hard to rise above it. This kind of stupid behavior makes that hard, honestly."

My jaw drops. "You don't like me? Why? What have I ever done to you?" I ignore the voice that tells me how easy my life has been compared to his, compared to every Marked kid in America. I mean, my dad's dead, and my mom, well, I thought she was dead, but that can be said of every single one of them. Plus, they didn't have an aunt or uncle to pick up the slack. Or if they did, they all died too.

"I met Wesley a few weeks ago now. He's a good guy, and I like him. He's smart, he knows how to get stuff done, he's funny, and he's worked flat out since he got here. He's done everything I asked and more. He lost his mom, his dad, his home, and a girl he loved, and he did it without whining. Even so, he spent every spare second telling me about this girl, a girl he described as prettier than anyone he'd ever met. He said she was kind, generous, and the smartest person he'd ever met. He said she acted ten years older than she was. I don't have many friends, but I count Wesley as a friend, and no matter how depressed he's been, he never once gave up. And if he quit, his surrender would only impact him. Yours would doom us all."

I struggle to sit up. Instead of helping me, Rafe holds out one hand, and thumps me with two fingers right in the middle of my forehead. "Sit back, princess. I know you think I'm being unfair, but I ain't done yet, so you can listen until I am."

I breathe in though my nose, and out through my mouth like my uncle taught me, but I can't quite school my expression into a calm one. He's monstrous.

"Your boyfriend and I had to talk quite frankly about your first kiss, and how it made him feel. It was more than I wanted to know, but I do know it. And then you finally show up a few weeks later, and he's right. You've got something in your blood that stopped Tercera cold. He's immune, but for some reason his blood doesn't do nothing for us. Talk about highest highs followed by lowest lows. We put all our resources into finding you because we're dying. Not like in the future, at some point, possibly, maybe, but literally, dying right now, in front of my eyes. My friends, the only family I have left are covered in festering sores, and their organs are giving out."

"I know," I say, "but—"

"No, princess. Not your turn yet. We finally find you, running away like a sad little girl from WPN, an army at your back. Wesley gathers you up, so worried, so concerned, and do you run, sobbing, into his arms? Nah, not you. You recoil from him like he's your dirty uncle trying to grope you at Thanksgiving dinner. Turns out, in the past few weeks, you dropped Wesley like a hot potato, and you're in love with some Sam guy. Well, here's the thing. There's absolutely no chance that you're so devastated you can't go on, not for some guy you didn't love three weeks ago when Wesley got Marked to begin with."

I open my mouth, but Rafe shakes his head.

"My take is that you didn't love Wesley and you don't love this guy. You're a spoiled little girl who's used to getting whatever she wants, and now you're seeing the world for the first time. Entitlement at its finest."

I collapse back against the pillows. He thinks I'm a whiny waste of space. What if he's right?

"Oh, now you've got nothing to say?"

I look at my hands, because I can't meet his eyes. My fingers are still stiff with cold, but they're warming up as I huddle under the blanket, and the lost volume flows back into my body.

"I wanna like you, honestly I do, but we've got literally hundreds of thousands of lives hanging in the balance here, and your little broken heart doesn't matter to me. If it hurts your feelings that we see you as a blood bag and not a person, well, I ought to be sorry about that too I guess, but I couldn't possibly care about that either."

Job stomps over next to me, and glares at Rafe. He drapes a blanket over my legs, tucking it under each of them. "Feel any better?"

He's talking to me, but Rafe smiles and answers him. "Actually yeah, I do. How about you princess? You gonna survive your latest temper tantrum turned suicide attempt?"

"I'm always glad to know where I stand with people." I pull the blanket up to cover my chest.

Rafe glances at the apheresis machine. "Even so, maybe keep that far enough away she can't reach the control panel, huh?" He spins on his heel and marches out the door.

"I'm sorry, Ruby. I only caught the end, and I was upset with you too, but you didn't deserve any of that."

I collapse bonelessly against the pillows and close my eyes again. "Actually, I think I did. I knew not to increase the volume. You can't power through blood loss."

Job sits on the edge of the bed and puts his hand on mine. "Your heart was in the right place. It always is. And you've never been one to throw tantrums. He doesn't know you at all. You love Sam, and it wasn't some kind of girlish infatuation. I know that, and if he doesn't get it, or if Wesley doesn't, then screw them both."

Job does not know how to talk angry, but his indignant defense of me brings a smile to my face anyway.

"Do me a favor?"

I nod. "Sure."

"Don't touch the machine again, okay?"

I snort. "Smart aleck." I eat the stew Libby brought me, and even cold, it tastes better than Defense rations. I'm swallowing the end of it when a knock booms on the door, and two guards enter, guns in holsters on their hips. I recognize one of them.

"Sean?" I ask. "Right?"

He grins at me. "We asked to be assigned to watch you, along with a hundred other guards, but Rafe thought you might appreciate a familiar face. I knew you were special last week from the moment I saw you. It wasn't coincidence that you evaded that net."

I roll my eyes. Everyone wants things to be preordained, but we make our own luck. "What are you here for?"

"Routine check, boss's orders. We'll be checking every morning and every night, and we'll be standing guard around the clock. Not always me, of course, but I'll take my turn."

I bite my lip. "That sounds miserable, I'm sorry. I don't think that's strictly necessary."

Sean says, "People are excited you're here, but they know there's only one of you, and that can be a hard thing to stomach. It can do weird things to people." He gestures to the guard next to him. "This is Dax. You'll remember him too, I imagine."

I bob my head. "Hey Dax. How's your shoulder?"

He frowns. "It's healing up nicely, thanks. I'm sorry to hear that guy who shot me didn't make it back."

It's big of him to say it. I know he wasn't a fan of Sam. "Thanks."

"We're gonna do a sweep of each room, if you don't mind," Sean says.

I shrug. "Sure. I'm kinda stuck here for now. Sorry I can't help."

"Not your job."

Sean and Dax stomp from one room to the next while Job fusses over me, forcing another glass of water down my throat. I collapse back and close my eyes, trying to ignore the noise for a moment. I'm warmer, but still shaky and light-headed. My new guards wave bye and head for the door, which slams shut a few times as they exit. I sigh in relief and lean back against the pillows behind me.

The sound of heavy boots approaches and my eyes shoot open again. Rhonda's stalking toward me. I didn't hear her come in over the generator's humming, but I hear when she stomps close enough. She sounds like an elephant with a sore tusk. Maybe I'll actually see one of those around here if I ever get out of this plasma center. "What's this I hear about you trying to kill yourself?"

I roll my eyes. "Rafe's exaggerating."

Job shrugs. "Well."

Rhonda shoves him out of the way and swings her legs up until she's laying down next to me. The machine beeps to signal it's done, and Job circles to take out my IV. Rhonda doesn't speak while he's removing the needle and tubing, but when he wheels the machine away, she whispers. "What's going on, kiddo?"

I mean to explain to her how I wanted to help, and I saw Libby and I wanted there to be more of my plasma to work with, as many antibodies as we can pump out. I want to help the people dying all around me. I wanted to do something good. I open my mouth to say just that, but when I look in her eyes, the lies die on my tongue.

A gasp wracks my body. "I know I'm whiny, and a spoiled princess, but it hurts so bad Rhonda." The tears flow again and I hate myself for them. I'm not Marked, I'm not dying, I'm not even sick, but I kind of wish I was. Because then I wouldn't be at fault for everything, and left with nothing.

Rhonda pulls me close. "Oh baby, I'm sorry. I'm so sorry. It's all been so fast and you don't have time for any grieving. It's not natural, and it's not fair."

She's stroking my hair when I whisper again. "I dreamed of him when I fell asleep—well, I guess when I passed out. I thought I was dying, and he was waiting for me, and I. . . I didn't want to come back."

She pulls back to look at me. "Oh Ruby, no."

I shake my head. "Or maybe it wasn't that, I don't know. It was so strange, like I was in a hospital, or maybe a prison, or a psych ward from Before or something. I had to look and look, and run until my heart nearly burst before I found Sam, trying one locked door after another, but finally I found him, and Rhonda, in my dream he wasn't dead. He wasn't in heaven, either. He was warm, and gorgeous, and . . .alive." I close my eyes. "I know how the Marked feel when they see me. My heart filled with so much hope, so much desire, and it all collapsed like a house of cards when I woke up and realized it was some stupid dream."

Rhonda stares at me one second too long this time, and I see it in her eyes. Doubt.

"What Rhonda? You're not telling me something."

"No, I'm not hiding anything," she says, "I'm just so sorry you're hurting." She tries to pull my head back toward her, but I resist. Her eyes looked just like this when Job and Sam ate my candy and she guessed. Her lips pressed in the same thin line when I dropped Aunt Anne's ring in the lake and she tried not to rat me out. Her nose scrunched exactly the same when she knew that Job broke my telescope, but he tried to blame a bird.

"Tell me right now. What're you unsure of?"

She puts her hand to her face and rubs her lips. "It's nothing, I swear."

I squeeze her hand. "What?"

"I don't want to get your hopes up, and Sam wouldn't have wanted me to tell you, not now."

"Tell me what?" My voice cracks, and I think about Sam's eyes, so real, his hand, so warm. "What is it? You have to tell me. I'm sick of people deciding what I should and shouldn't be told."

She wrings her hands. "Sam wasn't normal."

I narrow my eyes, ready to defend him. "What does that mean?"

"He... he was part of some experiments."

"What kind of experiments?" I narrow my eyes at her.

"Defense teamed up with Science. Mom and Dad spearheaded it. They should've experimented on us, Job and me, but they were afraid. They couldn't do it. John Roth volunteered for the trial. Losing his wife and his other son did something to him. He wasn't the same again, Mom said. He was cold and mean after his wife left. He wasn't much of a father to Sam, I don't think."

"Back to the point," I say. "Sam's dad John volunteered to be part of the experiments? How does that impact Sam?"

"John was too old. But Sam wasn't."

I grind my teeth. John Roth offered his only surviving child?

"I'm not sure what Mom and Dad did exactly, but Sam's fast, really fast, and strong. He's stronger than he should be, even for his size. He's also quiet when he wants to be, like freaky quiet. And his reflexes are out of this world amazing."

"I sort of already knew all that. I'm not sure how that helps, though." His speed and agility didn't help him evade my mom's shots in the back. I saw the blood, so much blood.

"That stuff was all a side effect of their real goal. They were trying to find a way to boost the human genes enough that they could fight Tercera."

"It didn't work, I assume."

"No," she says. "Or I guess they don't really know. They scrapped the whole initiative. They had several test subjects other than Sam. One of them came in contact with Tercera, and before you ask, I don't know whether it was by accident or not, but either way, it didn't work. The little boy died even with their enhancements."

I close my eyes. They die when we try to treat for Tercera, and they die when we don't. So many little boys dying here now with the suppressant failing. Dying slowly is supposed to be a mercy, but watching all these kids with sores and desperate eyes, I'm not sure I believe it. "Beyond depressing."

"Sam had already changed when they shut down the program."

"Changed how?" I ask. "Just the speed and strength?"

"He heals super fast, Ruby."

My stomach falls and my breathing picks up. "What does that mean, exactly?"

"I saw Sam get shot once," Rhonda says, "during a training exercise. He was teaching a new girl how to shoot. The kid thought the safety was on when it wasn't, and she shot Sam in the foot at point blank range."

I bite my lip. "And?"

"Sam was out running laps with the rest of his patrol a week later."

When I don't respond, Rhonda says, "Ruby, he should never have walked again. That's the only reason I know about any of this. I confronted him, and he told me to talk to Mom. He wouldn't say anything else, so I asked her over and over, finally threatening to ask John Roth before she finally caved."

My hands fist into balls so tightly that my nails cut into the skin on my palms. "You're telling me he survived on that bridge?"

"Six gun shots to his chest?" She shakes her head. "I don't know, Ruby. If it were anyone else, I'd say no way."

"But it's not anyone else. It's Sam."

"I didn't mention it before for a reason, even at the tree, when I wanted to tell you so bad."

"If you told me earlier, I'd never have left Texas City. I'd never have gotten into a car headed this direction, away from WPN, away from Sam."

"Sam's a fighter, Ruby. If he survived, he'll escape himself. I know it."

"And go back to the Unmarked, with no idea we're here in Baton Rouge."

She shakes her head. "He's not stupid. He'll search for us here, and he'll find you. He knew the Marked thought you were the Promised, and he knew they were gathered at the bridge. I don't know what happened between you two, but he's different than he was when he's around you Ruby, more complete somehow. I saw that much, even if I tried to ignore it. If he feels for you even half of what you do for him, he'll torch the earth to find you. If he's alive, he will make it back to you."

"I can't sit around hoping he turns up like a lost dog."

I know the alleged stages of grief: Denial, Anger, Bargaining, Depression and Acceptance. After my dad died, I talked and talked and talked about them with a friend of my Uncle Dan. We spoke on the phone at least once a week for six months, before Tercera burned the world to the ground. In the last twenty-four hours, I skipped right over Denial and ran straight to Anger. After all, I saw Sam die. Denial didn't have much of a toehold.

Until now.

"You have to help me, Rhonda. Promise me you'll help me go after him."

She shakes her head. "You can't leave here. Your blood, it's too important. We can't risk you for some ill-fated rescue mission."

"I agree." Job walks around, sets a glass of juice down on the table near me, and pulls up a chair. "I knew Sam was... different. I've seen the signs for years. I saw him slice his leg on a branch once, and there wasn't even a scab the next day. It healed entirely overnight. I wondered about it yesterday, but I know he would never have wanted us to stick around and get caught. Besides. Even healing fast, six gun shots?" Job sighs heavily. "In any case, Rhonda's right. You can't leave, not now. You have to stay here. I can't leave either, as much as I might like to. Maybe we can send Rhonda."

I shake my head, but I'm not going to bother arguing with them tonight while I'm recovering from hemorrhagic shock. In fact, if they won't support me, maybe I'm not going to argue with them at all. I can go alone. I will do exactly that if I have to, just like Sam would come alone for me if I were still stuck in Galveston.

"You coming to bed?" Rhonda asks. "I can help you walk to the back if you want."

I hold up my hand. "I'll be back in a minute. I think I'm entitled to a few minutes to sip my apple juice in peace while I process the information you two both had and didn't share."

"To be fair, Sam didn't share that information either," Rhonda says.

I pretend that doesn't sting.

Rhonda and Job both head back to the two rooms in the back of the building. I should sip my apple juice as quickly as possible and head back to the room I'm sharing with Rhonda, but I can't, not yet. I close my eyes and think of Sam, my Sam. He might still be alive. How could I have left him? How could I have given in so easily?

When I open my eyes, a movement near the door startles me. Wesley stands up, and takes a step toward me, his features hard to make out in the light of a single candle.

"They may not be willing to help you, but I will."

# CHAPTER 7

My heart stutters. "How long have you been sitting there?"

Wesley grins a sideways smile. "I snuck in just before Rhonda returned, and with Dax and Sean doing their sweep, well. I didn't feel like you needed more people to deal with just then."

I bite my lip. At least he didn't hear Rafe tell me I'm a waste of space, but he sat quietly while I described my dream, and how much I longed for Sam to be alive. Of all people, Rhonda and Job won't help me return to Galveston to save Sam, but Wesley will? Why would he do that?

He crosses the room slowly, his dark hair falling into his eyes. My hand itched so badly to shove it back that night during spin the bottle. It feels like years, but it wasn't even a month ago.

He gestures at the chair. "Okay if I sit?"

I nod.

"I ran over to make sure you were alright. Rafe wasn't very reassuring. I don't mean alive, but *alright*. When Rafe stormed into the main office, fuming, and said you tried to kill yourself—" Wesley chokes. "It took a lot of restraint not to punch him when he told me what he said to you."

I think of all the times Wesley's taken care of me. Bringing me something to drink on work projects, making sure I reapply sunblock, helping me with my greenhouse plants. I haven't been fair to him, not even a little bit.

"I wanted to talk to you, but Rhonda reached you first and you were sort of huddled. I thought I'd give you a minute to recoup. I followed Rhonda all the way over here at a jog, but I don't think she even noticed me. Given the way things are between us, I figured she'd do you more good anyway." He looks down at the floor and my heart constricts. I haven't been fair to him.

I reach out and put my hand over his. "You've always been my best friend, Wesley. I'm sorry I've been... distant. That was wrong of me. I know the past few weeks have been awful for you."

When he turns toward me, the wound in his eyes pricks at my conscience. "Can you answer one question for me?"

I nod.

"You've been mourning Sam. Everyone can see it, and I understand why. But when I saw you last, you were telling me you'd liked me for years. You told me if you were Marked, you'd meet me."

I bite my lip. "Was there a question?"

"Oh yeah, sorry. When you weren't Marked, and I left without you, I was basically dead to you then. Did you mourn me like this? Were you devastated, and I don't know, broken?"

I shake my head. It's not a fair question, but then nothing in life is really fair. Nothing's black and white. That's the biggest lie we tell children, that there's a right and a wrong, when really life is about darker and lighter, and doing the very best you can while painting in shades of gray.

Even so, I can't lie, not to him. "No. I didn't."

He flinches and nods his head a little too many times.

I can at least explain. "You weren't dead, Wesley. You were sick, and I thought I was sick, but you weren't dead. You had years ahead of you, and I was galvanized to make progress toward something that might save you. I read my dad's journals frantically in quarantine as you know, and I discovered he created Tercera. For the first time I found evidence there might be a cure. You're the reason I was so desperate to leave so I could find it. I wanted to go after it right away and no one would help me."

"No one except Sam."

I nod. "If you had died instead of contracting Tercera?" I shrug. "I don't know. Maybe I would've mourned the same way, or maybe not. For what it's worth, I'm glad you aren't dead."

"If I'd been there, and he'd been Marked, I'd have helped you too. I've always believed in you."

Even when I kept changing sections, and I had no idea what path to take, Wesley supported me. He never cared about my indecisiveness, about my hopping around. He never badgered me or minded my indecision. "I know you would have."

He bobs his head, pleased I've acknowledged it.

"But I don't get it. Why help me with this? Rafe won't like it, and he's not the only one. Even if you aren't Marked, aren't they your people and isn't he kind of your boss?"

Wesley's cheeks turn red. "He's the Marked leader. Like you just pointed out, technically I'm not Marked."

"That's not really the point," I say. "You know what I mean."

He rubs his forehead, pushing his hair back. "Yeah, I do. Rafe's gonna be pissed. They all are, if they find out their magical cure slipped their cage. I'll help you, but Rhonda and Job are right. It'd be way easier to send Rhonda and a team or something."

I shake my head. "That won't work. WPN won't let anyone else in."

Wesley lifts his chin. "What makes you so sure they'll let you inside?"

I shrug. "My mom knows I lied about the blood key, which means I might still be Solomon's daughter." I shudder. "I doubt he'd kill me outright, even though he's pissed."

"Paternal concern?" Wesley's eyebrows rise. "Didn't realize he had much."

"No, he doesn't." I bark a laugh. "I've been thinking about it since we left. He didn't give a crap whether I lived or died, not really. He had an idle curiosity maybe, and a mild desire to see his bloodline continue, perhaps. But no, I'm not operating under the mistaken impression my sadistic, possible biological father cares about me. I know he doesn't, but I think torturing and punishing people is more his way than outright murder, and he still thinks he can mold me into what he wants, assuming I really am *his blood.*"

"That's messed up. And not reassuring me that helping you to go back is smart, if I'm being honest."

"The main reason he won't kill me is that I infected him with Tercera before I left, and then I shot him with the accelerant."

Wesley slaps his forehead. "Once you tell him you have the cure, he'll let you inside."

I shake my head. "It's more complicated than that, and simpler at the same time. I've been thinking about how he kept Tercera in his drawer, along with accelerant. He's maintained power over WPN all these years, multiple ports with their respective leaders, and he's consolidated and maintained control over sophisticated regimes with limited communications and mobilization. I imagine there have been numerous power grabs. He's claimed he has a religious right to rule, and he talks about God's will a lot. According to him, the spread of Tercera was God's will, to eliminate the wicked. How handy would it be to have a bit of God's own will that you could use to remove anyone who violated your will from the power structure?"

Wesley's lips part as he thinks and then he exhales heavily. "You think he darted anyone who got in his way, and then denounced them?"

"I imagine if we poked around, we'd find that some of the darted individuals made their way here, if any survived at all."

Wesley nods. "I think we might. Todd came from WPN. He never talks about who he was or what he did before, but he's remarkably competent and well-educated. I could see him being ambitious enough to require elimination."

I shrug. "Either way, I doubt King Solomon will tell anyone he's been Marked. I imagine he'll be hiding in his rooms, laid up with an unnamed illness."

"Because if he's been Marked. . ." Wesley spreads his hands melodramatically.

"That means God's forsaken him, by his own rhetoric."

"In that case, his troops won't care if you're the cure. They won't even know he's Marked."

"Ah," I say. "That's where you're forgetting a piece of the puzzle. My mom took my dad's journal. King Solomon won't need to be told that I hold the cure in my own body. He'll have read that book, and when I show up, his people will welcome me back with open arms by his own edict. I'll even have some leverage to get Sam back if he survived, or even if he didn't," I choke a bit, "to demand my dad's journal. I imagine David Solomon will do most anything right now to gain access to a little of my precious blood."

Wesley leans back in his chair. "It's not a bad plan, but it starts with part B."

I groan. "I know. I've got to get out of here first."

"Which isn't going to be easy to do, you know. That's why you'll need me."

"Why would you help me?" I ask.

His mouth turns up in the way it always has whenever he's going to make fun of himself. "Yesterday, Sam was dead without a doubt. The day before that, I didn't even know you liked him. I thought he kind of annoyed you, which made me happy because he's like some kind of god to the people in Port Gibson. It bothered me he was so close to your family for a while, but you never mentioned him except in passing."

I think about how I saw Sam a month ago, two. More. "He did annoy me. Actually, maybe I was jealous of him."

Wesley tilts his head. "Huh?"

"He was Job's best friend, and he worked with Rhonda. We all grew up together, from before we joined the Unmarked. Our families go way back."

"And?"

"Well, Rhonda and Job were close, like this matched set. When my dad died and I went to live with them, I never quite fit in, not like they did. Then Sam showed up, and he wasn't even related to them, but he slid into the family like a duck into water. He played outside with Job, digging forts in the dirt, and shooting rabbits and squirrels. He and Rhonda ran and jumped and fought with wooden swords."

Wesley taps his mouth with his index finger. "I can't see you doing any of those things."

I shake my head. "I read inside mostly, or played piano,

or studied with my aunt, and played with the animals. I cultivated plants, even then. I'm not a warrior, Wesley, and I'll never be a warrior. I'm too tiny, and too uncoordinated. Sam though, he did everything they did easily. I was always the odd one out."

"You wished you fit in with Job and Rhonda like he did."

"Yep. He never talked much, which aside from piano and reading was kind of my thing. He never played games with me and Job. That was the only area where he sat out, and I interacted with the family on my own terms. I assumed he skipped games because he didn't want to lose. That's probably why I never thought he was very smart, if I'm being honest."

"But he is?"

I blush this time. "He's smart, yes. He was nervous around me I guess, and he doesn't talk casually, even now. I almost have to pry opinions out of him."

Wesley frowns. "You asked me why I'd be willing to help. That's why. You have a lifetime of memories with Sam, and a week or two of actually thinking of him romantically and *being* with him. Those memories are new which makes them all fond and sparkly. You'll probably start to forget anything annoying, and focus on the amazing stuff that never had time to tarnish more and more and more."

I open my mouth to contradict him, but he holds one hand up. "I'm not trying to pick a fight with you. I'm telling you that even though he's gone, he'll never really be gone if he's dead. Pair that with the fact that you're mad at me for nearly Marking you, and I don't have a prayer."

I shake my head. "I'm not mad about that, I swear. I forgave you before I even realized I wasn't Marked, and once I wasn't Marked, I had no reason to be mad."

He puts his hand over mine. "You may not even realize you're still upset and that's okay. You're right to be mad. It was careless of me to go to the Last Supper at all, and worse still for me to interact with you in any way. Selfish, careless, unfeeling. I was an idiot, and your resentment is justified. Believe me, I'm angrier with myself than you could ever be. With Sam gone, but remembered through the lens of a hero, I'd be up against a truly undefeatable foe."

"Sam isn't your foe, Wesley. Alive or dead, he's not your enemy."

"Oh you're wrong there, Rubes. Dear, smart, quiet, strong Sam is my enemy, because we both want the same thing. And I really hope he's alive, and we can save him. Because if he's here, boots on the ground, it's a fair fight, and one I hope I can win. Real men forget their socks on the floor of the bathroom. Real men fill the sink with tiny hairs when they shave. Real men eat a sandwich in bed and scatter crumbs that irritate and frustrate. I can't compete with a ghost, but I can compete with a man, even if he's a super human, genetically enhanced, ridiculously good-looking one."

I flop back against the pillows behind me. "Wesley, this isn't a contest. You're wrong about that. Sam and you and me, we're all on the same side. I want you to help me save him, but not if you're doing it so you can badger me with how annoying he is later on, or lord it over his head that you had to save him."

"I promise not to lord anything over anyone, but that's all I'm going to promise. Haven't you heard, 'all's fair in love and war?' Well, in case you didn't notice, we're at war with WPN, and I'm in love with you. I'm not planning to lose on either front, no matter what that takes."

# CHAPTER 8

I barely sleep. I want my sleeping pills so badly. Every time I close my eyes, I dream of Sam, or Wesley, or Sam with Wesley's face, or Wesley with Sam's voice. I walk to the bathroom to pee several times, and almost trip over Job every time.

"Oh, it's you," he says each time, as though he's not watching my every move.

When the sun's first rays finally light the sky, I sit up in bed and throw the covers back. I need to get out of here and start back toward Galveston. The only problem is, I haven't had a single idea for how exactly I can escape with guards posted everywhere.

Even worse, Rhonda and Job are watching me like squirrels guarding the last acorn tree. They came out and checked on me three times last night before I walked back to my room to sleep. And finally, if I do miraculously escape all the guards and my cousins, there's still hundreds or maybe even thousands of Marked kids tracking my every move. The guards are on duty as much to protect me from overzealous fans as to keep me put.

I sure hope Wesley had some ideas while I tossed and turned.

When I leave my room and walk down the hall, I notice Job's already hunched over a book, making notes on a yellow notepad. That guy's a machine.

"Morning," I say halfheartedly.

He bobs his head, but doesn't look up.

"What can I do today?"

He points at a stack of books. "I'm going to look through those this morning for anything about antibodies in treatment of active viruses, and the suggested treatment methods."

"Wow, you're a nerd."

He turns back to grin at me. "Nerds are in right now, or hadn't you heard?"

"And we have approval on all this academic studying? I had the distinct impression Rafe wanted us to start trials posthaste."

Job shrugs. "He just left, actually. I told him this afternoon we'd have a decision on a number of participants for our first clinical trial, as well as specifics on how far along we want each group in terms of disease process. I'm thinking with the amount of antibodies we have, we need three patients per category, maximum of eight categories, recently infected like newborns or like Wesley, infected in the last two months, infected over a year, and suppressed for years, all varied by the age of the participant, and the amount of the dose." He scribbles down a few things, and then turns to face me. "Any input on my categories? Do you think gender matters?"

"Uh, I haven't looked at any figures on antibody load or Tercera's viral load, so I can't really say how much should plan to give them. Are you looking at one treatment versus several small injections?"

He beams at me. "Exactly, yes. Standard protocols, but the numbers are making my eyes cross. I'm going to check Libby and Rose's blood later today. I've compared mine and Rhonda's to yours already. For some reason, even several days out for Rhonda and thirty-six hours for me, with virtually continuous exposure to the virus, your blood still has ten times the antibody load of ours. I need to figure out what exactly your dad did to make yours so much higher, and to keep it that way. I keep coming back to the article Mom showed me about the stimulation of CpG oligonucleotides, but of course, that article's back in Port Gibson."

"It's almost hard to listen to," I say. "You sound exactly like her."

He raises both eyebrows. "Her?"

"Your mom."

"Thanks!" He grins like I proclaimed him the smartest man in the world. I guess I kinda did.

I roll my eyes, and walk toward the door.

Job hops up, hands in his pockets like that will somehow make him look like he's taking a stroll and not making sure I'm not making a break for it.

"You don't need to play jailor," I say. "I'm only headed out to look for breakfast. I'm guessing eating is still on the list of items I'm allowed to do, my nutrition being key to my body's replication of said antibodies…"

Job has the decency to look chagrined. "They have a mess hall around the corner on the main street. It's for the Marked leadership mostly, but Rafe said we're welcome there. Probably because we're busy doing administrative, or, you know, scientific work."

"I'd be welcome even if I planned to sit around and stare at the ceiling. After all, we've gotta fuel my body's miraculous work, right?" I roll my eyes heavenward.

"Should I bring you food? It doesn't look like you're even stopping to pee."

He shakes his head. "I ate almost an hour ago. A pack of adult diapers would be awesome though, if you see a pharmacy. That was a brilliant idea."

I shake my head as I walk toward the front door. He's kidding, at least I'm pretty sure he's kidding. Something about Job's not quite right. I like making sense of things as much as the next researcher, but he's obsessed. Like mother like son, I guess.

I've always assumed my aptitude with science came from my dad. With an uncomfortable pang, I wonder where it came from. What if I picked it up from being around them, but I'm not really like them at all, because we aren't really related? Maybe that's part of the reason I left Science.

What if I'm actually genetically pre-destined to hatch, not medical viruses or their cures, but in fact, evil plans, murderous attacks and abusive torture of my loved ones? I shove my thoughts into the back corner of my head and walk out the door into the freezing cold air of Baton Rouge's winter. I wave at the two armed guards, who fall in a half dozen steps behind me. What's the protocol here? Do I chat with them? Is it rude not to? Or is fraternizing distracting them from their job?

The skin on my arms pebbles in the cold air. I should've grabbed my coat before launching from my new, homey, guarded plasma center hotel. I'm sure that's the reason I'm shivering as I reach the long brick building, and not because I'm worried about my conspicuous honor guard and my morally bankrupt parentage.

I wrap my arms around myself and push through the front doors. My lip curls when the smell of burned oatmeal assaults my nose, but my traitorous stomach growls anyway.

"Hungry?" Amir waves the guards away and offers me a bowl.

I reach out and take it, almost equally grateful for the dismissal of the guard and the food. "Thanks."

A groan from behind him draws my eye. Riyah hands him her bowl. "Oh don't worry about me. I'll go back and wait in line again so you can fangirl in peace."

Amir looks upward briefly as if asking for divine help in being patient. "Don't mind her. Seriously."

I follow him when he starts walking toward a table. "Why does she hate me? I didn't ask for your breakfast, I didn't even know there was a line."

He sets his newly acquired bowl down. "She's tired of us all hoping for some kind of way out of this. Riyah was born a pessimist and life has confirmed that worldview almost every day of her life. She thinks you're more false hope, since even if your blood can cure us, there won't be enough to go around. She thinks we'd be better off without you here."

I understand that sentiment, actually. It's exhausting to know so many people have pinned their hopes on me. False hope is more dangerous than no hope in many ways.

And yet, almost every face in this cafeteria casts pleading glances my way. "What do you think?"

Amir shrugs. "I think the world surprises you sometimes."

"How so?" I ask. "Flooding, famine and plague?"

Amir snorts. "Sure, I guess all that is true."

"What did you mean?"

He smiles. "My parents thought they'd never have kids. They were in their forties when my mom got pregnant, and then after they had me, Mom got pregnant with Riyah two months later." He throws his hands up in the air.

"And then they didn't even get to watch you grow into adults."

Amir frowns. "That's true I suppose. We can make plans all day long, but no matter what plans we make, we can't know how they'll turn out. Kids when you know you can't have any, and that miracle happens twice? My parents saved money like fiends, worried they'd die before we got married, or made it through college. And then they died when we were barely nine years old, but not from old age like they feared, or cancer. They died along with everyone else on earth, from a virus that killed everyone who had grown out of adolescence."

"How does that not scare you? You're like the only optimist left in a world full of pessimists. Except we aren't even pessimists. We're realists because when the world surprises us it's always bad."

He shrugs again. "I don't think there's such a thing as false hope, not really. There's just hope and despair, and we get to choose each day which one to cling to. I always choose hope."

I wish I chose hope. I wish I thought the world was full of possibility, as much good as bad. "The world needs more Amirs."

He smiles at me and I'm a little lighter for it. Amir eats his oatmeal quickly and stands up. When I start to stand, he holds out his hand. "No, please don't rush. I have another batch of new cows to integrate back into a local herd, so I can't stay. Such is the glamorous nature of the science affairs we manage."

"Hey, does that mean the other cows made it back safely?"

Amir nods. "All but one. WPN's strangely quiet right

now. Our sentries say no one's leaving or entering. We've been preparing for an attack, but they seem to be hunkering down."

Almost like their leader is incapacitated. I take another bite to hide my smile. The oatmeal's flavorless, and burned flecks are spread throughout, but it's food, and I'm glad to have it. I stand up. "Maybe I can help you? Or learn about your operations, at least."

He shakes his head. "Please, eat another bowl, and maybe drink a little more." He points at the line. "We're all allocated one drink per day, but I'm sure they'd be happy to give you as much juice as you can drink. Not all of us have succumbed to our worst fears. Most of us are overjoyed to have something, anything, to hope for."

For the first time, even though someone's encouraging me to eat and drink so I can make more plasma, more anti-bodies, more of the cure, I don't feel like he sees me as some kind of walking medication incubator. I don't have room in my stomach for any more fluids right now, but I appreciate his concern.

"Thanks, Amir."

I stay seated until he leaves the cafeteria. Once he's gone, I stand up to leave.

Wesley's voice stops me. "Done already?"

I shake my head. "I was going to look for you."

His smile makes it easier to breathe than it has been for days. "Here, take mine. I'll grab another bowl."

"Nah. I've already eaten, but I'll sit with you."

He hands me a glass full of juice. "Surely you've got room for a few sips."

"That's yours."

He raises one eyebrow. "You afraid you'll get cooties from me?"

I think about our kiss and feel a little jittery. "No, but—"

"Relax goof, I was kidding. I haven't had any of it. I'd rather you drink it."

"You'd think I was sick, not the other way around, with how everyone's treating me."

He grins. "Can you blame them? Everyone wants to keep you healthy. Try to enjoy the special treatment."

I slide over next to him and whisper. "Have you had any ideas of how we might escape?"

He takes a big bite and chews slowly. I'm convinced he does it just to annoy me, because you don't need to chew oatmeal.

"Well?"

He nods. "Actually, we've had a stroke of luck. Rafe gave me an assignment to return to Texas City in the truck you stole from WPN. It's our most reliable vehicle, and I'm supposed to bring back the last cache of supplies left at the hospital. Rafe thinks we might need them here in the near future. And there's one more cow that had its calf yesterday. He didn't want to move them both until today."

That is a stroke of luck. It puts Wesley headed down to right near where we need to go anyway. "How can you take me with you? Think Rafe would allow it if we ask?"

Wesley throws an arm around me and shakes his head. "Not a chance. He's not letting you out of his sight." He whispers in my ear. "But if you pretend to get upset with me right now for being too friendly, yell at me and storm out, I could act upset and leave with another girl. Maybe one who's wearing a hoodie and who people can't quite place. As long as you were somewhere isolated, researching maybe, or reading when I leave, who would suspect?"

I'm not a great actor, but I give it my best. I shove away

from Wesley and stage whisper as best I can. "Stop acting like you're my boyfriend. I don't like you like that, not anymore."

"Yeah well, the guy you liked for a whole entire week *died*, okay? You need to get over it, because I'm still here, and he's not coming back. Not ever."

My jaw drops for real. Wesley would never, ever say something like that. Lucky for me, no one here really knows him well enough to guess. "You may as well be dead for all I care. Leave me alone from now on, okay?"

I spin on one foot and march out, keeping my eyes on the door. If I focus on my path out, maybe I won't stumble and look like an even bigger idiot. I ignore my two guards, and all the other eyes on me as I walk the two chilly blocks back to the plasma center. At least none of them approach or touch me, maybe because of the guards. I shudder. I need to get away from here. I feel guilty about risking myself when they need me, but I don't see another way around it.

Job glances up when I walk inside. I grab three books off the top of his mountain of resource material. "I'll take these, okay? My head kinda hurts, so I'm gonna read them back on my bed. Can you just tell anyone who asks that I'm tired?"

"You can take a nap, Ruby. I've got this, really I do."

I shake my head. "I want to help." I couldn't sleep if I wanted to. I don't wanna see the Wesley and Sam show, not again. I carry the dusty tomes back to my room. Luckily, Rhonda's gone when I go inside. I glance at the window, and I notice it looks out onto another parking lot in the rear, probably the employee parking or the bay where trucks made deliveries of plasma donation supplies Before. At least I won't be seen sneaking out of a window as easily as I would from the main road.

Speaking of being seen, my coat has a hood to hide my uncommon mop of hair, but I worry the coat itself will be too noticeable. Everyone watched as I marched through town yesterday in my puffy, down coat. Unfortunately, it's all I've got and without a coat I'll be even more eye-catching.

I force myself to read through the table of contents of the first book to identify anything we might use. I slog through the four most promising chapters without finding anything helpful. I have no idea when Wesley's coming exactly, so I may as well try and make myself useful. I begin skimming the second book with a groan, but a few chapters in, I uncross my eyes in relief when I hear a tap on the window.

I wave at Wesley so he knows I heard him, and then walk to the door in the little office area I'm using as a bedroom. I poke my head out and call out to Job. "Nothing in this first book. The second has a few spots that have potential."

Job says, "Keep me posted. I've found a few good studies we can use to model ours, I think. And I have enough plasma to start now. It should last us at least three rounds with sixteen participants each. I'll want you to check my math, of course, but we won't likely need to pull more plasma this week. I think after yesterday you need a substantial break."

"I guess." I don't think the people living here in Baton Rouge will agree a "break" from the antibody farm is a good plan, but now doesn't seem like the best time to argue since I'm planning on ditching them entirely.

Satisfied Job won't check on me for a while, I grab my as yet unpacked backpack and cross to the window. The hinges on the window creak noisily when I lift it the first inch. Wesley and I both freeze, nose to nose, separated only by the dirty glass. A split second later Wesley ducks down, presumably in case Job heard and came to check on me. After a count of ten, I assume Job isn't coming and start to lift the window again. Every whining, scratching sound the window makes causes my heart to beat a staccato rhythm, but eventually I lift the window high enough that I can crawl through the gap. Wesley steadies me as I emerge.

He also holds out a darling, sapphire colored peacoat.

"What's that?" I ask.

He cocks his head and lifts an eyebrow. "I thought you'd want to change your outerwear. That huge down coat is totally last season."

I roll my eyes.

"Seriously, I imagine people will recognize that puffy thing." He glances at my dingy old coat disdainfully.

For some reason it annoys me that he's solving a problem I had already identified. I know it's irrational, but I yank the gorgeous coat out of his hands crabbily, and stuff my puffy jacket back through the window. The new one fits me perfectly, and the bright, combed wool, with a double row of shiny wooden buttons transforms me into a new person. It's even topped with a hood that will cover up my hair and face. In spite of my baseless annoyance, I manage to squeak out, "Thanks. I really like it."

He shrugs and takes my backpack.

"Where's your bag?" I ask.

"Already in the truck."

We walk along the alley until we reach the main road. Wesley reaches his hand out and holds it over mine, hovering suspended in air. Close, but not touching. His eyes seek mine out and he angles his head, as if to make sure I remember the plan. "Go ahead. I remember I'm supposed to be your new, pity girlfriend. Whatever."

His warm hand covers mine, and our fingers interlace smoothly. It feels right, like popsicles in the summer, like popcorn and an old movie on a Saturday night, like the sound of generators whirring, like swimming in the big drainage-basin-turned-pond off Bridewell Lane. Like everything about home that I miss now I'm here in Baton Rouge.

If Wesley wasn't Marked. If I had gone with him. If my dad hadn't created Tercera, and I hadn't gone off to try and save Wesley, maybe we'd be walking down main street in Port Gibson right now, on our way to our respective Paths, respectable Unmarked citizens. Maybe Sam would still be there too, and I'd never think about how he doesn't have much to say, but he's thinking about everything all the time. I'd never want to let go of Wesley's hand to ease the guilty ball forming in the pit of my stomach. I wouldn't have to grit my teeth and hold onto it anyway.

I need to do this to get back to Sam, so I do it.

I'm not paying attention to anything around us, but I feel Wesley's hand stiffen and he swears.

I look around, but I don't recognize anything concerning. "What's wrong?"

"My friend Mike's walking up ahead. He helped me out when I first arrived, and he's gonna want to know who I'm holding hands with. He'll recognize you for sure."

My hand shakes, and my breathing picks up, until Wesley spins me around and pushes me back against the concrete wall of the paint store we're walking past. His head leans down and I realize what he means to do. He's going to kiss me, because his friend won't interrupt that. If we're kissing, they won't look too closely, they'll walk on by, and hound him for the details later. Wesley's face lowers over mine, hovering in front of mine exactly like his hand did. Asking permission without asking. Time stands still. His hair falls forward in the way I used to swoon over.

He won't push it. I can stop him. I should stop him, because it's not Wesley's beautiful mouth I want on mine, not anymore. I should turn my head, or say no, or come up with another plan like tying my shoe. I should stop him right now before his lips touch mine. Before it's too late.

I don't stop him.

I think about how last time he kissed me, I prepared first. I spent days dreaming of it, imagining it, and then that night, I did my hair, picked my outfit, and I even borrowed lip gloss. Shiny lips, and gobs and gobs of expectations. This time, I know this isn't going anywhere. It's not important how I look, or what I'm wearing, because this means nothing. Except when his lips meet mine, a shiver runs from my mouth down to the pit of my belly. Instead of kissing me, and then letting me go, like he did in that dark shed, we're standing in daylight on a busy street. When Wesley's mouth opens a little, mine follows his lead. His arms wrap around me and draw me closer, and I sigh into him.

For some reason, his words from last night zing through my head. "Sam is my enemy, because we both want the same thing," and "I'm in love with you."

He meant those words, I can tell. His lips aren't simply pressed against mine in some game of make-believe, they're worshipping me. His arms aren't wrapped around me, they're cradling me. His body isn't next to mine, it's molded against it, supporting it.

I wrap my arms around Wesley's waist and for a moment, just a moment, I lean into him. I let myself kiss him back. It feels good not to think about anything else for one short second, but then I realize it's been more than a minute or two. I've let the world disappear for too long.

I push on Wesley's chest and he stumbles back, his eyes hooded, his lips swollen. He glances up and down the road, and then a lazy smile takes shape. "I guess they're gone."

I cock one eyebrow. "I guess they are."

He gestures up the street. "Well, should we be on our way?"

I stuff my hands in my pockets this time and start walking. Wesley doggedly follows, sliding his arm through the crook of my elbow. A moment later we turn a corner and head down a side street. "Truck is right up here. I don't know why you're so pissy. We gotta maintain appearances or we won't get out of here to save dear old Samuel."

"Oh?" I ask. "Is that what you were doing back there? Worrying about saving Sam?"

"Is that what you were doing?" He shrugs. "Can I help it if I'm talented and convincing? There are no small roles, you know, only small actors. I'm not a small actor, and I always rise to the occasion." He smirks.

Before I can craft a biting retort, I notice movement up ahead, a mother sitting in a rocking chair in front of a picture window, holding a swaddled baby. It's pristine, like a print from Before. The mother leans over the child, a tiny hand clasped around a single finger. When I notice the mother is Libby and the child is Rose, something in my heart eases.

Until Libby looks up at us. When I saw her last night, the Mark was gone, her forehead beautifully clear. The sores on her arm and neck were healing up, the weeping gone, the skin turning the shiny reddish-pink of new skin. Today, the Mark's back. My eyes shoot frantically to Rose, whose forehead is still free of any rash. But the fact remains, even with a liberal dosing of my blood, Libby isn't cured. She's still dying.

I stop dead in my tracks and shake my head.

I left Sam back at WPN because I thought there was nothing I could do to save him. I knew if I escaped the island, I could help the people here. Now Sam might be alive, and nothing on earth could have made me leave his side if I knew that at the time. But I'm here now, and if he were able to talk to me, I know what Sam would say. He'd tell me that he can take care of himself. Or even if he can't, my duty isn't to any one person, not now, even if that person is him.

My head begins shaking, and my mouth dries up like a tumbleweed. I couldn't speak a word if I wanted to, but Wesley understands.

He pulls me against him and our fingers interlace again. His hand squeezes mine tightly. His breath ruffles the hair on the top of my head when he finally says, "You aren't going with me to Galveston today, are you?"

I'm so sorry, Sam. I'm always sorry, always a disappointment. But no, I'm not.

The babies here need their moms, and I'm their only hope. As much as it pains me, and as much as I love Sam, and I really do, I can't walk away from them, no matter the pain it causes me.

# CHAPTER 9

I hear shouting before I even walk through the door of the plasma center, which isn't a good sign.

"-could you not know where she is? And you didn't think to mention that Ruby thinks her boyfriend isn't dead until now? Once she's already missing? Your recklessness borders on stupidity. Frankly, I'm assuming you're involved in her escape."

Rafe whirls around when Wesley and I walk through the door. He stands with his booted feet spread wide, and his fists clenched at his side. His head pivots around and when he recognizes me, he breathes a huge sigh of relief and his hands unclench.

"I haven't escaped." I frown. "You can pull the bamboo shoots out from under their fingernails, oh esteemed leader."

Rafe fumes. "Where have you two been? Job said you were in your room, but your window was wide open and your bag was gone."

Wesley holds his hands up, palm out. "You need to calm down, dude."

Rafe steps toward Wesley, the muscles in his arms quivering. He should look silly with his mohawk, his combat boots, and his baby face, but something about his eyes frightens me. Resolve maybe? Determination?

Rafe enunciates each word. "I am calm."

Wesley's shoulders square and his hands ball into fists, which really isn't helping anyone cool down.

What's wrong with boys?

I step in between them. "We were leaving, Rafe. There's no point in lying about it. Wesley was going to give me a ride as far as Texas City. Sam might be alive, and I couldn't let that go, not without going after him."

Rafe grabs my arms and shakes me. "You stupid little princess. Even knowing how badly we need you, knowing you may be the only person who can save all of us, a hundred thousand people relying on you, and you'd risk your life?" His grip is tight, and in addition to rattling my teeth, my arms ache where his fingers press into them. "You'd risk all our lives because your boyfriend *might not* be dead?"

Wesley throws the punch over my right shoulder and when his fist connects with Rafe's face, his hands release me. Rafe flies backward and slams into a metal table covered with instruments, which clatter noisily to the ground. Seconds later, Rafe launches himself at Wesley. I jump back against the wall, trying to stay clear of the two brain-dead idiots pounding on each other.

"Job!" I point at them in frustration. "Do something."

He throws his hands up in the air. "What am I supposed to do about it?"

"I don't know," I say, "but you're a guy. Don't you know what to do?"

Job splutters. "I've never hit anyone. I have too much sense for that."

We both look on, horrified, but unsure how to stop it.

Rafe handles himself well, but Wesley's got thirty pounds on him. He's wiping the floor with Rafe's ridiculous mohawk when the door opens and people stream inside. Rhonda, combat boots thumping on the tile floor, followed by Todd, eyes wide as saucers as they take in Wesley pounding Rafe to a pulp on the tile. Three more people follow, and two boys I don't know in black coats and black pants stand on either side of a thirty something man with a neck tattoo. A tattoo of a cross, of all things.

Wesley drops Rafe and sits back. "Uh, we were having a minor disagreement, but I don't think we needed all of you in here."

Rafe sits up and wipes the blood from his lip on his sleeve. He spits red all over the floor. "What's going on?"

Todd glances from Rafe to Wesley and back. He shakes his head once and rolls his eyes. "We have a messenger from WPN, sir."

"Sir?" Neck Tattoo scoffs. "This kid's your boss? How the mighty have fallen."

Todd swears and steps toward him menacingly. "One touch and you can stay right here with me."

Neck Tattoo flinches backward satisfyingly.

Rafe stands, leans against the wall, crosses his arms, and glares at Todd. Rafe's going to have an impressive black eye, but somehow it makes him look tougher. "What's the message?"

Todd shrugs. "He won't tell me. He said his orders are to talk only to the leader of the Marked."

Neck Tattoo looks down at Rafe, and for the first time I understand the phrase 'looking down your nose' at someone. Neck Tattoo stands a few inches taller than Rafe, which means he towers over most of the Marked kids, literally looking down at them. He thinks because he looks his age and he's healthy, that he's better. Which means he buys into David Solomon's propaganda, that WPN citizens are somehow chosen of God, and anyone infected with Tercera deserves it.

He's a moron.

The Marked may look like kids, but they're really late teens or early twenty somethings. They watched their parents, their caretakers, the government, and the leaders of the world die. The ones who survived picked up the broken pieces of what remained and crafted a world out of it. They look like kids, but they run their own organization, one that feeds and clothes and cares for hundreds of thousands of people. They grew up fast, but their bodies don't reflect that growth, not physically.

Rafe isn't a kid. He hasn't been a kid in a decade. But this guy can't see past his body, his stature and his disease, which is what makes Neck Tattoo the smallest, sickest person in the room.

"King Solomon would like to make you an offer. He's holding the prisoner known as Samuel Roth, whom you left for dead."

My heart lurches in my chest, but I bite my lip so I won't speak. This message is for Rafe, not me.

Neck Tattoo continues. "Our excellent healers worked a miracle to save his life and continue to care for him, even as we speak. His father runs the Unmarked. They're willing to provide a handsome ransom for him, but King Solomon doesn't want a ransom. He doesn't care about the Unmarked, and WPN doesn't need their money or their resources. King Solomon wants for nothing."

Rafe stares at the man, eyes wide, head cocked sideways. I expect him to say something, but he doesn't open his battered mouth, or even so much as grunt. I already know how he feels about the idea of wasting resources or risking my life to save one person, even if it's a person who's dear to me and strategically valuable.

And at the end of the day, the Marked might benefit from supplies, but the only thing they all desperately need is my blood.

Even so, hoping Sam's alive and hearing that he is are vastly different. My heart cracks in my chest and then knits back together. Hope soars inside of me that it might be true, but despair follows closely on its heels. Because if he survived, that means I really did abandon him. He's being 'cared for', which probably means he's being mistreated horribly. He's valuable, but that doesn't guarantee anything, not with Solomon. I believe that he doesn't care one iota about a ransom, and I've seen firsthand that he wants for nothing.

Actually, that's not quite accurate, although Neck Tattoo has no way of knowing. Solomon wants something badly. He wants me, and not because I'm his daughter.

I wonder how quickly Rafe will turn him down.

"And?" Wesley asks. The left side of his jaw is puffy and the knuckles on his right hand are bruised and swollen.

Neck Tattoo cocks his head sideways and shifts his gaze to study Wesley. "Who are you to be asking me questions? I don't answer to you."

Rafe growls. "Out with it, idiot. What does your king want from us?"

Neck Tattoo frowns. "King Solomon offers you two boons today, as he's in a generous mood. He's willing to release this Samuel Roth into your care. You can trade him to the Unmarked for whatever supplies and materials you may need. He's also willing to cancel all plans for the Cleansing, or the ritual removal of all Marked persons from the Earth. He believes God may be willing to grant you a reprieve. His daughter actually pleaded for clemency for the Marked recently. After careful prayer, he wants to offer you that opportunity."

Rafe lifts his chin, his eyes flashing dangerously. Faster than I thought possible from anyone but Sam, he whips a gun out and crosses the room to where Neck Tattoo stands. He shoves the barrel up against Neck Tattoo's head. "I've heard about this Cleansing. Your boss intends to murder every single one of my people. He's doing this to make the world pure again, to remove the virus that threatens your more valuable lives. Your boss thinks we're nothing, and that if we don't agree to his terms, we'll just roll over and die, does he?"

Neck Tattoo swallows slowly and we all watch as his Adam's apple bobs. "He doesn't believe there's anything you can do to stop it, no."

"Is that so?" Rafe cocks his gun. "Is that what you think?"

Neck Tattoo narrows his eyes and his nostrils flare. "I think you can shoot me, a lone man who came to deliver a message, but that's not the same as facing off against an entire army of properly equipped and well-nourished men bent on ending a threat to their families and livelihood, especially since God stands with us."

I watch the muscles in Rafe's arm work as his finger tightens and releases on the trigger, but after two more big breaths, he steps back and lowers his arm. "Your precious king offers us these two boons . . .if what?"

Neck Tattoo swallows again, eyes darting intermittently toward the gun resting at Rafe's side. "King Solomon will promise not to proceed with the Cleansing, and will give up any plans to do so in the future."

"Not much of a sacrifice since we're all dying anyway, but you've mentioned that. Get on with it." Rafe angles his hand to showcase the gun, cocked and ready even if it's not shoved against Neck Tattoo's temple anymore.

"He will also surrender Samuel Roth."

"Are you a wind up toy?" Rafe snorts. "You've said all this. Solomon won't try to kill us without provocation, and he'll give us a prisoner we can trade in exchange for a few muffin tins, or some cases of supplies." Rafe shakes his head in disgust and steps back. "For those great prizes, *what does he want in return?*"

"Something small," Neck Tattoo says. "Something easy. He wants a face-to-face meeting with his only daughter who you stole from him. Ruby Solomon got into a fight with her mother and ran off a few days ago, and you snatched her on the bridge before she had time to consider what she was doing and come back home."

I'm staring right at this idiot and he has no idea who I am.

Rafe quirks one eyebrow. "Why would she run away with Marked kids, and if she did, why would he want her back? Won't she be Marked?"

Neck Tattoo shakes his head. "Her father prayed for her safety, and he's sure she's remained unharmed, even in the midst of this terrible affliction and danger." Neck Tattoo gestures around the room. "His power and faith are that great."

"Apparently the Mark only appears on people God has forsaken." Rafe growls.

Neck Tattoo shrugs. "I only know what King Solomon says."

I choke off a laugh so I can form words. "I'm confused about why this little princess would fight with her mother and run away from a chance to be heir to such wealth and power. Perhaps your king isn't as wonderful as you think."

Neck Tattoo smiles a toothy smile at me, but there's no joy in it. "Clearly you've never met her. The daughter's an ingrate and a brat. King Solomon recently found out she's alive, and he showered her with presents. Unfortunately, she couldn't follow basic rules. I think he's better off without her, but the King wants what the King wants, and only God can fully understand at his level. He wants to help her, maybe it's to do God's will. Or it could be because his wife couldn't have any more kids, so he's got a soft spot for this one. God spared her life in all this madness, so there must be some kind of purpose in it, even if I can't see it."

I can't even. "So it's an fair trade in your mind? King Solomon's daughter, for a random prisoner, who we can ransom to the Unmarked for a small fortune?"

"He's hardly a random prisoner. He's the best marksman we've ever seen and God worked a miracle in sparing his life. Possibly to get King Solomon's daughter back. I don't know." Neck Tattoo squints at me, finally glancing up at my forehead. He curses. "You're her, aren't you? You aren't Marked. Even though you're here, in this place, and His Royal Highness said you couldn't get it. He said his prayers would keep you safe, and thank the Almighty, they worked."

Solomon's so full of crap, I can barely believe anyone listens to a thing he says. I roll my eyes. Rhonda barks a laugh.

Job bangs the table before laughing heartily. "Her father's certainly keeping her safe, and he's probably up in heaven. Maybe Solomon's not so much delusional as truth challenged."

I love Job.

"You're right, Neck Tattoo," I say. "Your King Solomon thinks I'm his kid, the ungrateful brat who doesn't accept any discipline. My name is Ruby, only I prefer the last name Behl to Solomon."

Neck Tattoo's entire demeanor changes now that he knows who I am, or who he thinks I am. "One clarification, your highness." He bows to me, like he literally bends his body in half. "He doesn't require your commitment to stay in Galveston with him. He wants to talk to you in person, but that's all. After that you're free to go. He said you care about this Samuel. You can leave Galveston with him, but only if you talk to King Solomon personally first. He wants the chance to apologize to you. He knows your life has been hard, and he might have come down a little too sternly. He wants a chance to get through to you, to explain. He wants you to know what he's offering for your future."

"He's trading someone he knows is important to me as a prisoner and demanding I return. And he's doing all that so that he can show me how much he loves me?" My face couldn't be full of any more skepticism, and still Neck Tattoo seems to notice none of the inconsistencies.

Rhonda crosses the room to the door. "Is that the entire message?"

Neck Tattoo glances at me. "Should I answer her, Your Highness?"

Oh good grief. "Yes, yes, answer anyone who asks anything."

He nods. "That is the entire message. Your father wants me to stay with you to ensure your safety and your speedy return. I'm entirely at your disposal until we reach Galveston safely."

My safety? More like Solomon wants his walking cure to make it back alive, at which point good old Wannabe Dad will be the biggest threat to my survival. Will Neck Tattoo help me against him? I think not.

"I have one more question," I say. "When does my loving, devoted father require my presence?"

"I don't understand," he says.

Wesley grunts. "She's asking how long we have to decide."

"He sent me with a vehicle, and the trip shouldn't take more than eight hours. He will allow two days for the Marked rabble to make up their minds. If he doesn't hear from them within three days time, he'll assume you're being held against your will, and he'll launch the Cleansing now. The new primary aim will become freeing his daughter. The destruction of the infected will be a secondary, albeit important, goal."

"So basically," I say, "send me and he'll give the Marked a little present of my boyfriend. Don't send me and he'll come take me. That sounds about right."

"You don't know him well enough yet to interpret his meaning, Your Highness. I assure you that he has your best interests at heart. Once you hear him out it will all become clear."

Arguing with Neck Tattoo is pointless. I shake my head at Rhonda.

"I'm sure this will require some discussion, which will not be improved with your presence," Rhonda says. "I'll show you out."

Neck Tattoo bows. "If I'm allowed, I'll stay with Her Highness to ensure her safety. I promise not to say a single word."

I laugh out loud. "You most certainly aren't needed for that. As you already mentioned, I'm protected by God himself. I'm sure additional body guards aren't necessary. Follow Rhonda, please. And I can't bear to think of you as Neck Tattoo for another second. Please tell us your name."

He bows. "My name is Arthur Fenton, Your Highness."

"Stop calling me Your Highness," I mutter.

"As you wish," Arthur says, "but I'd rather stay, if you'll allow it. Better safe than sorry."

I shake my head. "I won't allow it, and I spend all my time being sorry lately. I'm used to it."

Arthur's brows draw together. "I don't understand."

"Oh forget it. Just get out, I don't need you here."

After a few mournful glances my direction, he finally follows Rhonda outside.

No one speaks for a full minute after he leaves. Not that it matters. I already know Rafe's position on this particular point. Solomon's word isn't at all reliable, so his assurances he won't Cleanse the Marked are useless. The only thing we stand to gain is Sam, or from Rafe's perspective, whatever ransom his dad will pay. My stomach lurches at the thought of what Solomon might do to Sam if we turn him down, but I know Rafe won't care.

When I think about Libby's Mark returning, I can't even blame him.

"Obviously we aren't going to take his deal," I say. "And I know you were pissed earlier, but Wesley and I came back because I saw Libby, and her Mark is back."

"What?" Job leaps up. "When?"

I shrug. "It was gone yesterday. We all saw it. I doubt she has a lot of mirrors, but when we walked by today, we saw her rocking Rose. Rose's forehead is clear, but Libby's Marked. Again."

Job closes his eyes. He looks as sick as I felt. He pinches the bridge of his nose. "Well, that's why we're going to set up a study group. We're going to test various treatments and see what we can develop. In the meantime, we'll work with Rhonda's blood, Wesley's and my own as well, to see if we can boost our antibodies so we'll have more than one person's immunity to work with. Even now, we might be able to distill enough antibodies from our plasma to boost our trials."

Job paces back and forth so frenetically I can barely follow what he's saying. "This is a setback, sure, but we knew this was complicated. We still have a lot to learn, but we'll do whatever it takes. Right Ruby?"

I nod because I will, but it hurts to think of Sam waiting for me to come for him. What will Solomon do when I don't? Will he really attack us, or will he die before he can make good on his threat? Three days... plus the last two. How long can he survive with the virus and accelerant administered in quick succession? I wish I knew.

Can the Marked withstand a well planned attack from several sides? And the question I worry about the most, will Solomon kill Sam when Rafe refuses, or ransom him to the Unmarked? My heart pounds so loudly, I can hear it in my ears. I do know one thing for sure. Sam would never forgive me for leaving these people to die when I might otherwise be able to save them.

"Solomon's infected and dying. Wounded animals lash out, so we need to assume he's going to attack immediately when we deny his request," Rhonda says. "Todd, what plans do you have in place? If I were Solomon, I'd use fire to flush you out of the city. Do you have an evacuation plan if he does? It's a dry year."

Todd grunts. "Baton Rouge is surrounded by waterways. We should prepare for the possibility, because you're right, that does sound like him, but I don't think it'll come to evacuation."

Rafe walks to the door and reaches for the handle, but his hand hovers over it. After a moment, he drops his hand, turns back around slowly and faces us. "We should prepare for an attack, because Solomon can't be trusted. But you're wrong in your guess about my decision. I'm not willing to give Ruby up, but with a large enough escort, and with Solomon's public assurances she doesn't need to stay, I think it's worth the risk to send Ruby to Galveston."

Wesley puts his hand up to his ear. "I'm sorry, I must've misheard you. I thought you said we should take Ruby down to see Solomon like he asked. You did know she shot him with Tercera, right? He's Marked. He wants her blood to heal himself, plus he still believes she's his daughter. He might say he won't detain her, but that lunatic does whatever he wants whenever he wants to do it, even when he doesn't have what he believes to be a justifiable claim."

Rafe nods, "There are risks for sure. Even so, I think the upside is worth the danger. Solomon can have a vial of blood straight from her arm if he must, but he can't keep her. Surely once he's healed, he will understand we need her back."

"You think this will really stave off the Cleansing?" Rhonda asks. "Because I think we've got fifty-fifty odds that his death halts the cleansing, and if we send Ruby like he wants, he might not die."

"If his word is good, and we can avoid an all-out war, that's great," Job says. "But I agree with Rhonda. We should let him die. The longer he waits, the sicker he gets, and the less likely he can make good on his threats. His death will cause total chaos within WPN, and they're unlikely to attack us in the wake of something like that, at least not anytime soon."

Rafe shakes his head. "If we risk sending Ruby back, we have a guarantee he won't attack. Even if his word isn't worth much, his people must hold him somewhat accountable."

Wesley drags his hand through his hair. "That's the beauty of using God, right? He can change his mind whenever he wants and claim it's God's will."

Rafe sighs heavily. "I've made my decision. You can keep debating the benefits back and forth, but for me, the risk benefit scenario has shifted."

"Why?" I ask. "Twenty minutes ago you were pummeling Wesley because we thought about doing what you're planning to do now. Why the reversal?"

Rafe scowls at me. "Everyone calls me Rafe. It's been my name ever since my mom died, but my real name is Raphael."

A memory bumps at the corner of my mind. "Raphael. I know that name."

Rafe's smile is grim. "My given name is Raphael Roth. You've been talking about Sam for days, and I never realized . . . Samuel Roth is my big brother."

# CHAPTER 10

"I hate to be the voice of reason here," I say. "Believe me, I do. But did any of you hear what we said earlier? Libby's Mark is back. My antibodies didn't heal her. I may have the key to immunity against Tercera, and we may even be able to develop my antibodies into something that works as a treatment, but we may never find out if I traipse right into crazy King Solomon's hands and you never see me again."

Rafe raises one eyebrow. "He says he only needs to talk to you."

I snort. "Snakes bite, it's what they do. You can't believe a thing his talking puppet says, because you can't believe a thing *he* says. He's beaten his wife for years, and she goes running right back to him." I shake my head. I can't talk to Rafe with all these people around, not about Sam, not like I need to. "Why don't you step into my office for a minute."

"What can't you say out here in front of everyone?" Rafe narrows his eyes at me.

"Remember I offered you the courtesy of discussing this alone," I say. "You've completely flipped your position on this since learning Sam's last name, and if you're making this decision because you finally have family, if this is a personal decision for you, then you're the worst kind of hypocrite."

Rafe flinches.

"You don't even know if we're talking about the same person," Rhonda says. "You look nothing like the Sam we know."

Rhonda's wrong, but I don't correct her.

"A simple test would tell us whether it's the same Sam," I say. "He told me about his brother. He said Raphael left with his mom, and Sam wished he had, too, but he stayed with his dad."

Rafe's jaw drops. "That's right."

I collapse into a chair. It's been a long day and it's not even close to lunch yet. "He said you went to see someone just before that, someone special to your mom. Who was it?"

Rafe's mouth forms an O. "He told you about that?"

I nod. "You think I want to save Sam because of a childish infatuation. You think I'm flighty. You think I'm a spoiled princess. You're entitled to the decision, but as a flighty princess whose life will be on the line if you deliver me wrapped in a bow back to my wannabe birth dad, I'd like to make sure you're actually pursuing your brother. Who did you go to see that day, the day your mom filed papers against your father?"

Rafe's face drains of blood. "We went to see my Uncle in prison, a prison on the beach. My mom loved him a lot, but he wasn't a very good man I don't think. Now you tell me something notable about that day."

I know what he's asking. "Your Uncle was Marked. He touched you and your mom. Sam got in trouble for asking Chaz a rude question, and he was pouting in the corner.

126

That's how he escaped being Marked, and why he went with your dad instead of staying with you and your mom. He went to Disneyland and you and your mom…"

Rafe closes his eyes. "He'd be Marked if he hadn't acted so rotten. Except he wouldn't be here with me. He was too old. He'd be dead."

"Look, I don't mean to be patronizing here," I say, "because I'm sure you know a lot about your brother, but eleven years is a long time. And if I know anything about Sam at all, it's that not much can stop him when he makes his mind up to do something. If he really is alive, and I trust Solomon so little that I'm still not positive, he probably won't need our help to escape. He's going to heal as much as he can, and then he'll escape. But he'll be smart about when and how he attempts it so he is positive it will succeed."

"Now that I actually support you going, you've changed your mind?" Rafe glances at Wesley and then back at me. He frowns and mutters, "Your girl's not very devoted is she, Wes?"

Wesley looks at Rafe's black eye, which has swollen up pretty badly by now. "You really aren't making good decisions today. Feel like going a few more rounds, huh?"

Job raises his hand, honest to goodness, like he's in class and wants the teacher to call on him. I grin a little bit. No one else even notices him in the back of the room. "What's up, Job?"

"Uh, I know no one's mentioned this, but I've been thinking about it. Ruby told me this morning that I sound like my mother, and I'm trying to fill her shoes as well as I can. It's hard because she trained me, but at the end of the day… I'm not her. She's so much better at all of this stuff. Any chance she might show up sometime soon?"

We need her badly. Job and I are the best we have, but we're way out of our depth.

Rafe sits down and puts his head in his hands. "I sent a team to our settlement at Hermanville, but I don't expect to hear from them quickly. I don't have many vehicles and I didn't have enough to spare for that. They took horses."

Job groans. "This should be our top priority. My mom should have all of Donovan's other journals too, and without those—"

My dad's last journal. It's the piece I forgot about in my zeal to do what Sam would want, not what I want.

I leap from my seat. "That's it, you're right. We should go to Galveston, but not just for Sam. We may not know where Aunt Anne is, but we need my dad's data. His journal's full of his notes and equations and technical details from his work on my antibodies. I only had time to really read the last paragraph. But he mentions that virus that eats other viruses, which became his main focus after he found it. Maybe it has more in there about that, like how he developed it, or where he found it initially."

Job's eyes light up. "Worst case, it should contain something about how he boosted your antibody production, and maybe details about how he created the antibodies in the lab in the first place."

"So voilá, we're all in agreement?" Rafe asks. "We're going to Galveston?"

"Heck yes we are," Rhonda says.

"Umm." Rafe clears his throat. "We are, but you aren't. I need you and your brother to stay here. Job, so he can start the tests he's been working on, and you Rhonda because I need the two of you as insurance."

I scratch my head. "Insurance against what?"

"I can't have you rejoining the Unmarked while my back is turned," Rafe says. "I know you say you want to help, but I know how we look. Now that you've been here, you'll be wondering whether we're a lost cause. You said yourself, your blood would keep every Unmarked citizen safe, and immunize them from Tercera. You could do that right now. Eliminate the threat that's hung over them for more than ten years, and do it at your leisure. Your blood works perfectly as a passive immunity, but not so well as a cure. Plus, it's home for you."

I clench my fists. "You think I'd abandon you, all of you? Leave you to die and run hide in a hole somewhere?"

Rafe shrugs. "You and Wesley snuck away this morning."

"I did sneak away." I scowl. "You didn't catch me, but I came back on my own."

He nods. "You did. Still, just in case you have second thoughts, or would that be third thoughts? If that happens again and Libby and her baby aren't on hand to guilt you into doing the right thing, well. I think I'll keep your cousins here to make sure you don't get confused about the right decision."

Wesley puts his hand on my arm. "Ruby always does the right thing."

He doesn't know how wrong he is, but I appreciate the support all the same.

"When do we leave?" Wesley asks.

Rafe grins and glances at Todd. I had forgotten he was even here. "That's cute. He thinks the two of them are going alone."

"I figured that, too," I say. "Who else is coming along?"

Rafe says, "Oh, just me and about fifty other soldiers."

"We can hardly sneak up on WPN with fifty people," I say. "They'll be watching that bridge closely."

Rafe sighs. "Fine, twenty. We can fit that many in two vans."

"What about my new guard dog?" I ask. "I think we're supposed to take him along."

"Indeed you are. For the record, this would be far easier if he didn't already know who you are." Rafe shakes his head. "I guess we'll make do. He's not going anywhere. We'll keep him locked up, and borrow his big, new truck."

I glance at Wesley. "We'll be taking the borrowed vehicle, and you'll bring your men behind us somehow?"

Rafe sighs. "Something like that, except you'll be riding with me. Your decoy will ride in the borrowed vehicle. Your dad may be a diabolical genius, but I didn't get to where I am by not thinking."

Wesley and Rafe work with Todd and Rhonda on the details, and I spend the rest of the day holed up with Job, trying to do the most I can to help before I leave him. Again.

I'm exhausted when Wesley and I climb into the van heading for Galveston the next morning. Waking up before the sun even rises makes me crabby. Wesley and I sit shoulder to shoulder, surrounded by some of the toughest kids I've ever seen. I wish Rafe's tactical team prioritized showering a little higher, but they seem nice enough otherwise.

The warm press of bodies, combined with my early start, and the lull of the car over the bumpy road proves too strong to resist. I fall asleep against Wesley's shoulder at some point, and wake with a jolt when the van stops moving.

"What's going on?" I ask.

"Pit stop," Wesley says. "Refueling the vans. You should get out and stretch your legs while you can."

I glance out the window and already a handful of guys are peeing into the weeds along the side of the road.

Luckily their backs are to me. Eww. I think about staying in the van, but ultimately the urge to move prevails.

I climb out and look around. A sign for the Lone Star Alligator Processing Plant proudly proclaims it's the 'Best Meat Processing in Texas.' I shudder. Did people Before really eat alligator? I guess a few things have improved.

"Where are we, anyway?" I ask.

Wesley leans against a tree. "Near Winnie, Texas, or so they say. It wasn't much more than a blip Before. It's a ghost town now."

The sun's almost directly overhead. Its rays warm my face enough that I optimistically slip out of my coat. My skin immediately pebbles in the cool air, but I close my eyes and breathe in and out slowly. The sunlight eventually heats my arms and the goosebumps dissipate.

"Did you get a nice nap?" Wesley asks.

I nod. "Sorry about falling asleep on your arm."

He shrugs. "Why were you so tired? We didn't have to get up that early."

I open my eyes. "I stayed up most of the night with Job, helping him wade through some research he found on oligonucleotides. They're pretty complex and it was a bit of a struggle for both of us. I wish we knew where Aunt Anne was. I feel bad they're stuck with the B team. The Marked deserve better."

"I know you feel pressure," Wesley says, "but you don't have to stay up all night. You won't do anyone any good if you work yourself to death."

"It's nice to do something other than provide bodily fluids." I glance back at the kids stretching all around us, and when I speak, it comes out as a whisper. "They're all circling the drain Wesley, and we're running out of time."

"You're acting like it's your fault somehow, and it's not. It might be your dad's fault, either dad actually. It might be

131

your aunt's fault even, since she sat on the information she had about your dad's lab for so long, but any way you slice it, none of this is your fault."

"If I saved my dad ten years ago like I should have, or if I'd remembered anything about what he did to me when he injected me. If I'd listened to you earlier and never gone to WPN, if if if. There are so many ifs, and all of them touch on me in some way. Maybe no one thing is my fault, but it's hard to shake the feeling that if I had done better in any way, this might have gone down differently."

He leans against a tree trunk. "You can't live your life like that. You can't change the past, none of us can."

"I know that, but I can't help thinking about my parents, and how I might have been doomed from birth."

Wesley slides down next to the tree and pats the ground next to him. "What does that even mean?"

Of course he doesn't get it. "Your dad loves you and he loves your mom, and he's a little hard on you maybe, and you have struggles, but he has his crap together. He runs Port Gibson as well as he can, serving others and providing for you guys."

"I guess so." Wesley's eyebrows draw together. "But what does that have to do with—"

"Your mom's a great lady, too. Dedicated to your dad and to you. She spends all her time working to better the lives of everyone in Port Gibson."

"I won't argue with you there. My mom's the best."

"My mom, on the other hand, is a mess. She lets her husband beat her, and she chose him over her own daughter when she had a chance to do the right thing. Not to mention, she left her first husband and got pregnant in the process. No one knows for sure whose baby I am."

"You could get a blood test, you know. We've lost a lot of tech since the Marking, but I'm sure Job could test your blood or hair against Solomon's. Or his own, for that matter."

I throw my hands up in the air. "I don't know whether I even want to know. My options are a wife-beating, sadistic and probably sociopathic dictator who undisputedly annihilated hundreds of thousands of government workers to grab power, leaving millions and millions without guidance or resources. He uses God to suppress his people, for heaven's sake. Or, if door one isn't appealing enough, behind door two, I have a mustache twirling scientist who developed a virus, and possibly released it. That virus wiped out the majority of the population of the Earth over a period of just a few years. Don't even get me started on how he almost certainly stole me from my mom, and potentially my dad to spite them, and kept me in hiding for six years. I've been over it a million times and I honestly can't decide which father would be worse. I'm leaning toward David the name-changing Thomas-wannabe-Solomon, but Donald Carillon slash Donovan Behl is a disturbingly close second. Taking a kid who isn't yours. . . I mean. These are my options for parents, Wesley. How could I not be profoundly messed up?"

Wesley takes my hand in his and squeezes it. "You aren't your parents. You're nothing like any of them actually, other than the scientific brilliance bit."

"You haven't met her yet, but I'm the spitting image of my mom."

"Wow, she's good looking. If you end up saving Sam and reuniting in a blissful sea of romantic contentment, it's good to know I have options. . ."

I slug his shoulder and he winces and rubs it. "Go easy on my gorgeous body, lady. You already broke my heart."

"Knock it off," I say.

He shrugs. "All I'm saying is, that fake kiss yesterday

was about the happiest I've been since. . . Well, since the day I got Marked. Which should've been a crappy day, if you think about it. Instead it's one of my best memories."

"Doesn't hurt that you didn't actually *stay* Marked."

He shakes his head. "I didn't know then that your blood would save me. I thought my life was ending, and I still walked around smiling like a moron."

"Until I didn't show up at the tree."

He shivers. "That was a cold few days. I waited two full days, you know, even though at that point I was grasping at straws. I'd have waited a third, but I heard some guards talking. They said you weren't Marked even though I was. I'm selfish enough that it was a very low day."

I close my eyes and lean my head back against the tree. "I'm sorry I hurt you Wes."

"No."

When I open my eyes, Wesley's face is only a few inches from mine. He pokes the space between my collar bones with his finger. "You're lugging around this Santa Claus sized sack of guilt. I won't have any part of it. I refuse to allow you to add me to that burden."

His blue eyes, full to the brim with care and concern for me, crack a corner of my heart I didn't realize was still intact. I've felt nothing but pain for so long, the idea of feeling something good pulls at me, tugging and tugging. A few weeks ago, Wesley was my world. A few weeks ago, he was the only thing I wanted.

I move toward him slowly, so slowly, and this time he's the one who has the opportunity to pull away, or to stop me. He doesn't take it either. When I press my lips to his, his large hands grab my shoulders and pull me up to my knees, bringing our bodies together from mouth to knee.

He deepens the kiss, and I moan.

A throat clearing behind us brings me back to my

senses like a curtain thrown back in a dark room at mid-day.

"Pardon me if I'm confused here, but weren't you just in the pits of despair over my brother's absence?"

I feel the full force of Rafe's contemptuous scowl before he turns on his heel and heads back toward the van.

I collapse forward, hands clasped, arms pressed against the cold ground. "I really am just like my parents."

Wesley puts his hands on the back of my shoulders and tugs me back up. "You aren't, and that's the problem."

"What?"

"You're one of the best people I know Rubes, but you're seventeen. It's too young to know who you are yet, much less who you love to the ends of the earth. You've been through a lot in the past few weeks, and you blame yourself for all of it. That's why until further notice, my lips are off limits to you."

I know Wesley's face well, probably better than I know my own. He's smirking, but he's serious too.

"What are you talking about?"

He shakes his head. "You kissed me because you feel guilty and you're trying to punish yourself by ruining your life. I should've pulled away, because you only kissed me to inflict pain. I'm selfish enough that I ignored what I knew, because I wanted to kiss you."

I shake my head. "I wasn't punishing anyone."

He grins, but his eyes don't look happy. "You still don't see how fantastic you are, and until you do, until you want to kiss me because you think we'll be epic together, I'm locking these babies up." He pretends to turn a key over his lips and tosses it over his shoulder.

"You're crazy. Besides, when he hears about this, I doubt you'll need to worry about Sam anymore."

"See? What you just said proves my point. My favorite

thing from Before was fireworks on the Fourth of July, and that kiss we just shared, that was better for me. My heart is all aflutter, and you're only kissing me to ruin your life. I love you, Ruby, I swear I do, but that's messed up."

He stands and walks back to the van leaving me to stew.

Somehow, I managed to upset three guys with the same kiss. The one I kissed, the one I'm going to have to tell about the kiss, and his long lost little brother. Ugh. When I reach the van, I climb into the row behind Wesley. It's a more comfortable place to sit, stinky kids or not. At least none of them psychoanalyze me.

The sun passes mid-day and begins its descent. Rafe's plan is to have two crews of ten on either side of the meeting spot, just on the mainland side of the 45 bridge over to Galveston. The problem is, WPN randomly places trip wires on the 45 leading up to the island. To avoid them, I'm afraid we'll be doing a lot of walking. Sam and I missed them by accident when our car ran out of gas the last time I came down. We're hoping to avoid them intentionally this time.

"Hey Todd," I ask, "how will you know where to stop the caravan?"

"I've seen them placed as close as twenty miles from the entrance to the bridge," Todd says. "Once we get just past the furthest I've seen, we'll hide the vans. We'll go the rest of the way by foot. We have until tomorrow morning to reach our places, because that's when fake Ruby and fake Wesley are gonna drive the last fifteen miles."

A fifteen-mile hike in one day?

I groan.

Rafe smirks. "It's gonna be fine, princess. You'll see."

I always wished I had a little brother or sister, but I'm really starting to hate him. Maybe I wasn't so deprived after all. After we hide the vans, we all grab backpacks with basic supplies, first aid, and camping gear.

"Let me take that one." Wesley's voice surprises me, since I figured he was still mad.

He takes the bigger bag from me. Each pack has a sleeping bag, but the larger ones hold tents too. "It's heavy and you've been giving blood lately. You shouldn't try to carry it. You can share with me, and I promise to be a perfect gentleman."

I probably ought to insist on carrying my own, but I'm tired just thinking about fifteen miles, and I really don't want to sleep under a tent with kids I don't know. "Thanks."

The first few miles aren't so bad. My heels are calloused by now, and they don't bother me a bit. But my pack is heavy even without the tent, and eventually my shoulders start to ache. The sun beats down on us, and when we take a break around the halfway point, I take off the new blue jacket Wesley gave me and knot the sleeves around my waist.

Last time I made this trip, Sam and Rhonda practically ran circles around me. Wesley's in almost as bad of shape as me. He's panting in between swigs of water. "You need to drink." He points at my canteen. "We'll refill tonight, but if you don't drink enough..."

I haven't needed to pee in seven hours so I know he's right. "I know, my blood matters, my plasma matters, volume depletion, blah blah blah." I yank my canteen over and take a drink. "I hate being some kind of blood bag for everyone. I feel sorry for cows."

"Cows?" Wesley cocks one eye.

"I'm sure when they don't make enough milk, farmers are like, 'here, drink, eat, rest up. Try to do better when I come juice you in the morning.' I know exactly how they feel."

Wesley glances down at my chest and chuckles. "You do, huh?"

I throw my canteen at him.

He catches it, which isn't very satisfying.

"My point is, I miss people wanting me for, I don't know, for myself I guess." Which sounds idiotic. I mutter, "Not that anyone did."

"I always wanted you for you. I still do."

I blush. "You know what I mean. I wish my dad didn't make Tercera, and no one died, and that I had nothing to do with the cure."

Wesley nods. "Hopefully we can leave the world a better place for our kids than our parents did for us."

"I sure hope so. I don't think we could mess it up worse, at least."

Before he can badger me to drink any more, Todd shouts for us to get moving again.

The last five miles are horrific. Only watching Wesley struggle keeps me going. His bright red face, hair soaked through with sweat, and dragging feet inspire me. If he can keep going, so can I. When inspiration strikes, I can't help myself. I scoop up a handful of pebbles and stuff them in my pocket. Every few hundred yards I toss one at his leg or his arm. He brushes at his extremities like he's been stung every time, glancing around spastically for the culprit.

It gives me something else to think about, until he catches me doing it just as the sun's setting.

"You little punk. I should've known it was you." I have no idea where his energy comes from, but he takes off chasing me. I've got zero left in my tank, so I barely run twenty steps before I'm winded.

His hand swings out at me and snags my arm, and he

spins me around toward him. My body crashes into his, but he doesn't go down. The setting sun's rays bathe his face in golden light, his hair falling over his eyes, his strong jaw jutting out in defiance. "You owe me an apology. This hike was hard enough without thinking an army of disappearing cockroaches were trying to eat me."

"Disappearing cockroaches?" I shudder. "Thanks, now I won't be able to sleep at all."

"I'll protect you from them. I mean, didn't you see my moves? I'm gifted, clearly."

I think about him, jumping right and left, swatting at the air, and spinning around to see where the pebbles were coming from. I giggle.

"You think it's funny?" His head leans down, moving closer to me, his arms holding me tight against him.

The corner of my mouth lifts. "Yeah, it was funny. Thanks for distracting me."

"I'll distract you anytime, any place."

A shiver runs down my spine, and I realize I shouldn't be standing here, not now. Not with Wesley. I stiffen up and step backward. "I think we're getting close. We better not fall too far behind, though."

I jog to catch up with the others, but now I'm intensely aware of Wesley jogging beside me. When we finally reach a spot Rafe and Todd agree on, I practically collapse where I'm standing. I offer to help Wesley put up the tent, but when he shakes his head, I don't press it.

"You two are sharing a tent?" Rafe lifts his eyebrows, but doesn't offer any other opinions.

If I maintain a careful distance between Wesley and me while we eat dinner, and if I lay my sleeping bag down as far from his as I possibly can, even if it's only ten inches away, well, I hope he doesn't take offense. At least he doesn't comment.

The only good thing about walking fifteen miles is how exhausted it leaves me. Even plagued with doubts about seeing Solomon tomorrow, and guilt over kissing Wesley, I drop off to sleep minutes after I lay down.

I dream about Sam again that night, stuck in a room with a black door. I bolt upright in the middle of the night, but before I can lay back down, Wesley's sitting up next to me, one arm thrown over my shoulder. "Are you okay?"

I nod wordlessly.

"Bad dream?"

Another nod.

He pulls my sleeping bag next to his and pats it. I lay back down and go to sleep, back to back with Wesley. I don't remember any dreams after that.

Dawn, as usual, comes too early. My eyes burn a little bit when I wake up, either from exhaustion or the campfire smoke, I can't tell. We're all up and headed for the bridge right on time. We find a good spot, behind an old house on the bay, and settle in to wait.

It's not too long before the truck Solomon sent his messenger down with drives up to the edge of the bridge. Of course, now it's loaded up with my decoy, the Marked girl named Amanda, and fake Wesley, actually a kid named Robbie. Wesley taps his fingers on the side of the stilts of the house while we wait.

I don't know what Solomon will do when he realizes they aren't me. The muscles in my neck tense up, and I use my left hand to massage them. I hope Amanda and Robbie aren't shot because of me. Shooting the messenger seems like something he'd do.

If he sends people to seize them, there isn't a lot we can do, either. We can pursue, but we'd be headed right into the lion's den if we do. No, Rafe will make me stay here either way. If I knew Solomon a little better, I'd have a closer guess, but I have no idea what nefarious plan he's laid in place.

Eventually a single, red pickup truck heads down the I-45. I can't hear what anyone's saying from here, but a man climbs out of the truck after it stops and approaches Amanda and Robbie. He knocks on the window. He talks to them, and then gestures wildly. A moment later, a woman in black pants, and a thick black coat with the hood up climbs out of the car. She crosses to the truck and waves her hands around wildly too.

Amanda passes her walkie talkie to the woman. I guess they've discovered she's not really me.

I hear the distinct bleeping noise of the call from the walkie talkie.

"Rafe here. Over."

"Rafe," a familiar voice says over the walkie, "My name is Josephine Solomon. While I understand your reticence to trust us, we meant no harm to any of you. We very much mean to honor our offer. Whether you believe us or not, I'd very much appreciate the chance to speak with my daughter. Is that possible?"

Rafe holds the walkie out to me, but his eyes are full of questions. The biggest one is, do I want to talk to her?

I don't quite know the answer. Part of my heart lurches at the sound of my mom's voice. I'm surprisingly glad she's okay. I worried Solomon would kill her when she went back. Another part of me, though, that part rages. Sam may not be dead, but she didn't know about his miraculous healing powers. My own mother didn't care whether she caused my boyfriend's death. She was in such a hurry to abandon me and rush back to her abusive husband, she didn't care who she hurt. The broken hearted part clashes with the furious part and I freeze while my heart locks up in a stalemate.

Rafe beeps the walkie. "I've made the request. I'll let you know her answer in a moment."

I appreciate that Rafe never rushes me. He doesn't even look at me. He leaves me this choice at least. Eventually pragmatism wins the day, and I reach for the walkie.

"Hi Josephine."

"Ruby, darling, I'm so happy to hear your voice."

As conflicted as I felt when I was trying to decide whether to talk to her, once the conversation starts, anger and bitterness grab the wheel. "Wish I could say the same."

"I'm sorry, so sorry sweetheart, that your friend was injured in the confusion."

I roll my eyes. My friend? And injured is such an insufficient word to describe being shot six times in the chest and left in a pool of his own blood. "We have a counter offer to present."

Silence for a count of ten. "What do you want, Ruby?"

"I'll give your abusive husband what he wants." I refuse to call him my father. I will not. "I'll give him a blood sample, straight from my arm if you insist on seeing it, and in exchange I'll take Sam and your assurances there will be no Cleansing. In other words, you'll return my boyfriend to me, the one who survived your brutal and unprovoked shooting. I don't even want to hear about the miraculous nature of your healing, as I'm sure you know it had nothing to do with his survival. But giving my boyfriend back, and agreeing not to butcher hundreds of thousands of innocents isn't really enough for what you want from me."

My mom's vowels are clipped. It's hard to tell when talking through a walkie, but she sounds upset, terse even. "If I caused your boyfriend's injuries, then certainly you'll own up to causing your father's. In any case, I'm not sure what more we can offer you. What else do you want?"

"I need my dad's journal. You stole it, and I want it back."

"You dropped it when you ran away from the awful thing you did to your own father."

She yanked it out of my arms. I grit my teeth. I'm not going to argue about this with her. "It doesn't belong to you."

"It doesn't belong to you either, darling. He isn't really your dad, you know."

Wesley puts a hand on my arm.

"What?" I ask him.

"You said you infected your... er, Solomon, with Tercera, right?"

I nod.

"And the accelerant?"

I nod again. "I don't know how it will really work back to back like that, but yes."

Wesley shrugs. "I doubt he has much time left. We could wait until he dies. Your mom might be more reasonable without him."

Rafe shakes his head. "If he dies, our leverage dies with him."

True. The only thing they want from us is my blood. If the person they want it for dies. . . Sam's caught in the middle. I hate this whole thing, and David Solomon for putting me in this position.

I press the button on the walkie. "Will you give it to me, or not? It's a small request, and he needs my blood. You know that."

The truth is, I have no idea whether my blood will heal Solomon or not. He's been infected for days, not minutes like Wesley, or hours like Rhonda. With the accelerant added to the mix, well, I don't know. But I know he's desperate. I hope it gives me enough bargaining power to outweigh the risk.

"Has your blood worked to heal Tercera on anyone else?"

I sigh. I don't like lying to my mom, but strictly speaking, this isn't a lie. "Yes."

Josephine says, "I need to check with him."

Of course she does. Apparently seventeen years of marriage and complete devotion for that entire time don't buy her much autonomy.

"Fine," I say. "We aren't the ones on a timeline." Also not strictly true, but want her to know she's the one asking for favors here.

We watch as she walks back to the truck she arrived in, and drives back down the bridge.

As the sun climbs in the sky, we wait, and then we wait more. Finally, an hour or so shy of midday, a truck returns. I think it's the same one because it's red, but other than the color, all WPN trucks look the same.

A woman all in black with her hood down emerges. It looks like my mother. When I hear the beep of the walkie, I lift it back up.

"Your father agrees to give you my ex-husband's journal, since he assumes you want it in order to help your new friends. He's a man of God and of course he supports anything that might heal those children."

"Did you bring it?"

"He has one stipulation, darling. He wants to see you himself. If you come to the island to give him the blood sample, he'll let you and Sam leave without pursuit this time, with the journal safely in hand."

I can't help shuddering every time she calls me darling. Thankfully she can't see me through the walkie. "Solomon doesn't believe I'll give him my blood?"

"It's not that he doesn't trust you, darling, it's that he wants the chance to see you, to make amends. We both want to explain things. We've had so little time with you, and so many intervening factors, confusions, and deceits. We don't blame you for any of this of course, and we'd like an opportunity to make things up to you."

Every time she says we, I want to jump through the walkie and smack her in the face.

"Will you give us one last chance to see you, to apologize?"

I turn toward Rafe, who shakes his head. No. Todd shakes his head, too. Wesley grabs my hand and shakes his head so emphatically, his hair flies into his eyes.

They may all agree it's a bad idea, but I know Solomon well enough to know, if I turn this down, he'll send his armies out to force us. I could jump in the truck we stole from WPN and tear down the road, but we can't all fit in that truck. Solomon will kill anyone he can reach, possibly even me. And if I die, there's nothing to prevent him from carrying through with his initial plan to pursue and kill every Marked kid left. Although, if I die, it might be a moot point for them anyway.

In the end, it's an illusory request my mom's making. We don't have a choice, not really. Thanks to Rafe's wise plan, we're stuck here without transportation, near the most powerful and vindictive man alive.

"Sure Josephine. I'll come, but only for the day."

"Of course, darling."

I hand the walkie to Rafe. "In my experience," I say, "if you really treasure something, you don't need to say it."

The more she calls me darling, the less I believe it.

# CHAPTER 11

I stomp my foot. No one's listening to me, and they're all wrong.

"I'm going in alone. Trust me, Solomon is erratic and dangerous. Anyone who comes with me is disposable. If you're Marked, they think God found you unworthy, which means you shouldn't be kept alive. They're afraid of you too, and they'll be itching to pull a trigger. In fact it's worse than disposable. You'd be a liability."

Todd nods his head slowly. "She's right. If you go onto the island Marked, you may as well say your farewells now."

Wesley's voice is so soft I almost don't hear him. "I'm not Marked. And if I'm risking my life, well you already saved it once. You aren't going to face that man alone."

Rafe scowls. "I still think I should go. Wes doesn't look very formidable." He lifts his shoulders. "Sorry man, nothing personal."

Wesley smirks. "Says the kid with a mohawk? I've got forty pounds on you, and I'm better with a gun."

Rafe's utterly earnest tone sends a shiver down my

spine. "You've got no idea the things I'm capable of. She'd be safe with me." He's never reminded me more of Sam. "But I'm Marked, and she's right. I'm no use to her with a bullet in my head."

"Besides, the Marked need you," I say. "But I'll take Wesley."

Wesley smiles, and I can't help notice the irony. He's smiling that he can go with me somewhere we may both die. He's smiling at being able to help me retrieve my boyfriend.

Ultimately, he's only coming so I won't have to face my personal nightmare alone, knowing there's nothing but danger and misery in it for him. Rafe's right. I don't deserve a friend like Wes.

Rafe tries to hand him a silver handgun, but I put my hand on Wesley's arm and shake my head. "The first thing they'll do is take away any weapons we bring. It's pointless. If you insist on coming, you need to know it's only for moral support. You still okay with that?"

"Of course."

There isn't much else to do, so I incline my head toward the bridge and Wesley nods. Before I've taken two steps, Rafe clears his throat.

"Yeah?" I ask.

He looks at my shoes and shuffles.

"Rafe, did you need something?"

He makes eye contact and then kicks at a dead tuft of grass on the ground. He looks like an armed fugitive one moment, and a scared child the next. "Just in case something goes wrong, or you know, whatever. Can you tell my brother I love him, and I'm not mad anymore?"

"Of course."

Rafe sighs in relief and holds up one hand. "Good luck."

When I turn back toward the bridge, I think about how

many people's lives are resting on this trade going well. It's a lot of pressure. If we get that journal, it'll be worth it. If we don't, well I don't envy Rafe the task of returning to the Marked empty handed. We didn't exactly announce our intentions when we left.

"Just breathe," Wesley says. "It's going to be okay."

I wish I believed him. My mom looks as nervous as Rafe did by the time we reach the base of the bridge. She steps toward me, arms outstretched. She's lost her mind if she thinks I'm going to rush up and hug her. A memory of the smell of peppermint and her arms around me like a vise grip surfaces from the last time I saw her. My heart lurches dangerously, so I shove the stray memory away.

She glances at Wesley curiously. "Who's this? Another boyfriend?"

I roll my eyes. "Wesley's been my best friend for years. He insisted on coming for moral support."

She frowns. "You don't need that to visit your own flesh and blood, Ruby."

"Pardon me Josephine if I don't quite see it that way. When I last saw you, you ordered your men to shoot my boyfriend. Six gunshots in the chest later, here we are."

She flinches. "I didn't."

"Okay." This isn't going well, and this is the Solomon I like best, the reasonable one of the two. When no one moves or speaks, I raise my eyebrows. "Are we going somewhere?"

Josephine jumps as though I startled her. "I'm sorry, you're just so beautiful. I get distracted looking at you, thinking of all the years I missed." Her face flushes and her voice drops to a whisper. "Thank you for coming."

I'm not saying you're welcome, because she isn't welcome. I don't want to be here. She twisted my arm, and

149

I resent it. Maternal feelings seventeen years too late don't change that. "I'm ready to go when you are."

She sighs dramatically and gestures to the truck. I walk over to it and Wesley follows me. We won't all fit on the front seat, so I climb into the back and Wesley climbs in right next to me.

"Our driver today is Peter. What's your friend's name?" Josephine asks.

Oh good. I guess she's decided I need to be enrolled in Proper Manners 101. "Wesley Fairchild. His dad runs Port Gibson." I have no idea why I added that last part, except she seems to put a lot of importance on power and influence.

"Wonderful to meet you, Wesley."

"Nice to meet you too, Mrs. Solomon," Wesley says. "Your daughter told me you look alike, but nothing prepared me for this resemblance. You're practically twins."

Josephine blushes. "What a lovely compliment. I like your friend, Ruby. He's certainly much politer than your other boyfriend was." She frowns.

Was? Why would she say was? "Where is he? Sam, I mean."

She turns back to face the road. "I'm sure you're both starving. We're going to meet your father for lunch."

She acts like we came all this way for a garden party. "I'm not here to lunch with you. I'd rather skip the niceties and get on with it. I want to see Sam, give Solomon some blood, and get the heck out of here."

"Be patient, darling. All in good time."

I clench my fists, but Wesley places a hand over mine. I force myself to breathe in and out.

Eventually the truck crosses the bridge, turns right, and slows in front of the same enormous, white colonial David

Solomon drove us to last time I came to Galveston. The four pillars on either side of the double front doors are even larger than I remember.

Wesley lives in the biggest house in Port Gibson, but even his jaw drops at the sight of this monstrosity. "What a spectacularly beautiful mansion."

"It's not a palace," Josephine says, "but we find it comfortable."

I didn't need the subtle reminder that her husband considers himself to be a king. Wesley hovers a few inches behind me as we climb the long stairway up to the front porch. "I'm not going to fall," I whisper. "Stand down lieutenant Wesley."

"I'm being supportive," he says.

I scowl. "Quit it."

Ignoring me entirely, he catches up and walks alongside me toward the doors.

Josephine hands her dark coat to a lady in a gray uniform and turns toward us. Without the jacket to obscure her form, her fitted black slacks and pink sweater set showcase her trim figure. Pink pearls circle her neck. She clasps her hands in front of her stomach, and waits for us to surrender our coats as well.

Josephine says, "We'll be taking lunch in the garden room, Ralph."

Oh good grief.

We follow a man in a full suit, presumably Ralph, around the corner to the right, and down a hall toward the 'garden room.' I've never been in a palace, but naming rooms seems like a palatial thing if I ever heard one.

Ralph stops outside glass doors, opens them and says, "Her Royal Highness, Queen Josephine Solomon, Her Majesty Ruby Solomon, and Her Majesty's companion,

Wesley Fairchild, son of the ruler of Port Gibson, an Unmarked Settlement."

I can't possibly roll my eyes far enough back in my sockets. He's announcing us? For real?

Sam will be sitting in this room, I know it. I wring my hands, unaccountably nervous as I walk through the doors, and my stomach ties in knots. I expect to walk into a room full of people, but when I finally enter, other than two walls full of windows and blooming plants on every surface, only one person sits in the room. It's decidedly not Sam.

"Darling." Solomon smiles when we walk in the room. "It's so wonderful to see you again." He's wearing a suit like his butler, also black, but with a red tie. My heart falls when I notice his cheeks are pink, and his eyes bright. I hoped to find him on his deathbed, lips white, skin pale, and sores weeping everywhere. I notice he's wearing a crown, and it comes down just far enough to cover up any Mark he may have on his brow. Maybe he's putting on a show, barely holding it together. Perhaps he can't stand up without help.

He rises to his feet smoothly, and I suppress a muttered curse.

"I hope you found the ride into town comfortable?" he asks.

Did that dart even work? Or maybe my dad's journal provided another cure? Is he sick at all? Maybe we never had any leverage, and I walked into his stronghold like a moronic lamb to the slaughter.

"Excuse me?" I ask.

"I was saying, I hope your ride onto the island was a pleasant one. I trust Arthur took good care of you?"

My mouth drops open. Solomon's acting like I arrived in a carriage, and this is some exciting affair of state. "I came as quickly as I could, but you know, these royal balls take up so much time. The princes all fell madly in love with me of course, but not a one of them could slay a dragon, so here I am, still single." I bat my eyelashes and fan myself melodramatically with my hand.

Solomon frowns. I doubt he's accustomed to being mocked.

Josephine's voice is a little too high when she says, "Isn't she hilarious?" Her fake laugh cheese-grates across my nerves. She crosses the room and sits next to King Solomon. "Look, darling, we've saved you a place right here near the head of the table."

"Glad to hear you saved it for me, with so many people clamoring for a seat."

Wesley clears his throat and whispers, "A little politeness might not hurt."

I shove my anger down a little, grit my teeth and lie. "What I meant to say was, thank you so much, Your Royal Highness. I'm so happy to be here again, and I'm absolutely famished. I can't say how pleased I am to eat lunch with you." Because if I did that would be a big fat lie. I hope my smile isn't too forced looking.

I walk toward the front of the room, and try to pull a chair out, but Ralph beats me to it. I stumble back, unbalanced a bit by him shifting the seat in front of me.

"Uh, I'm sorry. I thought I was supposed to sit there, but I don't do fancy parties much."

Solomon's eyebrows lift. "He's pulling the seat out for you, my darling. It's done in polite company, or didn't the royal ball you recently attended have butlers?"

I blush, which I hate. That's probably why my anger slips free again. "The ball I went to prized female empowerment over outdated formalities." I bite my lip. This man still has Sam, who I haven't even seen yet, and Solomon doesn't look a bit ill. Either way, he could end me if he chooses. I need to remember that. I sit down, and lower my voice. "Thank you for having patience with my learning curve. It's a lot to take in. New family, new house, new people, new rules."

Wesley circles the table and sits to my left. "I'm delighted to meet you, King Solomon. I've heard a lot about you, and I'm absolutely dazzled by the idyllic community you've created here."

"God created everything you see here son, but I'm happy to hear you recognize the majesty in it."

Wesley smiles and it doesn't even look forced. He's much better at this than me.

"Ralph, please tell them to bring the first course," Solomon says. "I think we've all worked up an appetite."

I want to demand to see Sam, but I bite my tongue again. "What are we having? It smells delicious." I really hope it's not roasted baby ducks, or some other villainous food. A mental image of Solomon carving chunks off a bleating baby goat and eating them raw has me shaking my head to clear my thoughts.

"Clam chowder," Josephine says. "We recently got some clams in from our port city in Tampa, and they're delightful. Have either of you ever had it before?"

"Never with fresh clams. I can't wait to try it," Wesley says.

I try not to think about the hundred thousand Marked kids starving while Solomon eats soup made from shellfish shipped from the east coast. I try to act normal, excited even, but my hands shake slightly with barely contained rage.

"How about you, Ruby?" Josephine asks, while women in grey uniforms place bowls in front of each of us. "Have you ever eaten clam chowder?"

I think about the gelatinous cream based mush I've had in the past from old cans. I don't think it really counts. I shrug. "Not that I recall."

She claps. "Oh what fun. I get to watch one of your firsts."

She missed my first steps, first words, first everything. Part of me seethes that she's acting like she's actually a mother, but part of me softens. She seems genuinely excited to experience something with me. That kind of joy is hard to fake.

Turns out, I like clam chowder, and the crusty bread they bring with it is even better.

Solomon wipes his mouth with a napkin and sets it on his lap. "Ruby, all joking aside, I owe you an apology."

This should be good. "You do?"

"I overreacted badly when I thought your opening of the safe meant your mother had been unfaithful to me. I should never have let my anger take over like that. Although I know this doesn't excuse my behavior, I think it was a case of an old wound that hadn't quite healed. I hope you'll accept my apology. Although I didn't physically harm you, I did harm to your mother in front of you and I'm sure that was quite upsetting and distressing to watch."

"I'd say she had it a lot worse than me."

He compresses his lips. "I can never make that up to her. Luckily, she's a Godly woman and has been generous enough to forgive me. I don't know what I did to deserve her, but I've been blessed."

It's godly to forgive the unforgivable? I don't think I'll ever be Godly. "She is a forgiving woman." It's the best I can manage.

"Better than I deserve," Solomon says.

A lecherous hag would be better than he deserves. I meet his eyes. "We agree on that."

He clenches his napkin. "I'm sorry you felt you needed to act as you did. Of course I don't blame you for defending yourself and your mother. It was exactly what you should have done. In hindsight, I recognize the nobility in your behavior."

"Thanks," I say. "I was raised to stand up for myself."

"Although." He blots at his lips. "If you hadn't deceived me, none of that would have happened." He takes a bite of soup. "But I'm sure you weren't taught any better, and your mother has helped me to see that." He inclines his head. "So, I've forgiven your rash actions. I think your education is more to blame for that than the Devil's influence."

"Uh thanks," I say. "I'm glad to know the Devil hasn't taken full control of me quite yet."

He stares at me intently, but incorrectly decides I'm not mocking him and nods. Apparently in his mind, the matter is now settled.

I make small talk about the commerce and trade channels of the various WPN ports until the second course arrives, grilled swordfish. I take a dutiful bite, and it's better than I expect, but I've waited long enough. I try my hardest to be diplomatic this time.

"This swordfish is fantastic," I say. "I really wish Sam could try it. Any chance he could join us? If there isn't any more, I'm happy to share the rest of mine."

"I'm delighted you like it," Solomon says. "It makes people who aren't accustomed to eating seafood sick from time to time."

I narrow my eyes at him. "How are you feeling, *Dad*? You seem fine. Swordfish agrees with you?"

"I've been better." He glances around the room. Ralph's standing near the door. "Please leave us, Ralph. I'll call for you when we're ready for the third course."

Ralph bows and exits, pulling the doors closed behind him.

"Now that you ask, darling, I can tell you. Thanks to your assault with that dart, I've contracted Tercera." He removes his crown, exposing the rash on his forehead. He leans toward me, and places his hand on mine. As he extends his hand, his suit coat pulls back and I notice the edge of a sore on his forearm. So he is sick, and it's progressed to the point of second year symptoms. "You don't seem nervous at the prospect of my touching you, darling. Why is that, I wonder?"

I snatch my hand back and roll my eyes. "Ready to talk for real at last? Then no, I'm not nervous. My dad made sure I couldn't contract Tercera."

"Yes, thanks to your carelessness in fleeing after you assaulted me, you left Donald's journal. We know you've been supercharged with antibodies. What we don't know is whether it will treat my illness now that it's established. Do you happen to have the answer to that one?"

I'm walking a fine line here. I wonder how long they'll insist I stay after he takes my blood. "We've treated a handful of individuals, and they have all responded positively to the antibodies in my blood. Wesley here was Marked prior to treatment. He was the first recipient of my blood, ingesting it actually, and he's been clear of any rash for weeks, despite constant contact with those actively infected with Tercera."

Solomon's eyes fly wide. "You knew about your immunity before you came looking for the safe?"

I shake my head. "I didn't, no. His treatment was. . . inadvertent."

Josephine sighs. "I bet that's an interesting story."

Wesley grins. "Let's just say I was Ruby's first kiss, and we got off to a bumpy start."

Solomon frowns. "Now I want to hear the details. And I'd like to get to know you a little better too, son." He places his fork on his plate. "And I'll admit that I'm confused. I thought Samuel Roth was your boyfriend?"

"It's complicated," Wesley says.

"I see that," Solomon says. "Luckily, we have some time to sort through all of this."

Uh, no we don't.

"No offense," I say, "but we're actually in a hurry. One of the reasons I asked for Donovan's journal is that Job's running tests on my blood as we speak. The data in that journal would help a lot. I'm happy to come back for a longer visit soon, but I'm needed to aid in a solution to the infection of the Marked as soon as possible. I'd love to donate some blood to you, collect Sam, and head back to Baton Rouge. Some of them are quite sick, and with the suppressant failing, they're running out of time."

"Yes, yes, we are aware of their problems," Solomon says. "Young people are always in such a rush. For now, try to enjoy the sliver of time we've got together."

I slam my hand on the table. "Enjoy my time here?"

"I assure you, we'll provide the best food and accommodations," Josephine says.

My hand fists on the linen tablecloth. "I've asked and asked, and no one's answered. Where's Sam? Is he being treated? Is he on a respirator? I'm a big girl and I can take it, whatever his status, but I don't want swordfish, or chowder or steak, or a big, fat slice of chocolate cake. I want to see him. Right now."

Solomon sniffs. "I don't believe I've heard any kind of apology from you yet for your role in all of this."

I stiffen. He wants me to apologize for what? Making him beat my mom? I seethe inside, but I remind myself he's holding all the cards.

"Uh, I am sorry. I shouldn't have deceived you with my blood swap."

Wesley says, "Ruby told me she was scared, afraid to face the truth of her paternity. After what she learned about Donovan Behl, she was afraid, and she thought Job's blood would surely open the safe. She didn't want to know whether her own would yet."

Solomon takes a bite and chews slowly. "Is that true, Ruby? Were you afraid to face the truth?"

I nod. That much at least is true. "I still am, if I'm being honest."

"Honesty is good," Josephine says. "But I assure you that I have no doubt. I never have."

"Why did you think my blood would open the safe, then?" I ask. "Or did you assume I'd fail?"

"I thought you'd fail," Solomon says. "But I planned to remove the safe forcibly afterward."

Josephine shakes her head. "I assumed it would open. Donald was a geneticist. He'd have known you weren't biologically his after a simple test, and he might have added your blood sample to the safe, allowing you access. That's what I assumed happened when your blood worked. Or when I thought it did."

Solomon beams and reaches for his wife's hand, pulling up short when he realizes he'd Mark her, presumably. He sets his hand down and settles for saying, "You're so brilliant, darling."

I frown. Why hadn't either Solomon or I thought of that possibility that night? He could have given things a lot more thought before beating Josephine. Although in the journal entry, Dad said he didn't know if I was actually his daughter biologically, and he didn't care.

I realize Solomon's sidetracked me again. "No distractions this time. Where's Sam?"

Solomon shoves his chair back from the table and reaches below for a black box. "Call me paranoid, but I think I'd like my blood sample first." He sets the box down next to his gold ringed salad plate, and opens it. A silver syringe rests inside a velvet lined box. How perfectly, melodramatically corny, like everything in his opulent and impractical life.

He reaches for my arm, but Wesley stands up, reaches over me and blocks his hand. "Where I'm from, we were taught to ask permission before assaulting someone's body."

Solomon shakes Wesley's hand off of his arm with a snarl. "My, my, you certainly have found plenty of boys willing to threaten violence on your behalf. Perhaps you should recall that an entire city stands ready to act at my beck and call."

"Would that be true if I knocked that crown from your head in front of them?" I ask.

Solomon's cheeks flush bright red.

Before he can repeat the beating from a few nights ago on me, I reach over and pull the elastic band out from the box, where it rests under the syringe. I shove my sleeve up and loop the band around my own left biceps, knotting it tightly. I grab the syringe next and plunge it into my own vein in the same hole I used for Libby, Rose and Job.

I have easy veins to find, or so I've heard. I ignore the pain, and pull back on the loop with my thumb slowly, filling up the entire thing. I rip the elastic band off with my teeth, and pull the syringe back out. I slam it down into the case and shove a napkin against my arm as tightly as I can manage. "How's that? Satisfied?"

Solomon nods. "Do I inject it in my arm?"

I shrug. "We've had some success with oral transmission, but only in early cases. I'd recommend intravenous, myself."

"Do you mind helping me?" Solomon asks.

I do. I mind a lot. This much blood could be used for dozens of tests. It seems wasteful to let this monster have even a single drop. I can't exactly say that.

"I'd be happy to help," I say, "but I would like to know where Sam is. Any chance you'll ever answer me? It was part of our bargain. And I've fulfilled both my parts. I'm here, and I've given you my blood."

"After you've injected me, I'm happy to take you to see him. He's not in good enough shape to come and sit through a meal with us, I'm afraid."

I bite my lip. "Will I be able to take him home with me?"

"Oh you'll be able to take him wherever you'd like once we're through with our visit." Solomon's smile seems oddly sincere.

"Can you help me tie this?" I ask Wesley, indicating the linen napkin on the inside of my elbow.

He rolls his napkin into a long line and I remove mine, recoiling at all the wasted blood soaking it. He ties his long, skinny one tightly around my elbow. The puncture wound is small enough. It should be fine soon.

Once the makeshift bandage is secure, I hold the syringe out to Solomon. He shrugs out of his jacket, and rolls up his sleeve. There are two sores on his arm. The one I saw is quite small, but the one near his elbow is larger and already weeping. It looks painful. I suppress a smile.

I inject Solomon's arm with my blood, begrudging him every last drop. After I finish, he sits back in his chair and sighs. "How long until we'll know whether it's working?"

I think about Libby and Rose. "The others showed significant improvement within twelve hours. None of them had been accelerated, and I'm not sure how that will impact the results. I've never seen any data on it."

He grunts, and then yells out quite loudly. "Ralph, call Adam, Dave, Paul and Derek. I'd like my daughter and her friend escorted to the Grey Room, please."

Sam.

My hands shake, but I stand and smooth my hands down my jeans. I breathe in and out deeply. If he's okay, this was all worth it. The apologizing, the blood donation to save a monster, the long trip, leaving Job alone to work on the cure, all of it.

Four men in matching grey uniforms with hair cropped close to their scalps walk through the door, salute and bow to Solomon. I notice he's donned his crown and suit coat again. I assume none of these men know their precious king is Marked. It wouldn't do for them to think he'd fallen out of favor with God, I suppose.

The men aren't military, but they look like they're formed from the same mold. I imagine an assembly line like they used Before, plopping men out, both soldiers and guards, some going down a line for grey guard uniforms, some for dark navy military uniforms. Same hair, same build, same training, different color clothing. I shake my head. I need to focus.

I stand up, my chair legs scraping on the wooden floor. Wesley stands too, but his chair makes no sound. He's had more practice with fancy furniture and fine flooring.

"I'm ready. Thank you for taking me."

The four men bow to me as well. As I leave the room, I notice Josephine and Solomon have both risen and are following. "Oh, don't let my eagerness ruin your meal. Please stay."

Solomon shakes his head. "I wouldn't miss this."

Josephine's twisting her napkin in her hands frenetically. It worries me, but I have no idea what it might mean. I close my eyes and imagine the worst. Sam on a ventilator, Sam barely breathing, his heart damaged, pale and sickly.

He's still Sam. I won't care. I didn't only like him because he was strong. But if he survived six shots to the chest, he can survive anything. I'll do whatever it takes to get him home safely.

No one speaks as we walk down the halls, and then leave the enormous house via a back door. We climb down a large set of stairs behind the house.

I glance back at Josephine. "This is the right way to the Grey Room?"

She swallows and nods nervously, glancing at Solomon as if for confirmation.

"Uh, okay. Where are we going, exactly?"

"Just up here Ruby, don't fret," Solomon says. "He needed care and equipment we couldn't provide as easily in our home."

That makes sense.

We walk across a two lane road behind the non-palace, and fifty feet down another small street. It's only a hundred steps to the ocean from here, and I don't see another soul anywhere. Quite a difference from the bustle of the other WPN streets I saw last time I came. Finally, we stop in front of a long, brick building with only one window on the front, high enough that I couldn't reach it, even if I jumped. No sign, no address, no mailbox, nothing to indicate it's an active residence of any kind.

What is this place? "This is it? Sam's in there?"

"You'll find what you're looking for inside," Solomon says.

I fold my arms. "And if I say I don't want to go in there? Will you bring him out to me?"

"Ruby, be reasonable. If you want to be stubborn, I'm

163

more than capable of taking you inside forcibly. I thought you wanted to see him, and were prepared for whatever you might face."

"I do and I am." I listen quietly for any sign of medical care. Beeping machines, whirring, or the sound of nurses walking up and down the hall. I hear nothing. A tweet of a bird, the wind in the palm trees. Distantly, I can make out the sounds of waves crashing. Maybe it's sound proofed so the patients aren't disturbed. Maybe they keep it secluded for that very reason.

Something feels wrong, but Solomon's right. If he means me harm, there's not much I can do about it. I'm weaponless, and so is Wesley. Plus, he's already got my blood. "Fine. I'll go inside."

Solomon inclines his head and one of the guards unlocks the door. Why is the door locked from the outside? My heart jumps into my throat, but it's hammering so hard at the prospect of seeing Sam I ignore it.

I rush into the doorway, expecting a hospital bed with Sam lying prone on top of it. Wesley cries out, but with four guards, even if I hadn't already run through the doorway, there's nothing I can do. I stare down a white hallway, the only light in the building streaming in from the open doorway behind me.

It's the hallway from my dream. Rows of doors stretch out in front of me, all of them white. The tile under my feet alternates white and black, just like the floor that went on and on in my nightmare.

I spin around. "Where's Sam? Where are we?"

A short, stocky guard with greying hair shoves Wesley inside behind me. He puts an arm around me and drags me further inside.

"I thought you might benefit from some time in WPN's

prison block, such as it is," Solomon says. "As you can see, you have the place to yourself right now. We have very little crime in Galveston. We raise devoted, God fearing people here. The only crime comes from outside forces."

I shake my head and pull away from the guard, who stinks like body odor. "Josephine, what's going on?"

She frowns. "Your father didn't find your apology very convincing, and I'm afraid I didn't either."

"Why bother lying about your plans to let me go? You obviously had no intention of doing that."

"You're so melodramatic. What they say about teens isn't the slightest bit exaggerated, sadly," Solomon says. "As to the lying, I will let you go if you still want to leave, once you understand what it means to be my daughter. If you can learn to behave properly, you'll be free to go."

"What about Sam?" I ask. "Is he even here?"

Solomon barks a laugh. "Sam's dead, my dear. I can't believe you haven't figured that out yet. He had enough value that when he still had a heartbeat on that bridge, we tried to save him. Extraordinary measures and all that, but six shots to the chest? No one could survive that. I'm delighted you believed me, though. Perhaps I can convince his father, and get a ransom from the Unmarked too."

I collapse to my knees. "Why? Why make me sit and eat lunch with you, believing he's alive all that time? Why the charade, the lies?"

"Two reasons, really. A punishment for your poor behavior, of course, but also a fatherly lesson. You've been lacking in guidance for seventeen years, so I have a lot of ground to cover. Pay attention. I abhor teaching the same thing twice. Disappointment stings more when it follows on the heels of hope."

"You're a maniac," I say.

He sighs. "Not at all. Merely brilliant and dedicated to

repairing the gaps in your education. I've illustrated this for you in a way you'll likely never forget. You see, you're far more upset about Sam's death now that you believed it had somehow been avoided. Elevated disappointment follows when hope is squashed."

"I hate you," I say.

He grins. "You'll need to work on more creative attacks if you want to wound me. That one's pretty cliché."

"Hand me a weapon and call off the guards and we'll see how creative I can be."

He snaps. "You *are* my daughter, you know. I knew it the second you tricked me back at the Palisade Palms. I've always been too clever for my own good. It's my primary failing. I spend a lot of time on my knees asking God's forgiveness. But don't worry. I'll discipline that cleverness out of you, now that we have you back. There's a bonus lesson in here for you too, you know."

I want to spit on him. Or shoot him with a real bullet this time.

"The second lesson is in betrayal. Familial betrayal cuts the deepest, of course. You reminded me when you tricked me and then shot me. I needed that reminder not to trust anyone, other than the Almighty."

He points and two guards grab me. One grabs my right arm, but the other grabs me at the base of my neck, pinching me and pulling my hair at the same time. I cry out, and Josephine winces. They drag me through the first door on the left side and toss me onto a white cot. The one who held onto my neck yanks out a chunk of hair when he finally releases me. I whimper and curl into a ball on the cot, one hand to my stinging scalp.

Solomon's voice carries through the walls. "I think you need the time alone, but your mother worries about you. She insists you have the nicest room, the one with a window, and two cots. She's a good woman, so I've decided to humor her."

Two more guards drag Wesley into the room, and toss him on the other cot.

The door shuts with a clang and the guards lock it behind us.

I should be furious with Solomon, with my mom, and most of all, with myself.

I should be, but my heart has no room for anything but despair. I collapse into a heap and sob. You'd think I'd be used to it now, but somehow, losing Sam the second time hurts even more than the first. I hate that Solomon's right. Disappointment is worse on the heels of hope.

# CHAPTER 12

I'm not sure how long I cry, face down on my cot, before Wesley finally approaches me. I'm guessing a while. He doesn't say a word, but he does sit down next to me, put an arm around me and pull me against his chest.

It helps to know someone else understands, and that someone else cares. But as soon as the hurt eases, I feel worse for taking comfort from someone Sam can't stand. Sobbing and crying and whining are things I usually detest, so I breathe in and out and in and out and I force myself to stop. I sit up and wipe my eyes, breathe in and out a few more times and downshift my gasping sobs to streaming tears. Eventually the tears transition to hiccups.

I didn't make the selfish decision to come for Sam alone. Rafe wanted to save him too, and Wesley, for his own reasons, agreed. We all knew I might be held here, and it was a risk we took. My job now isn't to cry and moan, and throw a fit. That's the sort of juvenile behavior Solomon expects from me. I need to do something he won't expect instead.

"Can I say something. . . controversial?" Wesley asks.

"I'm really not trying to stir things up again, believe me, but I feel like I need to ask."

"Go ahead."

"Do you believe him? I mean, if we take him at face value, he lied about Sam being alive to get you here. What if he's lying again now? He might not even think it's so bad, since it's a lesson or whatever."

I shake my head. "I don't know. I don't think we can believe anything he says, and I'm not sure where that leaves us. He had a reason to lie about Sam being alive. To get me here. He has no reason to lie about him being dead, at least, not that I can think of."

Wesley shrugs. "To hurt you. Or in his twisted mind, to teach you a lesson?"

I flop back on the cot. "Let's assume initially that he's telling the truth. If he is, our major issue is that we're prisoners now. The Marked need us, and we can't get away."

Wesley nods. "True enough."

If I focus on getting out of here, I can stop thinking about Sam long enough to be useful. That's a far cry better than sitting around bawling.

"We only really have two weapons in our arsenal. First, Solomon may need more of my blood at some point, and he wants to keep me alive for that. Second, none of his people know he's Marked. He may not be Marked by tomorrow, and may in fact be immune hereafter, but he'd have some explaining to do if someone sees him with a rash, especially since he didn't tell anyone about it."

Wesley grunts. "That doesn't even address the fact that he became Marked by the Tercera he kept on hand for who knows what nefarious purpose."

"Sadly we don't have a way to prove that. I left the dart guns and darts at the Palms. I doubt his people will be keen on trusting my word, not based on his messenger Arthur's opinion of me."

"We'd need to be able to reach his people for that to matter at all." Wesley taps his lip with his index finger. "And once his rash is gone, no one will believe us."

"These guards certainly won't believe anything I say." I frown. "I think the first thing on our list should be checking out of this prison cell. We were stupid enough to walk right in here, without any proof Sam was alive or even present. Maybe we're smart enough to sneak back out."

We both stand up and examine our surroundings. WPN doesn't have many prisoners, which means this cell hasn't ever been tested. The only window is ten feet or so above the ground floor. I leap up in the air toward it and Wesley snorts.

Even standing on a cot, I doubt Wesley could reach it. The room itself is small, with only two cots, a small table and two chairs. The table protrudes from the wall on an iron arm. The chairs are bolted into the tile floor on all four feet. A small door in the corner leads somewhere other than the main hallway.

I open it, and the door itself barely clears the edge of the toilet. A roll of toilet paper sits on the top of the toilet tank, and a small, metal sink opposite the toilet is the only other thing in the bathroom. No soap, towel rack or towels. I step back out. I suppose I should be glad we have a toilet in a separate room with a closing door.

"We seem to be alone in here," I say. "What about the window?"

Wesley squints. "We might be able to smash it, possibly with a leg from one of the cots, but I'm sure there's a guard outside, if not in the hall. If we go that route, we need to be ready to deal with an immediate, and possibly lethal, response. Though I doubt your sweet father would give them orders to kill you, at least not until his rash is gone for good."

I swear.

"They've gotta feed us, I assume," Wesley says. "That may be our best way out."

I shake my head. "Sneaking out won't help. There's an island full of ignorant zealots between us and the bridge. What we need is an ally here who will help us. Someone we can convince to side with us by telling them about Solomon's duplicity. Someone close enough to see and believe us."

I wrack my brain, but other than the guards, no one comes to mind.

Wesley sits in one of the chairs, tapping his fingers on the table now instead of his lips. "What about your mother?"

I groan. "Relying on her help is like asking a dog to bite its own master. Useless idea. Or maybe you've forgotten that her betrayal is what got Sam shot?"

Wesley stands and begins pacing. He's tall and the room's small, so watching him pace reminds me of my aunt's Newton's cradle, four little metal balls that swing back and forth on a pendulum. Nowhere to go, nothing to do but click and clack, click and clack tirelessly.

"One of the things I had to learn in Administration," Wesley says, "was how to identify and spot women and children suffering from abuse. They don't act like you or I would, and it's not their fault, either. If Solomon's been abusing your mother for years, well, she could've wanted to help you, but maybe she couldn't help herself much less anyone else. In fact, she might not even know that he's wrong."

I throw my hands up in the air. "See? Useless."

He shakes his head. "Not useless. I wish I'd paid better attention, but actually there are a few things I remember about what motivates abused women to finally escape their abuser. Things that might help us if we could somehow foster the occurrence of one of them."

"Like?" I ask.

"First, a truly awful assault, one that leads a victim to believe they might actually die at the hands of the person beating them can result in the victim fleeing." Wesley runs his hand through his hair. "We can't really count on that, though."

I sigh. "I really doubt she'll help me, and I think he's too smart to do anything very awful to her right now. I've drawn too much attention to it."

Wesley sits down next to me. "It's not about smart or dumb. It's about trained behaviors. His brain is warped, and it's twisted hers up, too. The next thing I remember likely won't help either. Sometimes women leave if they discover the man's having an affair. Beatings they may feel they deserve, but they frequently won't tolerate infidelity. And for some reason, men who abuse physically are commonly unfaithful."

"Ironic, given she left my dad for him."

"Yeah, that's true. But people rationalize things, right? Anyway, there were others, but I can only think of three. The first two are hard to manipulate, but we may be able to use the last thing I recall. The number one impetus for abused women to flee an abuser is fear of irreparable harm to their child."

That hits me like a slug to the gut for some reason, and tears spring to my eyes. Again. I wipe them away. I won't cry for her, not right now, not when her concern for me has only gained me two things. A cell with a window, and a cellmate to plot with. She doesn't deserve my compassion or my pity.

Besides, Wesley's wrong. She doesn't give a crap about me. The last time she had to choose between us, she raced back to Solomon. "She doesn't even know me, Wes. Besides, Solomon brought me here, by his own words, to hurt me. If my mom was against him harming me, she'd have done something then."

Wesley sits on his cot. "Technically he said he brought you here to teach you a lesson. He didn't bring you to do you physical harm. In fact, has he physically harmed you a single time since you met him?"

I nod. "He slapped my face minutes after we met."

Wesley nods. "There's a difference between beating someone and disciplining them and I wonder whether that crossed the line. Or at least, she'll see things like that, right? Abusers spin things, and rewrite the narrative, all while undermining a woman's sense of worth. The abused women rewrite history frequently, especially strong personalities, because they can't accept they might be . . . Well, weak, or easily taken advantage of, I guess."

"Okay, which makes our plan what exactly?"

Wesley shrugs. "I don't have one, not really. But if we wanted to get your mom on our side, Solomon would have to beat her within an inch of her life, which I know isn't ideal, or cheat on her, which seems unlikely to happen or be revealed out of the blue. The only other option is. . ."

"He'd have to beat me, severely. So that it's clearly not a matter of discipline, but an actual attempt to physically harm me."

Wesley winces. "I guess so, yeah. I'm just spitballing here, obviously."

I guess if my options are to take a beating by a dictator, or rot slowly in here while a hundred thousand Marked kids waste away and die, well. It's not gonna be fun, but bruises and broken bones are still better than widespread death and destruction.

I drop my face into my hands and mumble. "At least it shouldn't be hard to get him to beat me senseless. I seem to have a natural affinity for pissing Solomon off."

# CHAPTER 13

Josephine brings us dinner in a basket later that night. Several kinds of sandwiches, soup in a ceramic tureen with a lid, several kinds of fruit, and a large carafe of ice-cold milk. I think about refusing all of it, but if we do get out of this, Job's going to need my blood. I need to be eating as well as I can so I can produce all the antibodies the Marked may need upon my return.

Wesley, Josephine and I eat in painfully awkward silence.

Wesley widens his eyes at me several times, suggesting I bond with my mom. After all, unless she cares about me, she's not going to flee my dad for hurting me. I want to win my mother over, but I don't know how to do that. It's not like I've ever studied how to be charming to a parent.

"It's too bad you don't have a piano in here," Wesley says.

"Oh?" Josephine raises her eyebrows. "Do you play?"

He shakes his head. "Ruby does, and she sings."

I close my eyes. It's like a horrible chapter out of *Pride and Prejudice.* Next thing I know, he'll be telling her I've got four thousand pounds a year.

"I'd love to hear you play once your father lets you out." Her smile is forced and I make myself return it.

After I've eaten one turkey sandwich and another roast beef sandwich, and drunk a full container of milk, Josephine shoves a bowl of orange slices into my hands.

"Oh, thanks," I say. "But I think if I eat another bite I might pop."

"You don't eat nearly enough," Josephine says. "You look as fragile as a bird, like one good yank could break your wrist."

I'm heartily tired of people calling me puny, scrawny, and commenting on how I must not eat enough.

"She's always been like that." Wesley's eaten even more than me, but he stuffs the end of his second banana into his mouth with a grin. "There's never quite enough to go around in Port Gibson, and she always shares whatever she has with everyone else."

"Not here," Josephine says. "Here we have more than enough, so eat up."

I eat the orange, one section at a time, savoring the burst of tangy juice as it explodes on my tongue.

"Thank you for dinner, Mrs. Solomon. I appreciate it," Wesley says. He pats his stomach, right on top of his six-pack, and I can't help rolling my eyes. "I can't remember the last time I ate this well."

"Speaking of that." With a grin on her face, Josephine pulls out a box from behind her back. When she lifts the lid, I see two slices of dark brown cake.

I gasp. "Is that chocolate?"

"Ruby, darling, we took over ocean ports. One of those is in Tabasco, Mexico. That region has always been responsible for more than seventy percent of Mexico's chocolate. That's why we travelled so far to re-settle it. Most of the trade takes place by ship, but your father and I fly down at least once a year. I'd love to take you the next time we go. It's a beautiful place." She runs a hand over my hair, pausing to pull on a curl. I want to bat her hand away, but I don't.

As stuffed as I am, I'd never turn down chocolate in any form. Josephine hands a plate with a large slice of three layer chocolate cake with chocolate frosting to me, and another to Wesley.

I lean back on my cot, trying to make room in my over-full belly. Even though she said cocoa isn't rare here, chocolate's so valuable in the rest of the world that suspicion takes hold.

"Why are you bringing us cake?" I ask. "Is there some kind of hidden lesson in this? Did you secretly make it using cockroach flour, or lace it with some kind of laxative? I can already anticipate the moral Solomon will mouth over me while I'm cramping in misery. 'Gluttony always results in misery.'"

Josephine shakes her head, but I plow ahead. "Or maybe you're just trying to keep my energy up in case Solomon needs more blood?"

Josephine frowns. "I'm your mother Ruby, and I love you."

"Oh, and that's why you let Solomon toss me in a cell? As long as I get to keep my friend along and there's a window, it's fine? I can definitely see how much you two love me."

Wesley says, "I think Ruby's wondering whether King Solomon knows you're here with chocolate cake and sandwiches." What I really want to know is whether there's a crack into which I can drive a wedge.

"I told him I was bringing you food." Josephine's eyes

look anywhere but at mine, and I know she's not telling me everything. I doubt Solomon knows she's treating us to the best meal we've had in weeks, aside from the chowder and swordfish banquet from earlier today.

Wesley puts one hand on hers. "Did he know you were bringing us cake? Oranges? Of course neither of us would like him to . . . Well, we'd hate if this made him mad at you."

She tries to scoot her chair closer to mine, and frowns in dismay when it won't move. "Darling no, don't worry about me. You're in a cell, it's true, but try to think of this as an extended time out. You're our only child. We want you to have the world, such as it is now. Your father hasn't had any practice with teaching and managing children. We're doing the best we can with limited experience all around."

In Josephine's mind, locking me in here is evidence of some kind of tough love. Draw a firm line with the new daughter, because she's an errant, ignorant child who needs direction. What does that make Wesley? My security blanket?

I exhale heavily. "I don't need a time out Mom, and I am your child, but I'm not actually a kid anymore. You may not have seen me grow, but I'm an adult."

She beams at me. "Every time you call me Mom, I just. . ." She sits up straighter and adjusts her sweater set. "I know you aren't a child, I do."

"You sure? You cut the crust off my sandwiches."

She frowns. "I'll admit I still mourn for some of the things I missed, but I know you're grown."

"You need to treat me like an adult."

"You did throw a tantrum and infect your dad with a deadly illness a few days ago." She clucks. "We're trying to help you here, but we need you to meet us halfway."

I throw my hands in the air. 'We' this, and 'us' that. She'll never pick me. This entire plan is doomed.

"Thanks for dinner, really, but I don't need fancy meals, or stern talkings to. I need to get out of here and get back to the hundred thousand kids who are dying because of a mess you and dad, and Solomon, or his nefarious partner, or whoever else was involved, created."

She shakes her head. "We just want some time with you, and we need to make sure your blood cured your father, before we can even consider you leaving."

I groan. "How long before you're convinced?"

"Give us two weeks, okay? What difference will a few weeks make to those children?"

"That's at least two rounds of clinical trials," I say. "Job's been developing a plan, and I have no idea how much my absence will set them back."

"Clinical trials?" She shakes her head. "I've already missed seventeen years with you, and now you begrudge me two little weeks."

"Then come with me! Do you understand any part of what I'm saying? This isn't about you or Solomon, or making up for lost time, or teaching me lessons. This is about an entire group of people surviving or dying." I almost choke on the word, thinking of Sam, but I shove that thought away. "If you can't see the urgency in this, in my speedy return, we'll never, ever have a chance of seeing eye to eye."

Josephine sighs. "Ah, youth. I miss the passion, the certainty about everything. I do understand that you want to help them, darling. I even get why you're in such a rush. I'll talk to your father and see if I can help him remember what it was like to be young, to feel like if something didn't happen right away, you'd explode. How about four or five days instead of fourteen? Would that be an acceptable compromise?"

Because there's no way they'll release me until they can be reasonably sure Solomon's healed from my darts.

Which is what this is really all about at the end of the day.

My mom may care for me, and she may even love me in the way a little girl loves her favorite doll, or a beloved dog, but she doesn't love me like a daughter, because she has no idea what that even means. And Solomon isn't going to let me go until he knows he's healthy again.

"Just answer one question for me, please?" I ask.

She bobs her head.

"Is Solomon going to kill the Marked kids, or not?"

She frowns. "He gave you his word he wouldn't if you came."

"He promised me Sam could leave this island with me, too."

Before Josephine can answer, I hear a commotion outside, and the door to my cell bursts open.

"I did promise that, didn't I?" Solomon's wearing jeans and a dark sweater instead of a suit. "You don't forget a word do you? Even though I only included that promise to bring my daughter back to me, so I could fix the mess she created with her interference, her terrible temper and her insolence." He glances at Wesley. "I hoped when you brought this one along, it meant you'd replaced the Roth boy. If you had, I hoped you might eventually let the past go, and be willing to give your mother and I a chance."

I glance at Wesley, and he shakes his head. He's come to the same conclusion as me. My mom's not about to change course, no matter what I do. And yet, I can't quite give up on her, knowing what Wesley told me about abused wives. She may not have known me long, and I may not have a lot of faith, but something deep inside me longs for her to love me more than this man, this awful, terrible man.

I want to be enough.

"You never know," I say. "I do look just like her, maybe I take after my mother in other things, too."

Solomon's eyes snap toward me. "What does that mean?"

I stand up. "She hadn't even divorced my dad yet when she decided to take up with you, right? Isn't that what landed us in this mess to begin with?"

Solomon scowls. "You know nothing. About anything."

Josephine's face pales and her hands fist into balls on her lap. I change tactics. After all, Josephine's not the one I'm trying to upset.

"Although, she seems certain you're my father. You're the one who doesn't know. I've heard that people who cheat are the most paranoid about others doing the same. Is that why you're so quick to judge her? How many women have you slept with since calling yourself a king? I bet your subjects adore your crown."

His slap surprises me, knocking my face to the side in a bright flash. My eyes momentarily can't see and after I blink them several times and vision returns, my left cheek burns.

Wesley jumps up, but I hold out a hand. He's going to need to do far worse than slap me if we hope to make any progress. I glance at my mom. Her hand covers her face, but she's shocked, not upset.

Not yet.

"Watch your mouth. I won't allow anyone to talk like that about me, not even my daughter."

"I'm not your daughter." I sneer. "I'm nothing like you."

He barks a laugh. "Thank you for that perfect segue. I came down to share the good news. My guard took a hair sample from you as I requested, and the lab results are already back."

That guard did yank a chunk of my hair out, apparently on Solomon's orders. My stomach turns. Solomon's crowing.

No, no no.

"My wife never lied to me. She's been faithful to me for all these years, just as I have to her. You're my daughter, clever mind, filthy mouth and all."

I shake my head vehemently. "I don't care what the DNA test shows. There's no part of me that has anything to do with you. I'm Donovan Behl's daughter through and through. If I could scrub any trace of you out of my body, I'd scratch my skin off to do it. If it left me permanently disfigured, well, I'd count it cheap."

This time he slaps one side of my face, and then the other in quick succession. When I bring my hands up to block him instinctively, he knees me in the stomach. I double over, and then slump slowly to the ground. I don't try to disguise my moans. I want my mom to suffer right along with me.

"Daughter or not, speak to me that way again, and I won't be as forgiving." Solomon spins on his heel.

Josephine crosses the room and takes my face in her lap, stroking my hair gently. "Shhh now. I'm so sorry, darling, but you must be more careful not to anger him like that. He can't help himself when you're so disrespectful. You mustn't talk to your father that way."

"Joey."

Josephine stiffens and pats my cheek one last time. She slides away from me and stands up, glancing back apologetically.

"I'll bring you breakfast in the morning," she whispers, and then she scurries after Solomon.

So much for galvanizing Mom.

Wesley rushes to my side and picks me up, laying me back down on my cot. "What can I do? Anything?"

I'm still curled in a fetal ball, the pain radiating out from my stomach, but after a moment my stomach doesn't hurt nearly as bad, and I pull myself into a sitting position.

I bring my knees up under my chin. "Well, the way Plan A played out genuinely sucked. Feel like working on Plan B?"

# CHAPTER 14

Wesley's laugh warms my heart. "I love you, you know that? You quite literally took those punches and kept on swinging." He shakes his head. "Plan B, huh?"

I love him, too. I don't feel the same way about him as I do about Sam. As I did about Sam. Or as I do.

I'm a mess.

But I do love him. Wesley's always been there for me, and he and I are the same in so many ways. He doesn't wallow, he's a pragmatist, and he keeps looking for ways to deal with things.

Wesley's not the only one who's there for me, either. There's Rhonda, Job, Aunt Anne, Uncle Dan, and a whole host of friends back in Port Gibson. My heart aches for home, for my house, and my room. Why did I think I didn't have a place? Now that I've found my biological parents, all I want to do is flee as fast as possible and never look back.

Does Josephine really think chocolate and trips to Mexico compensate for who Solomon is inside?

"About that window," I say.

Wesley snorts. "I thought we ruled out the cot-stacking-window-smashing plan?"

"We did, but then my dad slapped me silly and my mom told me I needed to be more careful not to make him angry."

"True," Wesley says. "What exactly did you have in mind?"

"The only thing we still have going for us, writ large, is that no one knows Solomon's Marked, right? And everyone knows I'm his kid. He finally has an heir, albeit a disappointing one who needs quite a bit of spit and polish."

Wesley nods. "I'm with you there."

"So maybe if we smash the window and incapacitate the guard, we can walk right out of town."

Wesley scrunches his nose. "I think Plan A has more promise, if I'm being honest."

"Plan A crashed and burned. We're lucky we climbed out of the wreckage."

"I know." He pulls me close. "I don't think I can stand around and do nothing while he hits you again anyway."

I roll my eyes. "Look, I know it's not a great idea to try walking out, but it's all I've got, and I can't just sit here, not anymore. If my mom offers me one more piece of chocolate as if that makes up for the way he treats her…"

"Sneaking out the window isn't going to work," Wesley says. "And it's just gonna piss Solomon off even worse."

"How much angrier can he really get? Besides, if we make him truly furious, we're back to Plan A, right?" I grin.

"Fair point."

I climb off the cot and cross the room to the bathroom.

"Good thinking," Wesley calls after me. "We should pee now, before we try to race across town."

"Oh shaddup, smart aleck. I can't remember if there's a mirror or something shiny in here. I'd like to know how bad my face looks before I try and convince people we run into that I'm Princess Ruby and they should let me do whatever I want to do instead of trying to stop me."

No mirror. Of course not. A mirror could be smashed and used as a weapon. I curse.

Wesley grins at me. "Don't worry. You don't look so bad."

"Okay, if you had to pick one, does my face look like I'm too old to be climbing trees, or like I was shuttlecocked in the eye in a round of badminton?"

He laughs. "Shuttlecocked? I have no idea what that means, but it doesn't sound good. To answer your question, Rafe looks bad after our fight, but you look fine. Your cheeks look pink, but so far, no bruising."

That's good. "I guess my dad would be an expert at inflicting pain without leaving substantial marks."

"Next question," Wesley asks. "How do you plan to break the window, and once we do, how do we incapacitate the armed and presumably annoyed, if not outright angry, guard?"

Sam would never ask me any of these questions. He'd leap to the ceiling, kick the window out, and then use a bunch of weeds as a garrote to strangle the guard before he had a chance to breathe, much less cry out. Tears spring to my eyes, but I shake them off. I can't think about Sam. He's not here.

Wesley and I have to figure this out without ninja skills or super human strength. I rifle through the basket full of leftovers my mom left in her rush to abandon me when Solomon whistled.

"That soup tureen looks heavy."

Wesley sighs. "I doubt it'll break that window, though."

I shake my head. "Not for the window, but it should knock that guard out."

"Good call. Now about the window." He kneels down by one of the cots, arms braced to try and pull it apart.

"Wait, if we disassemble the cots to break the glass, how will we reach the window?"

He sits back on his heels and swears. "I guess you could stand on my shoulders?"

I imagine us wobbling back and forth, and ultimately falling to the tile floor in a crash. "I dunno, that seems. . . unreliable. Besides, how will you get up after I do?"

Wesley sighs. "Have you ever tried stacking cots? I doubt that will work any better."

"Let's say I do stand on your shoulders, smash the window, and then crawl over the shards to the other side."

"Okay."

"How," I ask, "do you think you're gonna get out?"

Wesley exhales. "If you take out the guard inside, too—"

"As opposed to bashing just the one in the head and sneaking off?"

Wesley throws his hands up in the air. "This isn't really my strong suit, escapes and whatnot. I'm more of a managing people and troubleshooting political minefields kinda guy."

I collapse on my wobbly cot. This is so not my thing, either. I refuse to think about Sam, though, because a meltdown hovers on the other side of that cliff, and it won't help us.

"I guess we can wait, and hope that once he's cured, God-loving Solomon will let us go? Maybe Mom can even convince him to do it in just five days."

That sounds stupidly optimistic, even to me. I don't think he'll kill me, at least not right away, but I doubt he's sending me back to donate blood for Marked kids either. Besides, if his Mark comes back, all bets are off. I wouldn't put it past him to keep me in this room forever for regular blood transfusions to hold his Mark at bay.

"What about the pipes for the sink?" Wesley asks. "Aren't they metal?"

"Pipes? What are you talking about?"

"For smashing the window. I know a lot about problems that crop up in town," he says. "Once I followed Mr. Edwards around all day."

Mr. Edwards is one of Port Gibson's two plumbers, the better one, in my opinion. I know them both from my time in Sanitation. "Why'd you follow him?"

"I think he wanted Dad to appoint him as head plumber. He spent all day complaining about Phil Nyugen's work. But the point is, I know what a P trap is. Do you?"

I shake my head. "I never studied plumbing. I was only in sanitation for a few months, but I actively avoided anything to do with pee."

"Not pee, but the letter P. They make the pipes in a certain way to trap sewer gas, and. . . Actually, you don't need to know all of that. It's gross. The point is, it's designed so that a normal person can take this part of the pipe off to check for hair and junk. I might be able to get it off, even without any tools."

I point at the bathroom. "Less talking, more plumbing."

Wesley ducks inside and closes the door to muffle the noise. Even so, I hear a clang and glance at the main doorway. If the guard hears us and comes to check, we're screwed. I bang on the door myself to cover the noise.

A moment later, a deep male voice asks. "Yes, Your Majesty? What can I do for you?"

Uh. What do I say now?

"Are you the jerk who yanked out my hair?"

He makes a choking sound. "No Your Majesty, that was Edward."

Another clang from the bathroom. I try to cover it up by banging on the wall again.

"Your Majesty, I'm right here. There's no need to bang on the wall."

"Uh, I'm upset. I want to talk to Edward. My scalp still hurts where he ripped out my . . . er, royal hair."

"Your royal hair?"

I laugh before I realize I shouldn't. I turn it into a cough.

"I'm sorry about your royal hair, Your Majesty, but Edward's stationed outside and must maintain his post."

Wesley pokes his head out, large pipe in hand and throws me a cheesy thumbs up with his other hand.

"Okay well, I have some select words I'd like to say to him."

Wesley points at the door and mouths the words, "What are you doing?"

I sigh. "That will be all, umm, non-assaulting guard whose name I don't know."

"My name is Adam, Majesty."

"Wait," I say. "You sound a little familiar, Adam."

"I showed you around your first trip here," he says.

I close my eyes. He was pretty nice. His steps recede slowly, and I hope I don't need to bash him over the head.

"Why would you call him over?" Wesley whispers. "I thought we decided we weren't going to win any of them over."

"I didn't call him over. You made so much noise in there that I had to cover for you. All I could think to do on such short notice was bang on the wall."

He slaps his forehead. "Nice cover, Your Majesty."

I slug him in the arm. "I'm sure you'd have come up

with something far better in this room, where we have nothing."

"Yes, your Highness. Whatever you say your Royal Fanciness."

I snatch the pipe from his hand. "Oh, and bad news. There's definitely a guard stationed outside, in addition to the one in here." The good news is that I won't even feel guilty when I bash Edward's stupid, hair snatching skull in.

Wesley grabs my cot and carries it over next to his. "So much for sneaking away. Do you want me to try and get out first so I can do the smashing?"

I shake my head. "I think he'll be less likely to shoot me, what with all my majesty and pomp. Besides, I have a score to settle with Edward. He yanked out a fistful of my hair."

"You ready to do this, then?" he asks.

I nod.

We stack the cots on top of each other. It's harder than I expect. The top cot keeps sliding, and at one point, the bottom cot collapses entirely.

"Everything okay in there?" Adam's deep voice makes me jump.

"Uh, yes," I say. "Just playing a game."

The guard clears his throat. "Well, keep it appropriate, or I'll have to come check on you. King Solomon wants me to put anything odd into my report."

"I'm sorry," I say. "I promise we'll be less . . . rowdy."

Wesley smirks, and I thump his shoulder again. He falls back on top of the cots with a crash, and I swear. There's no way Adam's walking away now.

Wesley shoves my cot back to the floor, and kicks the pipe underneath his. He sits down on his, tucking his feet underneath him to cover up the pipe. I hop onto his lap, and not a second too soon. Adam opens the door and stares from Wesley to me and back again.

He's tall with blonde hair and sparkling blue eyes. Even with his broad shoulders and dark tan, he's not as beautiful as Sam, but he's awfully close.

"No funny business," Adam says. "Your dad specifically ordered that. Your mom wants your friend here only for moral support. I'm authorized to move him one cell over if I think anything improper is underway." He narrows his eyes at Wesley pointedly.

I leap from Wes' lap and nod my head in what I hope is a penitent way. Adam glances from me to Wesley and back again, and after a moment, steps back out and locks the door.

We wait a half hour or so, until the light starts to disappear from the window. This time we stack the cots on top of one another, and Wesley braces them in place while I climb up on top. The whole thing wobbles alarmingly when he hands me the pipe.

"You scurry up first," Wesley says, "and try to smash the window as quietly as you can."

Quietly smash a window.

I sigh heavily. This plan is idiotic, but sometimes dumb things do work, right? At the end of the day, it's our only idea and I can't sit around and hope everything will all work out.

I stand up and for the first time, I'm eye level with the window. I raise my arm to smash the glass, and I'm bringing the pipe down forcefully when a face appears in front of me. I stumble back and fall off the cots, only spared from crashing to the ground by landing unceremoniously in Wesley's lap.

I might not have been so shocked by the appearance of a human face in the window I was preparing to smash if the enormous, beautiful, golden-green eyes I saw hadn't belonged to a dead man. The glass from the window shatters and shards fall all over me, the two collapsed cots, and a concerned Wesley.

I look up into Sam's gorgeous face. He's sitting on the windowsill, booted feet dangling into the room. My eyes search every inch of his body looking for damage, bandages, or some sign of injury. He's wearing a blue t-shirt that stretches across his broad chest as perfectly as it ever did.

"Sam!"

He grins back at me, his eyes twinkling.

"You look . . . completely fine," I say. "How's that possible?"

He shrugs. "I heal fast."

"What are you doing here?" I ask.

"I'm saving you, of course."

Seeing him is like discovering the sun hasn't set after all. Warmth spreads through my body.

"What else would I be doing?" Sam glances behind me and I know the very second he recognizes Wesley. "What the hell is he doing here?"

# CHAPTER 15

"Ruby was under the clearly mistaken impression that you'd been shot six times in the chest a week ago," Wesley says. "I came back with her to see if we could save what was left of you."

Sam leaps from the window, dropping a good eight feet to land in a crouch on the tile floor a few inches in front of Wesley and me. His landing doesn't make a sound.

"Why'd you jump down, man?" Wesley moans. "How are we supposed to get back up there now?"

I slide off of Wesley's lap and scramble to my feet. Sam stands at the same time, and quicker than a blink, his arms encircle me, lifting me up off the ground, swinging me around and setting the world back on its proper axis.

"I thought you were dead," I whisper. "And then I thought you were alive, and then dead again." My eyes tear up, even though I'm happy.

He snorts and his breath ruffles my hair. "I'm hard to kill, sunshine."

My heart sprouts wings and soars. "I'm so glad you're here."

I pull my face back from his chest and look up into his. He's so beautiful I might weep. His hair is back in a pony-tail again, but a few blond strands have escaped, and sweep across his chiseled jaw. I reach up to brush them back, and he leans down to kiss me.

His lips brush mine, and I sigh against him.

"How are you here?" I whisper.

He kisses me again, this time more firmly, and I mold against him, my hands curling against the hard planes of his chest, my heart beating in time with his.

"There are some things I should have told you," he says. "I'll explain later when we're away from here, but the short version is that I heal fast."

"I'm so sorry I left you," I say.

He shakes his head and puts one finger on my lips. His eyes follow his finger and his head bows back down toward mine. His lips graze mine gently, and then more insistently.

Wesley clears his throat. And then he clears it again.

"Not to break up this delightful reunion, but remember how the shattering of glass would bring down the wrath of not one, but two armed guards? Might we want to expedite the escape process?" Wesley's standing behind me, hands in his pockets, eyes on the wall.

"Why'd you bring this guy again?" Sam asks. "And wasn't he Marked?"

"Funny thing about that. Turns out me and Ruby's epic kiss healed me." Wesley turns around to face us so we can see his smirk.

Sam stiffens against me, and I want to smack Wes. "It wasn't our kiss. It was the blood from the split lip that resulted when our faces banged against our teeth."

Wesley shrugs and grins. "Oh fine, details details."

I shake my head. "Another detail. My dad injected me

with antibodies, so I've been immune to Tercera all this time."

Sam cups my face in his hand. "I'm glad to hear you're safe." He leans down to kiss me again and I melt inside like butter on a hot day.

Wesley sighs melodramatically. "Really with the kissing again? Your attention span is not long. Guards, man. We gotta get out of here. Didn't you say you came to save her, as opposed to say, joining us in chains?"

Sam straightens up and pulls me tighter against his chest. "It's been a long week. I think I'm entitled to a moment. I took out the guard in front before coming in through the window."

"Which still leaves another guard," Wesley points out.

"I try not to annoy people by repeating things. You might try to emulate me," Sam says.

"Excuse me if I get hung up on little things like armed guards." Wesley frowns.

Sam reaches behind his back and pulls a gun from his waistband. "I could take out that guy with my eyes closed." He tucks the gun back into his waistband.

"If you could have taken him out with your eyes closed, why not keep your eyes open, just for kicks, and take that second guy out? Then you could have come through the door, instead of leaping down through the window and stranding us all in this tiny box full of glass shards?"

Sam frowns.

Wesley throws his arms in the air. "But what do I know? It was just a thought."

Sam raises one eyebrow. "It upsets Ruby when I shoot people I don't strictly need to shoot, and we know the second guard. He was very polite to us on our last trip here."

I clear my voice. "I'm glad you didn't shoot Adam. He's nice."

Wesley gulps. "Fair enough. No one seems to care what I think, but I vote for leave now, smooch later."

Sam glares at him, leans over and kisses me one more time, lingeringly, before he straightens and drops his arms. "Ruby, you ready to leave?"

I smile. "It's probably a good idea. We were gonna stack these cots, and use them to—"

Sam pulls his t-shirt off, and I completely lose my train of thought. This time, it's not only his beautiful chest that distracts me. It's the six bright pink circles on it that I can't look away from. How could they have healed so perfectly in less than a week?

"Seriously, I feel like we're filming one of those old soap operas my mom loved," Wesley moans. "What possible reason could there be for you to take your shirt off? And can we talk about why you aren't wearing a coat? It's winter, for heaven's sake."

Sam bites the collar of his shirt, leaving his hands free, and leaps four feet vertically in the air. He pulls up to the window sill, and drapes his shirt over the glass, and then he drops back down to the ground. "The shirt is so Ruby doesn't get cut up crawling through the window."

Wesley sputters. "I'd have loaned you my jacket, you insane body-building high-jumper. But I guess, any excuse to get naked, right?"

Sam ignores him. "You were saying about the cots, sunshine?"

"Uh," I say, "We were gonna stack them and try and climb up to reach the window. It was working, for the record."

Sam grins, and picks me up. He sets me easily on his

shoulders like I'm a toddler. "If you stand up, I think you can scramble over. They built this holding facility at the end of the inhabited area since they like to pretend everyone here is so perfectly behaved. The upshot is that very few people are around. I doubt anyone will notice you climbing out, but I'll be right behind you if someone does."

"What about me?" Wesley asks.

I climb up to the window and glance back at Wesley and Sam. They're glaring at one another like dogs, circling slowly as though they're about to face off gladiator style. Even the thought of the two of them fighting makes me giggle. "Sam, can Wes climb the cots like we planned?"

Sam grunts.

"We aren't leaving him here, so don't even suggest it."

Sam grits his teeth. "No cots." He grabs Wesley, who's skinny, but still has a good foot and seventy pounds on me, and tosses him up to the window ledge.

I scramble to the side, and dangle from my hands, ready to drop into the bushes outside, but Wesley's voice carries faintly. "Uh, what now?"

"Pull yourself up kid, geez. Don't tell me you can't do a single pull up, because that would be pathetic."

I drop to the ground, the bush simultaneously cushioning my fall and scratching my calf. I bite down on a whimper.

Wesley's bright red face appears over the edge of the window, and I breathe a silent sigh of relief. Apparently he can do at least one pull up. He drops down more gracefully than I did, which makes sense. He has twelve inches less to fall, after all.

A moment later, Sam leaps down after him. He crouches near me and lays a hand on my knee. "Where are you hurt?"

"How could you possibly know that?" I ask.

He grins down at me and kisses my nose. "You whimpered when you landed, you've got a slightly elevated heart rate, and there's a faint smell of iron from your blood."

He pulls my jeans up and looks at my scrape.

"You can hear my heartbeat?"

Sam shrugs.

"That hardly seems fair." I yank my pants leg back down. "Apparently I have no secrets, but I'm fine."

"That's my girl," Sam says.

"Rubes, you ready?" Wesley asks.

I stand up and nod. "Let's go."

I head down the road in front of the prison, slowing down to check out the slumped figure of Edward, the hair pulling jerk. He's unconscious, but breathing. Sam's a few paces ahead of me, and I jog to catch up to him. He takes my hand in his, and I suppress a ridiculously girly giggle.

Sam heads up the street purposefully. He's right, there's no one else around. In fact, the only other lights anywhere near come from my parents' palatial white house. If it weren't for a nearly full moon, we'd be stumbling around in the dark, or at least I would be. Sam guides us down near the water, a solid fifty yards from the house. "Hopefully anyone who sees us will assume we're out for a romantic evening stroll." He winks at me.

"What will they think I'm doing?" Wesley asks.

"I forgot you were there." Sam shrugs. "Huh. Maybe they won't notice you. But if they do, they'll probably feel bad for us. Third wheels suck."

I squeeze Sam's hand. He needs to cut Wesley some slack.

A few blocks past Solomon's palace, Sam cuts down an alley way, and toward the main road.

"What's the plan here?" Wesley asks.

"I thought we'd head back to the abandoned bridge Ruby and I used to get here."

"How do you know your way around so well?" I ask.

"Yeah," Wesley asks. "Haven't you been in a hospital bed for the last week?"

"I heal fast," Sam says. "I've been for a few walks around town, and I have a good mind for directions."

"You haven't been a prisoner?" I ask. "Solomon lured us here with an offer. He'd trade a visit with me and a dose of my blood for your safe return."

Sam frowns. "I haven't seen Solomon, but your mother reassured me I was a guest. I was treated quite competently for my injuries. I still have a bed in the hospital."

"How'd you know to rescue Ruby, then?" Wesley asks.

"I heard a rumor that Solomon, who everyone believes is your dad, by the way, had imprisoned you as some kind of discipline. I knew you Marked him, so I had my doubts about the nature of it."

"I think in his mind, he's trying to teach me proper behavior, or at least that's the story he's publishing to the community at large. It probably doesn't look great to say the king is tossing his daughter in jail. Mostly though, I think he's holding me until he's sure my blood has healed him."

"I can't believe they're giving Sam free rein, and they locked you and me in a cell," Wesley says. "They told us when they locked us up that the offer was a lie, and you really were dead."

Sam stops, and pulls me close, under the light from a streetlamp. "That's what you meant by dead, then alive, then dead again?"

I nod, mutely.

He crushes me against him again. "I'm so sorry. I don't know what I'd do if I thought you died."

My heart stutters remembering how I felt.

"I may not have been behind bars, but I don't really have free rein, either."

"At least you weren't being tortured," I say. "I wondered about that, once we heard you were still alive."

He cups my face in his hand. "I'm sorry, sunshine," he whispers. "That you had to go through that. I told you I'd keep you safe, and I meant it."

"I never should've left you." I shake my head against his chest. "I never would have if I thought there was any chance you'd pull through." Tears fill my eyes again. I blink to clear them, but one snakes down my cheek anyway.

He lifts my chin and wipes my tear away. "Job was right to flee when he did. You're an easier target than I am. I just wish you'd known I would come find you. If you hadn't come back, I would have escaped in the next few days."

"If I had known, I'd have stayed put and we could've left together," I say. "I'll never leave you again."

He grins. "That's a better plan. Plus, if you'd stayed on the island with me, we wouldn't have a gangly tag along."

Wesley harrumphs. "I'm still her best friend, oaf, even if you're the boyfriend."

Sam leans down and kisses the top of my head.

A shrill voice startles me. "Who is she, and who's the boyfriend?"

I look past the pool of light surrounding us, and squint at the shape beyond. A tall, thin woman with long, dark hair, wearing a long white coat strides into view.

"I said leave now, smooch later," Wesley mutters, "but does anyone listen to me?" He shakes his head.

Sam steps away from me with a guilty look on his face.

"Claudia, this is Rhonda, my sister. Oh, sorry, where are my manners?"

He gestures to me. "Rhonda, this is Dr. Flores. She's the one I was telling you about, who took such good care of me. She's the reason I'm still alive." He widens his eyes before turning back toward Claudia with a smile.

I hate her on sight.

Her ruby red lips part in surprise, and I realize my jaw has dropped. I snap it shut. Wait, did he just introduce me as his sister and say my name was Rhonda? What the heck is going on?

Then it hits me. Everyone's heard about Solomon's daughter Ruby, so he can't very well tell her who I am. Not unless he wants to march me back to my cell.

Dr. Flores puts a hand on her hip. "Mílagro, you're from the Unmarked, no? How's your sister suddenly standing next to you in the street all the way down here in Galveston?"

"I had no idea she was coming." Sam puts an arm around me, and pats my shoulder. "I guess there's trouble back home, with the Marked. You've heard the suppressant is failing, I assume."

"You never mentioned a sister." Dr. Flores arches one eyebrow. "Not in many hours of conversation."

Many hours? I clench one hand into a fist and stifle the desire to punch the perfectly groomed physician who nursed Sam back to health. I should be thanking her, but that's not happening anytime soon.

Sam shrugs. "We weren't that close growing up."

I grit my teeth. That hits a little too close to home.

Dr. Flores smiles at me, but it's forced. "Who's this man with her?"

Sam sighs. "That's her boyfriend, Wesley. He came with

her to find me. He's more like a puppy than a boyfriend, honestly. I'm always tripping over him." Sam bares his teeth in what I believe he thinks resembles a smile.

Judging by the smile on Wesley's face, he's really enjoying this. I wish I found it half as funny as he does. "We were so worried about you, Sam. Rhonda literally cried herself to sleep every night, snuggled up next to me. In fact, she had a nightmare about you once. I calmed her down eventually, but I don't think she's ever curled quite so close to me." Wesley's smile splits his face. He waves brightly at Dr. Flores. "It's wonderful to meet you. How fantastic that dear old Sam had such an attractive physician to take care of him."

"Your girlfriend doesn't look much like her brother, does she?" Dr. Flores looks from Sam to me and back again. "She's so small and pale."

"I've always thought they look strange together," Wesley agrees.

"She does look awfully familiar to me," Dr. Flores says. "You said you both came from the Unmarked settlement in Mississippi? Has she ever visited World Peace Now? I feel like I've seen her at some point."

I hate when people talk about me like I'm not even present. I narrow my eyes at her, but she's got to be thinking of my mother. We look so much alike, I should have known people would recognize it. What if she won't let it go?

"I've never been here before," I say.

Dr. Flores raises one eyebrow. "It really feels like I've seen you somewhere."

I panic, but Wesley winks at me.

"She and Sam don't look much alike, and they weren't close mostly because," he lowers his voice and Dr. Flores leans in to hear him. "no one talks about it much, but they have different fathers." Wesley smirks. "Sam's dad is kind of a big deal with the Unmarked, you know." Wesley whistles. "But Rhonda's dad, well, he's small and somewhat unimpressive after Sam's father. Everyone was surprised. It was kind of a scandal."

"You don't say." Dr. Flores smiles at Sam as if seeing him anew, and then raises one carefully plucked eyebrow again. "You said you were going on a walk, Samuel. How'd you even find your half-sister?"

"That's my fault," I say. "I heard he was in the hospital, and we were headed over there when we saw him on his walk. We should've insisted that he return to his room right away. I know he's recovering, but I've never seen the ocean, and he said he felt good enough to walk us down there. It's so beautiful in the moonlight."

Dr. Flores presses her lips together and glances at Wesley again. If she saw Sam kiss my head, she's struggling to process how we all fit together. I can't say I'm pleased Sam never mentioned me, but this is where we are. I notice a man in a beanie, and a woman with a blue scarf glancing in our direction, and I think about Edward slumped on the ground. As soon as Adam checks in and realizes we're gone. . . We need to get moving pronto.

"I'm so glad Sam's alright," I gush. "But we'd never have made it all the way down here to find him without my darling Wesley." I take his hand in mine and pull him close.

He looks around in confusion, but when I squeeze his hand, he catches up. "Anything for you, *sunshine*."

Wow, he's really enjoying this. He leans down and I realize he's about to kiss me. In front of Sam.

"Gross you two, I don't think I can handle any more PDA." Sam practically growls.

"Oh, mílagro, let them kiss. Young love is a beautiful thing." Dr. Forbes bats her lashes at Sam and smiles.

Wesley's a cat with an entire bowl of cream. He pulls me close, and I whisper, "You said your lips were locked."

He smiles. "That was before I saw you with Mr. Soap Star himself. I'm declaring my mouth open for service again."

He dips me, bringing his lips to mine slowly, so slowly I feel every heartbeat pounding like the beat of a drum. When his lips finally touch mine, my heart skips a beat, just like it did during our second kiss. Wesley presses my lips open, but before he can do anything more, Sam swears.

"I can't watch some stick figure maul my baby sister, okay? I think that's more than enough."

Wesley stands back up, pulling me up under his arm. "Relax, man, she's an adult. And believe me, it's consensual."

I roll my eyes. Enough idiocy. "Sam, we need to get going."

Dr. Flores clucks, "Going where, Samuel? You aren't cleared to leave, not yet."

Sam reaches his hand out for the stunning doctor, and takes her fingers in his. It doesn't look like the first time he's held her hand, and I can't help wondering whether he's kissed her.

Now's not the time to worry, Ruby. Drop it.

Sam says, "You know I'd love to stay, but Rhonda and Wesley need me. Rhonda thought I died, but once she got word I was alive, she made Wesley bring her straight here. They need my help. The Marked are attacking our town back home. I lead the Defense Path there, and without me, Port Gibson's falling apart."

Dr. Flores sighs prettily, her lips drawn into what looks like a practiced pout. "Samuel, you can't leave yet. Not until I can get the proper approvals. You know that."

I hate the way she says Samuel, in three evenly spaced syllables, like she's saying a prayer, or something.

Sam pats her face and I force back a snarl. "I appreciate all you've done for me, you know I do. You've bent the rules to let me go for walks, which I can't thank you for enough. You and I both know that God's worked a miracle, and I'm healed up. Please do me this one last favor. Let me go without waiting on all the paperwork. That could delay us days, if not more. You said yourself that while I couldn't let on how much I healed or how fast, I was entirely back to normal. You know I'll be fine."

"You're my mílagro, Samuel. I'll never forget it. You were my first answer to prayer, but sneaking away is a mistake." Dr. Flores shakes her head and her hair shimmers in a waterfall down her back. "You should all stay here where King Solomon will protect us." She frowns at Wesley and me. "All of us." Her voice goes flat, "Even your never-before-mentioned sister."

Sam tilts his head, his eyes pleading with her silently. A moment later she sighs. That I understand. I've never been able to resist that look, either.

"Fine. If you insist on leaving, I won't stop you. Please take better care of yourself this time. There's no guarantee of a second miracle, Samuel." She leans forward and presses a kiss to his cheek and I fume, but I don't move from where Wesley's arms hold me.

Sam steps away, and bobs his head down the way we were headed. "Thank you, Claudia. I'll take better care of myself, I promise."

Wesley uses the weight of his arm around my shoulder to drag me down the street toward Sam. "Close call," he whispers in my ear. "It's a really good thing not everyone here recognizes your royal countenance or we'd be toast."

I roll my eyes, but I don't pull away. Sam doesn't even

notice, practically jogging ahead of us. Wes and I pick up the pace and still seem to fall further and further behind.

Sam's given up the pretense of us taking a stroll. His eyes scan the streets as he moves from one corner to the next.

Wesley drops his arm as our jog transitions to a run.

"Does he always move this fast?" Wesley huffs when he speaks, and I don't blame him. We've gone nearly a half mile since the good doctor left, and we aren't Sam. Normal people can't run flat out for a hundred miles without breaking a sweat.

I moan.

Wesley groans right back at me. "I don't know how much longer I can keep up this pace before people start to wonder whether I'm about to pass out in the street. I'm pretty sure if they call a medical alert, our cover will be blown."

"I think he's worried about how much time we have left. That conversation with Claudia took awhile, and drew too much attention our way."

"Yeah, girlfriends are a real drag." Wesley wheezes. "If you weren't so hot, I might dump you."

Sam scowls at Wesley from way ahead of us. I forget how good his hearing is.

I whisper to Wesley, "Stop baiting him."

Sam glances back and motions for us to catch up.

"Short legs, remember?" I mutter under my breath, "We can't all have legs that never end like Doctor Flores."

Wesley rolls his eyes. "Oh, please. Are you jealous?"

I refuse to answer.

"Rubes, he was cozying up to her to get out of here. He used her to get out for his walk earlier, the one he took over to the prison to rescue you, remember?"

"I know that, duh. It doesn't mean I have to like her, though. Especially if he kissed her as part of this ruse."

"You'd be pretty hypocritical to be upset, since we kissed too."

I scowl at Wesley. He doesn't realize Sam can hear every word he's saying. "No, and I'm sure he won't be mad about that. It's his own doctor girlfriend's fault that we had to kiss."

Wesley shakes his head. "I'm not talking about that kiss, Rubes. I'm talking about before we even came here."

Sam stops dead in his tracks.

I glare at Wesley.

He throws his hands up in the air. "Umm, why'd Sam stop?"

"He heals fast, Wesley. And he's super strong, and guess what else?"

Wesley scrunches up his nose. "Super hearing?"

"Bingo."

When Wesley and I turn to face Sam, I feel like a truant child whose dad is angry she stole a cookie.

Before I have time to explain anything, a red dot appears on Sam's forehead.

"Ruby, darling, do you see that little red dot?" Solomon steps out from behind a parked car. "That's from the laser sight of a sniper rifle. Both your boyfriends have several well-trained snipers aiming at them right now. I can't tell you how delighted I am that you slowed down to argue over who you've been kissing so we could line up their angles."

Solomon turns to face Sam. "I'll take your gun, if you don't mind."

Sam growls, but he hands Solomon the gun he took from Edward.

Solomon lifts one hand. "Men, please. Come on out."

I watch in horror as a dozen men surround us, handcuffing Sam and Wesley.

One of the men glances at me questioningly.

"No, not her," Solomon says. "My daughter adores her boyfriends. Unless she's got a third I haven't met yet waiting in the wings, I'm sure she'll be quite polite while we've got them in custody."

# CHAPTER 16

Maybe if Solomon had been there for my tantrums as a toddler. Maybe if he'd been there for my stubborn refusal to eat anything other than Cheerios at the age of three. Maybe if he'd seen me devolve into the Tasmanian Devil when anyone else tried to tie my shoes for me before I left for pre-school. Maybe if he'd packed my lunch and put my hair in pigtails before sending me off to kindergarten. Maybe if he'd been there to clap at my kindergarten graduation, or to kiss my forehead before my first date.

Maybe if David Solomon had been there for these typical father-daughter moments, he might not have felt the need to lock Sam and Wesley in shackles in a cinderblock walled interrogation room at the back of the prison we just left, dismissing the guards so he could punish me without accountability.

Maybe he'd have loved me like a father should. Maybe, but I doubt it.

Solomon doesn't strike me as an average father in any sense of the word. There's no doubt in my mind that he's seething right now. Even though he has cause to celebrate, because he's not wearing a crown, and his forehead is Mark free. Even though his errant daughter stands next to him, cowed and penitent. Even though he rules half a million people, and flies to Mexico to eat decadent chocolate cake while the rest of the world has gone to hell.

Even with all of that, he's still not happy.

"Sit." Solomon points at a wooden chair he's placed between Sam and Wesley's shackles on the wall. I wince at the sight of their ankles and wrists bound by steel bands.

When I don't immediately move, Solomon glares at me. He's holding a gun, so I shuffle over to the chair and sit down.

"You should be celebrating, Your Highness," I say. "My blood has cured you."

His fingers fly to his forehead.

"Aren't you at least a little relieved?"

He frowns. "You don't seem the least bit penitent for breaking loose and running away. Again."

I drop my eyes. "I am very sorry, Your Royal Highness, I really am. If I wasn't sure you were cured, I'd never have dreamed of leaving Galveston, but there are so many other people who need my blood. They're all waiting on a cure, and with as advanced as their cases are, we don't have much time."

He shakes his head. "They don't need your blood. They're Marked and they're dying, but you didn't infect them. It's not your fault. Why should you be a guinea pig, or worse, a walking blood bank in Baton Rouge for a bunch of rabble? You're a princess, the heir to my throne. Royalty doesn't open her veins for the common folk."

My eyes fly to his. "Did you ever intend to release me?"

"Ah, now you see. You're my daughter, my only heir. I have great plans for you, for us actually, but none of them include sending you to slit your wrists regularly for a bunch of deformed, sore-covered, perma-children." He spits on the ground and begins to pace.

"They aren't deformed, and they aren't children," I say. "And they don't need to be removed."

"How would you describe someone who should grow, but doesn't?" He shakes his head. "The Cleansing wasn't born of fear, or hatred, darling, but from compassion. Those poor things are like mangy dogs, eking out an existence they never should have been condemned to maintain. The Unmarked scientists didn't do those children any favors when they developed the suppressant. They've forced them to suffer for a decade instead of dying as God intended, that's all."

I think of baby Rose, and her sweet mother. I imagine Todd's competence, one of Solomon's own former guards, and sweet Sean, with his scarred face and haunted eyes. Rafe's face rises in my mind, his mohawk bobbing in the sky, the rebellious act of a kid whose dad left him alone, and his mom and aunt died when he was far too young, leaving him to fend for himself in a horrifying world gone haywire.

They created something from the ashes of the world. Rafe protects his people, and he's made communities, and homes for them.

Solomon thinks they're deformed? He thinks they're mangy dogs? I shake my head. "What you don't get is that family isn't about blood. You think it is, but it's not. It's about choices."

He raises one eyebrow. "What does that even mean?"

A door opens and Josephine slips through. "Oh, you found her. I'm so glad." She sighs and presses her hand to her chest.

She's glad he found me? Why? So he can punish me

more? So he can beat me into the shape he prefers, like he's done to her?

I didn't want to hurt her when I was stuck in a cell, but now I do. "You shouldn't be glad he found me. I'm not. You aren't my parents, and you never were."

Her eyes widen, full of pain. "How can you say that?"

"Because I don't choose you, either of you."

Solomon scoffs. "You're such a baby. You can't choose your family."

"Maybe not usually, but my Dad gave me a chance. He knew the kind of person you are, and he stole me away. I'm grateful he did what I couldn't."

Solomon's face flushes. "You are my blood, you ungrateful wretch."

"I'm nothing like you, and I don't want to be. I want to be like Donovan Behl, and his twin sister Anne, and her husband Dan. I want to be like their kids, Job and Rhonda. I want to be like Samuel Roth, and Wesley Fairchild. They're my family in a way you never will be."

Solomon's nostrils flare. "You will not insult your mother or me anymore. We've given you a lot of leeway, and I've tried to be calm about your attitude and your behavior, but that ends today."

"It does? How?" I ask. "Tossing me in a cell again?"

He shakes his head. "You've earned quite the punishment, and I'll pair it with a teaching moment. Today's lesson will be on consequences. When you misbehave, your punishment is the consequence. You can't blame me for administering it, when you caused me to do this by your own actions."

He grabs the back of my chair and swivels it around, shoving it a few feet away from the cinderblock wall so I'm looking at Wesley, Sam, and Solomon simultaneously.

"Let's talk about cause and effect. It may be the most

important lesson I'll ever teach you. See, I could spare the Marked like I have for a decade, and they'll continue to plague me and my people. They hinder the repopulation and development of New America. Your mother has encouraged me to spare them, calling it mercy, but God has opened my eyes."

I have no words.

He continues. "It's not mercy to spare them, but it would be mercy to end their suffering. God clearly Marked them, and they deserved to suffer, but the term of their suffering has been fulfilled long since."

"I'm sorry," I say, "but I don't quite understand. What exactly did hundreds of thousands of young children do to deserve this suffering?"

Solomon grins. "That's an astute question, darling. I despise your attitude, but your wit, at least, does you credit. You see, unfortunately the sins of the fathers often fall to the children. The Bible's rife with examples of this, but Deuteronomy 5:9 springs to mind. 'I the Lord your God am a jealous God, visiting the iniquity of the fathers on the children, and on the third and fourth generations of those who hate me.'"

I shake my head.

"You disagree?"

I shrug. "I don't know the Bible, which I'm sure disappoints you, but I do know that a child isn't to blame for what her parents do." I stop short, blinking quickly. The words I spoke sink into my mind like sugar sinks into tea.

For the first time in my life, a weight lifts from me, like a spotlight shines directly on my heart. Those Marked children don't need to pay for their parent's mistakes, if their parents even did anything wrong, because they were children. They aren't culpable. The light fills me up inside, lifts me up, and I feel free, clear, and buoyant.

I wonder whether this is what God feels like, because in this moment, I know it truly wasn't my fault, any of it. My dad made some bad decisions and trusted the wrong people, but those people made the wicked decisions that led to his death, and to the subsequent release of Tercera. I didn't kill my dad, and he doesn't want me to carry that misguided guilt around anymore.

So I let it go.

Because Solomon's wrong. I'm not to blame for either of my father's actions, not his, and not Donovan Behl's. I'm not responsible for Josephine's mistakes, either. We've all been handed a world our parents broke, and we're stuck repairing the damage as best we can. That doesn't mean it's our fault, and if God exists, and if he's the light I'm feeling, he'd never punish a child for the mistakes of their ancestors. The Bible got it wrong if it says otherwise.

Solomon, oblivious and uncaring about my epiphany, says, "There's passage after passage that says the same, from Jeremiah 32, to Isaiah 65. I'll be sure to show them all to you. Lucky for you, your father's a man of God, so you have very few sins of mine to atone for."

I don't roll my eyes, but I want to.

"Those children, however, their parents were part of a modern day Sodom and Gomorrah that was consuming the world like a snake eating its tail."

That's when it hits me. "No matter what I said or did, no matter what things you promised me, you always planned to move ahead with the Cleansing, didn't you?"

Solomon smiles. "Now you understand. I'm not a monster, you know. Children need discipline and rules, they excel in a stable environment. I can eliminate the suffering of the Marked, while providing those things for more than a half million of our people. They deserve a world free of the blight of Tercera. Do you understand?"

I nod. I do understand. "That's why you'll never administer my blood to your people. And you'll keep a few dozen live samples of Dad's virus for yourself hidden somewhere inaccessible. That way if anyone questions you or defies you in any way, God can take care of them?"

"That wit." He shakes his head. "You're very bright, you know. You take one and one and put it together and come up with three. But how do I surgically remove the attitude, while leaving the wit intact?" Solomon lifts his gun and holds it to Wesley's head. "I think I've had an idea. This will be just the lesson for you, my smart but ignorant child. My witty and bright, but misguided and confused offspring."

Solomon glances down at Wesley. His eyes stare straight ahead, but the muscles in his arms and legs strain.

Solomon sneers at me. "You've been behaving poorly, hurting your mother's feelings, and acting out. It doesn't seem to help when I beat you, but you're empathetic, that's clear. You care a great deal for a bunch of riff-raff you only just met who would burn you at the stake if it would take away their just afflictions."

"They really don't care about you," Josephine says. "Not like we do."

"It's because we care about you that I was going to beat your boyfriends in your place," Solomon says. "I felt it might hurt you more to watch them suffer than to be harmed yourself."

I look at Sam's face, calm, clear, and unconcerned. Sam would gladly take a beating for me, I know it in my bones.

One glance at Wesley and I see the same look in his eyes. He'd rather take a beating than let me endure one, too.

Solomon's right, though. It will hurt me more to watch them.

"Don't," I say. "Beat me instead."

Solomon smiles. "I thought you might say that, which means I chose well, but I've had a bit of additional clarification from God while we stand here. A beating isn't a strong enough punishment. It won't make the lasting impression you need. You deserve swift and just punishment for your insolence, and your disregard for my authority."

He lifts the firearm and shifts it to his other hand. "Did you know I'm ambidextrous? It comes in handy sometimes, especially in cases such as this. It makes it easy for me to watch your face and inflict this punishment at the same time, without moving around and wasting time." He presses the gun against Sam's temple. "One of your boyfriends will pay the price for your poor behavior, and because I'm a charitable man, I'll let you choose which one dies and which one lives."

Wesley groans. "I've heard of shotgun weddings, but this is ridiculous. I'm not even her boyfriend, and you already shot that guy, like six times. Maybe we call it square."

Solomon drops his hand and raises both eyebrows. "So which is it? The funny one? Or the one who already almost died for you?"

In a moment of clarity, Wesley's words come back to me. An abused woman only takes action when she fears for her own life, or that of her child. Solomon, in his dark and twisted way, actually seems fond of me. He's killing Sam or Wesley to teach me a lesson, and to prove the lengths to which he will go, I assume. Slaps and knees to the stomach notwithstanding, he hasn't threatened me with any lasting or permanent harm. There weren't sniper rifles pointed at my head, or at least not that I know of.

I lunge for his gun without warning, and snatch it from his hand. I think about shooting Solomon, but if my mother freaks out and tells everyone we murdered their king, we'll never make it out alive. No, I need to get her on my side, squarely and completely. I think I know how to do it.

I step back and aim the gun toward my own temple. "I choose option C. Myself."

Solomon's lip curls up. "Go ahead. Your theatrics have gone too far. You value yourself far higher than I do."

I smile at him. "I'm your only heir. Try again."

He tilts his head and the corner of his mouth turns upward. "My only legitimate heir, yes. I have several other children, mostly younger to be sure, but also less recalcitrant. You're valuable as my legitimate heir, but ultimately like everyone else other than me, you're disposable."

Josephine gasps.

"Now that I'm cured, go ahead, Ruby. Save me the trouble of retraining you and shoot yourself. It will be a real tragedy, but I'll rally and move on. My people will be so proud that God is my strength."

My hand drops to my side. "Those children are illegitimate."

"Only while Josephine lives, which is what made you more convenient. I am quite fond of your mother, you know. She's so forgiving, so useful in many ways, and she's maintained herself impressively. She strikes a lovely figure at public functions, and she keeps my life steady, comfortable, and consistent. But if you force my hand, I can go back to my former plan. Your mother's aged quite nicely, and marrying a younger woman is such an embarrassing cliché. I've always planned to dispose of her after she passes her expiration date, and marry one of the mothers of my other children. Then voilá. Ready made heir. An heir I've controlled from start to finish no less."

"You're disgusting."

He leans casually against the wall. "I know just what I'll tell my people. My daughter, exposed to Tercera and buoyed up by my prayers for so long, finally succumbed due to her own wicked, rebellious heart. After she contracted the illness, I was prepared to perform a ritual sacrifice and ask God for a cure, but the virus has mutated. It drove her quite mad." He lifts one eyebrow. "Didn't you hear? It's got new neurological side effects in year one, now. People lose their minds and make rash decisions, including sometimes tragically taking their own lives."

My suicide would expedite the Cleansing, not to mention eliminating the Marked kids' only real hope for a cure in one fell swoop. Solomon's like a slippery eel, shifting and twisting every which way, but always on top. Except Josephine, my poor, abused, kicked-puppy of a mother, has crept up next to me while we talk. To Solomon she's nothing more than a prop, window dressing in every conversation. She's not a threat and never could be, but he hasn't been watching her face like I have.

Solomon just hit the trifecta of reasons an abused woman might finally leave her abuser. Threat to her child, risk to her own life, and prolonged and extensive infidelity.

I lift the gun back to my temple, keeping one eye on Josephine the entire time. Wesley's smiling at me from the back wall, proud of what I've done.

Josephine's pale white hand snakes out and grabs the revolver out of my hand. She looks at it with a mixture of fear and disgust, as I imagine she views herself. Slowly, so slowly, she turns it toward Solomon, her hand shaking violently, her lips parted.

Solomon straightens up, suddenly sensing the danger. His people may be right outside the door, but they trust this woman implicitly. She's been Solomon's unblinking left hand for more than seventeen years.

"Joey, what are you doing? Put the gun down, or hand it to me."

She shakes her head. "Not this time, David. I don't believe this is her fault. Maybe none of it is, and you've gone too far this time. And how could you cheat on me? How? After all the times you questioned my fidelity."

I only need her to hold Solomon still long enough that I can grab the keys from his belt and release Sam, who will eagerly finish off Solomon now that Josephine has shifted sides, but before I can creep toward him, it happens.

BANG.

Solomon reels back, the bullet hole in his chest leaking far less blood than I expect as he collapses to the ground. Time slows and it feels like I'm moving through water, the sounds distorted, the motions delayed.

I try to look away, but motion draws my eyes. Josephine walks toward David Solomon slowly, stands over him for a moment, staring at him blankly. The gun dangles from her fingers. I half expect him to reach out and grab her leg, taking the gun away. My heart races at the prospect, but I'm frozen in place. Unable to stop it, unable to react.

My mom's stricken face paralyzes me. What if David takes the gun back? What if he stands up and shoots us all? Who would stop him, with Sam and Wesley chained to the back wall?

I shake myself like a dog. Looking at my mom with a functioning brain again, I recognize the early signs of shock. Pale skin, rapid breathing, enlarged pupils.

The guards knock on the door, and Josephine doesn't respond.

"We're fine in here," I say.

"Sire?" a guard with a deep voice asks. "Should we come inside? Did you fire the weapon? Are you alright?"

Solomon doesn't answer, which gives me hope.

I sprint to the door and lock it from the inside, and then I scramble over to Solomon's body. I fumble with the keys on his belt as the banging on the locked door grows louder.

"Sire, why is the door locked?"

I reach down and press his chest, sticky with warm, wet blood. I recoil in disgust, but I need to check for a pulse. I force my shaking hand back, and feel around on his neck until I realize I can't find it because Solomon's heart isn't beating. I pull the keys out, gently take the gun from Josephine's limp hands, and cross the room to where Sam's being held.

"Sure," Wesley says, "unlock him first. I guess I know who you'd have chosen if it came to it. Although, I feel like you should have chosen him to be shot. I mean, if anyone was going to survive the tender ministrations of your insane father, I think we know who it would have been, and it's not me. It takes me a week just to heal from a paper cut. I'm just saying."

I unlock Sam while Wesley prattles on about how long it took him to heal from a broken finger. "I couldn't even carry the firewood for two months," he says.

"Shaddup, Wes." I sound annoyed, but my lips curl into an involuntary smile. I'm so relieved I want to collapse on the floor and cry, but there isn't time. Not yet anyway.

Sam takes the gun from my hand and crosses to the door. I unlock Wesley's hands and pass him the key to unlock his ankles. Josephine huddles near Solomon, tears streaming silently down her face. She holds his hand in hers, and rocks back and forth, murmuring something I can't make out.

Just as the banging and shoving on the door becomes so loud I expect the door to give way, Sam unlocks it. I watch as Sam blurs, using the gun's handle to knock the first guard's hands down. He kicks the gun toward me, and moves to the second guard. He disarms him too, fighting as quietly as he can, presumably to avoid drawing more attention. When I hear the boots of a third guard stomping down the hall, I'm sure Sam will need to fire a shot, and I resign myself to the entire militia coming down upon us.

I glance at Josephine to see whether she might be ready to make a statement, or calm them down. Sam's amazing, but no one person can take out an entire army.

Sam stands flush with the door, gun pointed just inside of the doorframe.

Solomon's voice shocks me. "Put your gun down before you enter, soldier."

I spin around, confused and horrified. How could he have risen from the dead? He didn't have a pulse.

A grinning Wesley smirks. I recall with overwhelming relief how much time Wes spent working on impersonations at home. Why couldn't he have done that when the guards came to the door to begin with?

The guard enters the room, his gun down at his side, and Sam strikes his arm, forcing him to drop the weapon. Within moments, the three men are bound and gagged with strips Sam tears from Wesley's jacket.

"Sorry about your coat," I say.

Wesley lifts the side of his jacket, surveying the damage. He'll need a new jacket for sure. "That's okay." He shrugs and points at Sam. "I'm just proud as peaches this guy kept his shirt on. It's already been a long day, what with being called the funny one, and a stick figure, and Ruby picking Sam to unlock first. I'm not sure I'd have made it through the self-esteem nose-dive that ensues when this one strips."

Sam rolls his eyes. "Let's go."

Josephine still huddles over Solomon. I'm surprisingly peaceful about his death, relieved and giddy even. In spite of my feelings, my heart goes out to her. I touch her shoulder softly. "Mom, we need to get out of here." When she doesn't acknowledge me, I repeat the words, louder.

When her face turns toward me, her eyes are glassy. "Ruby, darling, is that you?"

I swear. "Sam, can you carry her?"

"We might need his hands free," Wesley says. "She can't weigh more than 100 pounds. I think I can manage."

Sam lifts one eyebrow, but doesn't comment.

"I don't even want to hear it," Wesley says.

Sam shrugs. "I didn't say anything."

Wesley scoops my mother into both arms, and lifts her. She moans in protest, extending one arm, but doesn't stop him. The boys walk to the door to leave, but I need to check one more time. I can't handle Solomon haunting my dreams for the next ten years. If he pulls a Lazarus, I'm gonna burn down every church I can find, I swear. I stoop over him and press my fingers to his throat. Still no pulse anywhere.

I breathe a sigh of relief.

"We need a truck, or something," Wesley says. "I can't carry her very far. And our last expedition on foot didn't end as well as we'd hoped."

Sam grunts. "You're right about that."

No trucks are parked helpfully in front of the prison, but I see one a few hundred feet down the road, just behind Solomon's big, white palace.

Sam sees it too, and sighs. "I'd rather circle wide around his home base, but that might be too far."

I glance at Wesley, who's already perspiring. "What do you say?"

"Unless you wanna trade places and trust to my marksmanship skills, we need to find some wheels soon."

Sam nods.

"Oh!" I grab Sam's arm. "We can't leave without my dad's journal."

His eyes widen and he groans. "No, we can't. That thing's what got us into this mess in the first place."

I start walking toward the large, non-palace.

"Where do you think it is, exactly?" Wesley asks.

I point at the back door. "It's gotta be in Solomon's office, right?"

Sam whistles. "How are you planning to get in?"

"I was sort of hoping one of you had an idea."

Sam shakes his head.

"I'm the brains of this operation," Wesley says, "so I understand your reasoning, but I've got nothing."

"I guess we'll have to wing it," I say.

My mom shifts with a sigh, and Wesley's shoulders slump. "I was worried you were going to say that."

My mom's nearly catatonic form gives me an idea. "It's not much of a plan, but it's better than just waltzing in the back door like we own the place and rummaging around. Sort of."

# CHAPTER 17

I crouch in the winter skeleton of a butterfly bush at the base of the flowerbed next to the back door of my mom's house.

Wesley climbs the stairs as quickly as he can, shouting. "Help, help me! Quick, someone help!"

The back porch light was already on, but it takes less than ten seconds for someone to answer the door. I watch as Wesley's rushed inside. I hear a voice I don't recognize yell. "Call for a doctor!" Someone else says, "The queen! She's ill."

Sam walks through on the periphery of all the chaos. He glances down at me briefly before closing the door. He'll have left it unlocked for me. I tried to convince him to take my place, hiding and then sneaking in while everyone's distracted to grab the journal, but he felt he didn't have the best history with going back to retrieve the cursed thing. I can't fault him for that. Besides, I have the third most recognizable face on the island, so staying hidden as much as possible makes sense.

I count to one hundred, and then sneak up the stairs. I slide through the back door, and try to recall exactly where the office is in relation to the back door. I bumble into a library, full of rows and rows of leather books, and a music room with a grand piano, a cello, a violin, a harp, and an assortment of horns, but luckily no one's inside either room, thanks to the hubbub coming from the front of the house.

Wesley's voice rings out clearly above the rest. "She's in shock. She needs something to drink, and a warm blanket."

Sam's voice sounds more like a rumble than anything else, but I can make out a few of his words here and there, too. "Yes you, go get it!" and "Not in five minutes. Now."

I silently express my gratitude to God, if he really exists, that Sam and Wesley seem to be keeping everyone busy.

Third time really is the charm for me tonight. I stand at the threshold of Solomon's office, remembering the first time I snooped in here, when I found his dart gun with Tercera and the accelerant. I cross to the dark, heavy wooden desk and pull out several drawers before I remember the locked one. That's probably where Solomon would keep something small and valuable like Dad's journal. I pull a paperclip out of the top drawer, and straighten it out. My brief stint in Defense finally pays off. I can't shoot a gun with any accuracy, and I couldn't take down a ten year old kid with my roundhouse kick, but I know how to pick a basic lock. It takes three tries, and I break two nails, but finally I hear the click and grinding, and the drawer slides open.

The paternity test Solomon told me he performed rests on top, declaring in bold print that I'm his daughter, just as he said. My fingers grip it tightly, and I want to shred it into bits, and deny it forever. Once he's gone and his body's buried or burned, no one could prove he's my father ever again. This one little action, and it would be like we aren't related at all.

If the past has taught me anything, it's that lies rarely make things better.

Ostriches may stick their heads in the sand, but everyone laughs at their huge, feathered bodies just the same. I slide the paper into the top, skinny drawer of his desk. Beneath that paper are quite a few ledgers detailing wealth, favors, and debts owed to him from the leaders of the other WPN ports. Beneath that rests a dark, blood red book. I flip it open and discover lists and lists of secrets. Disgusting things, embarrassing things, criminal things. I shut the book and shove it to the bottom. Which is where I find a dark, hard bound, leather journal. I yank it out so fast that a stack of paper bound with twine flies out, too. The packet of papers slips to the glossy wooden floor with a plop.

I pull one of the papers in the bundle loose and realize it's a letter. I recognize Aunt Anne's handwriting. I look around the room for something to carry the journal and letters with. A tan messenger bag hangs on a hook near the door. I stuff the journal and the bundle of letters into the bag and slide it over my shoulder before walking back out the door. Here's where my pseudo plan loses its momentum. I have the ball in hand, but how do I get it across the finish line without being tackled?

I walk quietly to the back of the home, and rap on the back doorframe three times. The hope is that, even with all the chaos in the front over my mom, Sam will hear me. He and Wesley are supposed to sneak back so we can escape in the truck parked out back.

Sam may have heard my knocking. He may be on his way right now, but unfortunately he's not the only one who heard me.

A pissed off Edward, with a giant bump on the side of his head, turns a corner and locks eyes with me.

"Well, well, what are you doing back here?" He grabs my arm and yanks me down the hall after him. "Let's see what exactly you're trying to take when you disappear this time."

He wrenches my shoulder, and I whimper.

"You're hurting me," I say.

He stops. "I'd say you deserve it, given your poor behavior, Your Majesty."

I lift my chin. "Is it your place to decide that?"

He frowns. "No it's not, but I imagine your father doesn't know you're wandering the halls. He said he had some lessons to teach you tonight. I heard him bragging about the lesson he'd teach you, after I woke up and had to report you'd escaped."

I raise one eyebrow. "Was he pleased with you, when he discovered you let me escape?"

He shakes his head. "How'd you get out? We can't figure it out."

I smile. The longer I stand here talking, the more likely Sam or Wesley will head down this hallway. "I used the p-trap from the sink to smash the window."

"How'd you get to the window in the first place?"

I shrug. "Stacked the cots."

He looks at me dubiously. "Stacked them? Those flimsy cots? They're made to collapse when weight isn't evenly placed on top. We tried for two hours to stack them before deciding they were safe in that room."

I smile even bigger. Without Sam, Wesley and I would

never have both gotten out, but I'm not telling this guy that.

"Stop smiling like that. Even if you figured out how to climb those cots, what about me? I didn't hear glass or anything. Something just clocked me in the head, and everything went black."

I cycle my arm, trying to get him to loosen his grip. "I have a pretty good throwing arm."

"You threw something at me?" he asks. "What was it?"

"Soup crockery." I grin again at my fiction. "Pretty good, huh?"

He shakes his head. "I can't get over the fact I didn't even hear the glass break."

"Well, I'm sorry about the bump on your head, but I'm not escaping this time, in case you hadn't noticed. I'm at home, in my own palace." I raise one eyebrow in what I hope is an imperious fashion.

Edward frowns. "You shouldn't apologize to me. I'm a guard. You're the princess."

I sigh. "Where were you just *dragging* me, again?"

He lets go of my arm, and bows. "My apologies, Your Highness, but your mother is unwell in the front entryway. May I escort you to her side?"

Crap. I guess I can't really say I don't care to be there for that. "Uh, sure, yes."

Every step I take away from the back door feels like a step toward the executioner. These zealots are not going to take the news that their king was shot very well, and with my mom in shock, we look guilty. Really guilty.

"Not so hasty," a familiar, shrill voice says. "He's my patient. He and his sister's boyfriend brought her into this house, or so I've been told. Why are you acting like he's a suspect for some crime?"

I turn the corner and see a guard with gold stripes on his grey uniform facing off with Dr. Flores.

"Here's the daughter," says a gruff-voiced man with grey hair. "Let's see what she knows."

A dozen people turn to face me when I enter the absurdly large front entryway, Wesley and Sam among them. I glance around. My mom's lying on a settee with Dr. Flores standing at the foot of it. The men in uniform and the two women bow and murmur, "Your Highness."

The guard with gold stripes bows, and then bellows. "What happened to your mother, Your Highness? There seems to be some confusion. We can't locate your father, either."

"Who are you speaking to?" Dr. Flores asks. "That girl isn't the princess. She's Samuel Roth's sister, Rhonda."

The gold striped guard chuckles. "I don't know who you've been talking to, young lady, but this most certainly *is* Ruby Solomon, and we need some answers."

Dr. Flores shakes her head and opens her mouth, but Edward opens his mouth and speaks over her. "I escorted the Princess with those two an hour past." He points at Wesley and Sam. "King Solomon was with them. He dismissed us at the prison, but he was questioning the three of them when we left."

An older man with streaks of grey in his hair purses his lips. He smacks when he opens them again to talk to me. "Princess Ruby, my name is General Kovar. I'm your father's right hand man for all military operations. I assure you, we'll do whatever we can to help. Please tell us, what happened to your mother, and where is your father now?"

I glance at Sam, who wraps one hand around his back where I know he's got at least one gun tucked, silently asking whether he should go on the offensive. I do some mental math. Sam has at least three guns he took from guards at the prison, probably all stored behind his back. There are eight armed men in the room. He can likely take them out before they could react, but they'd all die. The two maids, and the doctor would be at risk, too.

I shake my head.

I open my mouth to tell them where they'll find Solomon and confess that he was killed at my hand, but before I can say a word, the front doors burst open.

"Seize them, all of them." One of the guards Sam knocked out stands at the front of the room. He and a cadre of other grey uniformed men stride into the entry hall, filling every available space.

General Kovar raises his voice. "I command the entire military, including the palace guard. You'll all heed my orders, or you'll face a court martial. Now Arnold, what are you talking about? Why should we lay hands on the Princess and her companions? Did His Royal Highness order it?"

Arnold stutters. "H-h-he's dead!"

The room erupts in fifteen different conversations, and two guards seize me, one on each side taking my forearm roughly. Sam disarms three guards and makes it across the room to stand just behind me. I can barely hear his whisper. "This doesn't look good, Ruby. It'll be easier to take them out and leave now, than after a trial. Say the word." I want to get out of here, but I cringe when I contemplate the death toll.

Even if Sam kills a thousand people to get me out, it might be worth it. After all, if I die, a hundred thousand Marked kids are doomed.

I glance at my mom, stupidly hoping she'll come to, and do something. Anything. She stares off into space as though she hasn't a care in the world.

I exhale painfully. "Fine," I say. "Get us out."

Sam's body tenses and his arms reach for guns, ready to eliminate my captors first, I assume.

Before he's fired off a shot, Josephine shifts on the silk covered settee. She glances around, dazed, and I shout at Sam. "Wait."

Josephine raises her voice louder than I've ever heard it. "Release my daughter, right this second. Stand down, every last one of you."

General Kovar, Edward and every other soldier in the room salutes and drops to a knee.

General Kovar looks up at Josephine and barks his question, "What's going on, Your Royal Highness?" His voice quivers, but he pushes ahead anyway. "Is King Solomon really dead?"

Josephine stands near the silk settee, having finally roused herself to action, but unable to move due to the crowd of people cluttering up the entryway.

"My husband was infected with Tercera as part of a conspiracy orchestrated by one of his enemies. We're still investigating who, but all of you have heard about the failure of the hormone suppressants. Right alongside that disturbing news, we've discovered that Tercera is mutating, and it manifests with erratic neurological symptoms in the first year."

Dr. Flores gasps. "Why were we not informed?"

Josephine turns a frosty glare on her, and the doctor shrinks. "I don't answer to you. We used medical care we trust, care we're certain isn't influenced by my late husband's enemies. You transferred from Miami, if I recall."

Dr. Flores frowns, her brow furrowed.

"Then it's true," the General asks. "King Solomon is dead?"

Josephine hangs her head. "The symptoms resulted in

paranoia and erratic behavior. He threatened his daughter and it terrified her. She tried to escape him, and he hauled his own daughter, her boyfriend, and her best friend into restraints. I couldn't reason with him. When he came to himself, and he realized he had almost shot his only child, along with both of her companions, he turned the gun on himself. Before I could stop him, before any of us could, he ended his own life." She brings one hand to her mouth, and the tears that leak from her eyes in that moment are real. No one could doubt this woman is grieving a devastating loss.

Her entire performance is brilliant, moving even. She stole Solomon's own lie to cover up her murder. I see my mother in an entirely new light, and I'm not sure quite what to make of her. Perhaps in this, Solomon was the perfect tutor.

"Go now," she orders the guards who burst into the room moments before. "Retrieve my husband's body, but take care. You'll see sores on his arms and legs, and other indications of his sickness. In light of that, he would want cremation immediately, no time to spare. I can't bear the thought of anyone seeing his body ravaged by the Mark, or the sores that appeared only days after infection."

"Your Majesty," the guard who called for my arrest says, "he was shot in the chest."

Josephine nods. "He was trying, even in his death, through the Tercera induced fog that clouded his mind, to kill himself quickly, to end the reign of terror of the disease that drove him mad." She shakes her head, and closes her eyes, clearly gutted. "He won't want to be remembered this way. We tell the people, his people and his devoted disciples, that he became gravely ill, and was called home by God. Honor his memory, even as I will seek vengeance from his enemies."

I can't keep myself from smiling. Without her tyrannical husband shoving her down, my mom's kinda magnificent. She's going to be a much better ruler than Solomon ever was. I'll need to make sure she's not moving ahead with the Cleansing before we leave, but she's so much more reasonable, I'm sure we can work something out.

Sam slides his hand into mine, and I lean my head on his shoulder. He kisses my forehead and I close my eyes in relief.

"You aren't Samuel's sister." Dr. Flores' voice is flat, her eyes flinty.

I smile at her. "What in the world makes you think that?"

She glances at our interlocked fingers, purses her lips and lifts one eyebrow.

"Why are you talking to my daughter in that fashion?" my mom asks. "You have no right to interrogate her. In fact, you have no right to speak to her at all, unless she's sought your professional opinion. You'll show her the proper respect. Immediately."

Dr. Flores' eyes widen and she inclines her head. "Yes, Your Royal Highness, as you say."

"Your services are no longer necessary here. You may leave."

Dr. Flores splutters, but bows and turns awkwardly to leave. I suppress a smile of smug satisfaction. It wouldn't be very royal. I may only be a princess for another day or so until we leave, but I ought to enjoy it while I can.

Josephine turns to address a small man wearing a black suit and spectacles. He combs his thinning hair with his fingers obsessively, as though it might have been blown out of place by a gusty wind.

"Robert, I'd like the coronation to take place immediately. We'll hold a memorial for my husband the morning after next. The coronation should follow the evening after. Send word to the Heads of Port, and let them know their presence will be required in two days, at sunrise. Tribute for my husband's widow, oaths to their new queen, and a coronation pledge will be expected. Let me know when you receive responses."

The small man bows and turns to leave, presumably to send word immediately. He stops and turns back before exiting. "Your Majesty, I only ask because I know they'll ask. What evidence do we offer to support the new queen's claim?"

Josephine's eyes flash. "Other than my word, and that of my late husband?"

He lowers his eyes, and I can barely make out his reply. "Your Majesty, while that is enough for nearly everyone, the Heads of Port may require. . . more. Nevertheless, I will do as you command."

Josephine seethes. "Very well. I have evidence, as it happens. A paternity test is in my husband's desk, clearly naming Ruby Solomon as his only blood heir. Don't offer the evidence unless the Head of Port requests it, and I'd like a list of everyone who demands proof."

Robert nods and departs.

Something doesn't add up for me. "Mom."

Josephine turns and takes my hand in hers, smiling at me. "What a trying night, darling. Dear, sweet Marisol can lead you to a room. And of course, you can share with your friends." She smiles at Wesley and Sam in turn. "Or you can each have your own lodgings, whichever you prefer. I swear you'll be safe here from now on. I won't sleep until things are in order for the coronation."

"Thanks. We'll all share one room, I think." I glance at Sam, who frowns at Wesley. I roll my eyes. "Yes, the blue room we had last time will be fine."

"Wonderful." Josephine kisses my cheek and pulls me tightly against her. "I'm sorry I checked out on you there for a moment. I think I may have been a little dazed, or perhaps overwhelmed by it all. I didn't know I had that in me, but I'm glad now. It's like I shoved an anvil off my chest, and I'm rising up toward air for the first time in two decades."

I smile at her. "Oh Mom," I say, "I'm proud of you."

She hugs me tightly against her, and the smell of peppermint surrounds me, just like I remember. When she releases me, her eyes still stare into mine intently.

"I am exhausted," I confess. "But I have a question first, if you don't mind. If I don't ask, it'll bother me all night and I won't sleep a wink."

"Of course darling, what?" Mom pulls me down onto the settee next to her and takes my hand in hers.

"Why would the Heads of Port, or whoever, ask for 'proof'? Why does a paternity test for me have to do with anything?"

She squeezes my hand and speaks in a low voice. "Darling, don't fret. I know your father's raving about other heirs, and my talk of enemies was distressing, but really, though your father had rivals, no one was unhappy. No one will threaten you, and no one knows a thing about any other children, nor will they."

"I still don't understand," I say.

Josephine glances from me to Sam and then to Wesley, clearly confused herself.

Wesley clears his throat. "I think Ruby's asking, who exactly is being crowned queen in three and a half days?"

Josephine's eyes widen. "Well you are, of course." She giggles. "I'm certainly not Solomon's heir."

I look from Sam, whose eyebrows almost meet his hairline, to Wesley, who drops into a deep bow.

"Well," he says, "let me be the first to wish you well, Your soon to be Royal Highness. May your reign be long and fruitful."

I wish I'd shredded that infernal paper when I had the chance.

# CHAPTER 18

I collapse on the four poster bed after eating dinner and taking a shower, finally clean and wearing clothes Josephine brought me from her own closet. Somehow she procured appropriately sized clothing for Sam and Wesley, too. When I flop backward, the fluffy duvet rises on either side of me, partially blocking my view of the room.

"Are you sure you don't want your own room?" Wesley asks.

"Actually," Sam says.

"Ewww," Wesley says. "I didn't mean the two of you. I meant, Rubes, would you like some space? It's been a long day. Or actually, it's been a long few weeks."

I sit up. "No, I don't. I want you both close. Josephine's assurances aside, I don't know who we can trust."

Sam sits in a chair next to the bed, making no move to be nearer to me. I feel the space like a tangible object between us, and I hate it. I think about what he heard just before Solomon's men captured us. About Wesley and I kissing, before the lip lock he had to watch to reassure stupid Dr. Flores.

We might need some private time, after all. Maybe that's why I was so quick to agree to the shared space. I'm not ready to deal with this conversation.

"We have time," I say.

A muscle in Sam's jaw works, and I realize that may not be true.

"Actually, maybe you should sleep in the anteroom Wesley, so Sam and I can talk. Do you mind?"

Wesley sighs. "Does that make me the canary?"

"Excuse me?" I ask.

Sam snorts. "Miners used to bring canaries in cages into coal mines. They sing almost constantly, which is apropos."

"Shaddup," Wesley says.

Sam shrugs. "You said it."

"I still don't get it."

"Because the canaries were so small, any toxic gases that existed in pockets in the mines killed the canary first. When it stopped singing. . ." Sam draws a finger across his throat.

I roll my eyes. "You aren't the canary, Wesley. No one's coming to kill us."

Wesley mutters, but he stands up and walks toward the door. Sam may be able to understand him, but I can't.

"Good night," I say. "Thank you for all your help and support over the past week. It means more than you can possibly understand."

He bobs his head and forces a half smile. "Night Rubes. Please get some sleep."

I grin. "I promise."

After the door shuts behind Wesley, I shove all the way back against the headboard, lean back against it, and gesture for Sam to come sit by me. He meets my eyes for a moment, but doesn't move.

"Sam, please talk to me. I can't read your mind, so I won't know what you're feeling unless you say the words. I could barely tolerate monosyllabic Sam. I fell in love with a man who knows how to use his words."

His implacable facade cracks then, and the hurt in his eyes stabs my chest.

I pat the bed beside me again and he stands, crosses to the bed and hops up next to me.

"You kissed Wesley before you came to Galveston?" He shakes his head. "Why?"

My head's pounding. I slept on the ground last night, then faced off with my sadistic father, donated blood to him, got locked in prison, had a chunk of hair ripped out of my head, escaped the cell, ran through a foreign city, confronted Sam's possessive private physician, got caught again and threatened, and learned my bio dad wouldn't bat an eye at shooting me, since he has kids all over the place. I threatened suicide, and then watched my mom shoot my biological father dead. Oh, and I almost unleashed Sam on an untold number of innocent people.

Why was all of that easier to face than this?

"It wasn't a big deal Sam, I swear. Everyone knew you were dead, okay? We all agreed no one could survive six gunshots."

"You sure moved on fast."

Tears well up in my eyes. "I didn't move on. I struggled with it a lot. It was a rough few days for me, dark days, desperate days. Until Rhonda told me what she saw."

"What she saw?"

"She told me you'd been shot before."

Sam leans back against the headboard. "I should've told you before that I was a lab rat."

"Why didn't you?" I don't tell him it hurt me, that

Rhonda knew it about him and I didn't. I don't admit that I felt betrayed, that I felt like I didn't even know him.

"I didn't want you to know," he says.

I hate the whiny note in my voice. "Why not?"

"I'm not. . . normal, okay?"

I twist around until I'm looking up into his eyes. His abnormal, golden greenish eyes. "I don't like normal. Normal's boring." I take his hand with mine and interlace our fingers. "And you're not a lab rat. Actually, I've been thinking of a few names, but so far my favorite is Super Sam."

He smiles at me, and it reaches his eyes this time. "Super Sam is corny. You'll be trying to stuff me into a lycra suit next."

"Your cape fitting is scheduled for tomorrow at noon. I was thinking black and red. Manly colors."

Sam laughs. "No cape, no matter the color, is manly."

"Healing from those bullet wounds was miraculous."

"It still hurt."

I lay my face down on his chest. "I'm sorry."

"I'm sorry you thought I was dead."

"I wish you'd told me," I say.

"I should have. I guess Rhonda told you how our parents experimented on me, and said I healed quickly?"

I nod my head. "Freaky fast, which explained a lot, actually. Your speed, your strength, your accuracy, your hearing and eyesight."

He shrugs. "I'm not sure anymore which of the things I can do came from the enhancements, and what I might've done without them."

I release his hand and turn it over, palm up. I trace his fingers, one by one. "I don't care, you know. Every part of you is perfect to me. I just want to know each part of you."

Sam leans toward me, our lips drawing nearer. My

heart accelerates like always. I wonder whether he can hear it. I hope he can. His perfect lips hover an inch from mine, so close I can smell him. Leather, gunmetal, sweat, and the woods. I breathe it in hungrily, but instead of closing the space between us like I'm dying for him to do, Sam turns away.

"If you think I'm so perfect, how could you kiss him days after you thought I died?"

I should come clean. I should tell him I kissed Wesley twice, and that once, the second time, there was no compelling reason. I had no real excuse, and I should be honest about it. Lies never help, and I know this.

But my head hurts, and I can't face a fight tonight. I can't deal with him leaving me, not now. I need Sam. I need things to be okay with us. I can't face a coronation, and a hundred thousand Marked kids dying, and everything else I have to do alone. I can't.

So I lie.

"It was for you, you big goofball."

His eyebrows rise. "What does that mean?"

"We hadn't gotten word from Solomon yet. I only had Rhonda's story about you healing from a gunshot in a week. I had no reason to believe you'd survive, other than an insane story and my own desperate hope, but I knew." I press my fist to my heart. "As soon as she said you'd been enhanced, I knew I never should've left. I should've thrown myself from the truck that day on the bridge, and crawled my way back to your side. But the blood. There was so much blood."

I choke back tears and push ahead. This is about me kissing Wes. "I told Wesley the next morning that I thought you were alive, and he agreed to help me escape."

Sam frowns. "Escape from what?"

"The Marked were pretty excited when I turned up. In

fact, if not for Rafe, I'd probably have been torn to shreds by all the people who were desperate for my blood."

"Who's Rafe?"

I pause. Do I tell him now? Or wait? I decide tonight's not the best time. "He's the leader of the Marked. But the point is that, while they're good people, and I think they really are, they weren't about to let me wander off on a suicide mission. They need me there for blood tests, and research studies and whatnot."

Sam nods. "And?"

"Right. Wesley said he'd help. He brought me a new jacket so I could keep the hood up and sneak off. He'd been sent to gather the last cow or two-"

At Sam's raised eyebrow I chuckle. "That's a story for another day. But the point is, he had transportation, and he was willing to risk Rafe's anger to get me to you. That should earn him a little credit."

"You kissed him as a thank you?" Sam sounds dubious.

"Sam, let me finish. We were sneaking away, holding hands because everyone knew I had yelled at him pretty loudly that morning to leave me alone. We planned that, too. Anyhow, everyone was supposed to think he'd found a revenge girlfriend, who obviously wasn't me since we'd gotten in a fight. It would fall apart if anyone took a good look at my face or saw my hair, but it was working. Until we saw his friend Mark or Matt or something walking down the street toward us. He pulled me up against a wall and kissed me, so his friend didn't stop us and ask any questions."

Sam frowns. "Had this guy met you? Would he know who you were? Did you even know that he really was Wesley's friend?"

I throw my hands up in the air. "Sam, let it go. I kissed him to escape so I could come to you."

"You didn't need to do that," Sam says. "I would've escaped and found you without any heroics on your part. It would've been easier than this mess, probably."

"Oh, please. I had no idea if you were even alive, and either way I needed the journal. Beyond that, if you did survive and were so badly injured you couldn't move, you'd have needed my help. And without me, the Cleansing would still have hung over our heads," I say.

"Solomon was dying before you came along. After he croaked, Josephine wouldn't have moved ahead with it."

"I don't think she'd even have been the next monarch. These Heads of Port sound like bad news. In fact, I think tomorrow—"

Sam takes my face in his hands and whispers. "You need to trust me more."

My heart aches. I should tell him. I kissed Wesley because I was afraid. Because I don't know what I want, or whether I'm good enough for him. Maybe Wesley's right. Maybe I was trying to ruin things.

Either way, I need to tell Sam the truth.

His golden eyes burn into mine, and something in my belly tightens. I can't lose him, not Sam, not my Sam. It was one kiss. It doesn't even matter. Why does he even need to know?

Slowly, one millimeter at a time, Sam brings his face down toward mine. When his lips finally cover my mouth, the butterflies inside my heart take flight, and the tightness in my chest eases. My heart speeds, and the exhaustion stretched over my entire body dissipates like water on a hot pan. I pull him closer and deepen the kiss. Sam groans satisfyingly.

"Not in a bed, Ruby, I can't kiss you in this bed. Not tonight, not with all of this hanging over us like a fog. I can't. Not if you want me to stay here and sleep with you, and I want you near me. I want to know you're safe tonight."

I exhale, frustrated, but he's right. I need sleep, and so does he. I put one hand to his chest. "Are you really alright?"

He smiles. "Wanna see?"

"Without Wesley here to complain?" I ask. "Absolutely."

He lifts his shirt over his head and tosses it on the floor. My fingers reach out, tentatively at first. When my fingertips touch the first of six pink circles, Sam inhales sharply. I move slowly from one entry wound to the other, brushing each gently, one at a time.

Two went into his lungs on the right side, and one into his lung on the left. One hit his sternum, and one hit a rib and glanced off, based on the shape of the scar. But the last. I gasp and touch the hole on the left side near his sternum, but not quite. "Did this one hit your heart?"

He takes my hand in his and pulls me up against his chest, my head resting against his pectoral muscle. When he talks, I hear the words, and feel the exhalation of air at the same time. "It nicked the top corner, or so Claudia says."

I lay my ear against his chest and listen to the beating of his heart, steady as a drum. "I'm glad you're okay. Actually, glad doesn't even begin to describe what I felt when I saw you again."

He beams at me. "Me, too."

I look downward, away from his eyes when I ask this, an unfair question I'm not sure I even want to know. "Did you kiss her? I won't judge, I swear." I cross my heart with my fingers. "But I think I want to know the truth." Even though I don't deserve it.

Sam shakes his head. "She tried a few times, but I

feigned a leg cramp once, and trouble breathing the other time." He grins sheepishly.

I frown. "Why didn't you just tell her about me?"

"I needed a way out, Ruby. I could tell she was infatuated with me. I'm pretty sure she found me attractive," he says.

I roll my eyes so hard I worry they might get stuck inside my eye sockets. "Ya think?"

"But more than that, watching my body heal was like a religious experience for her. She thought God worked through her to save me, and it made her willing to help me in ways she shouldn't have been. I planned to use her to escape, so I had to flirt with her, encourage her fascination. I actually felt a little guilty about it, but it was the easiest path back to you."

I lay my head on his chest. "I'm glad we made it back to each other. We belong together."

"Yes," Sam says, "let's not part again, okay?"

I agree entirely. I fall asleep that way, my face pressed to his chest, listening to the rhythmic beat of his solid, healthy, heart.

## CHAPTER 19

I joked about Sam's cape fitting, and I shouldn't have. Karma sucks. Since the Marking, we've lacked many things, but clothes aren't one of them. When everyone began to starve, no one cared about their wardrobe. Entire stores full of clothes are free for the taking in every city and town.

Even so, my mom stuffs all of us into actual fittings with seamstresses. Honest to goodness seamstresses who measure our waists, our thighs and our bust. Clucking and chirping. Later we have to go back and let the same women pin fabric around us, poking us occasionally.

Wesley grins his way through tuxedo fittings, food tastings, china and flower selections, and program details the next day. I actually enjoy watching him in his element, making decisions right and left with confidence and excitement. I'm delighted someone else wants to handle things. If one more person asks me about the colors, textures, or flavors for the coronation celebration, my head might explode.

Apparently preparing a coronation gown usually takes

months, so cramming it into three days results in a gaggle of panicked dressmakers. I finish my second fitting of the day and practically sprint for the Blue Room. Wesley may love this, but I'm beginning to feel like an overfed fox with starving hounds on my tail.

I duck into my room and nearly stumble over a brown messenger bag on my way to the bathroom. A book slides out when I kick it. My heart leaps into my throat. How could I have forgotten about my dad's journal? I only read the last entry once, and I glossed over it in my panicked escape last week. I pick it up and clutch it to my chest.

I wish Dad was here to answer my questions. I have so many I'll probably never find an answer to, but if this has the answers we need to glue the world back together, I'll never complain about his absence again. Or I'll try not to complain at least.

I open the first page and flip one by one through equation after equation, looking for any mention of a hacker virus, or anything like it. If my antibodies don't work, this virus my dad made that eats other viruses may be our only hope. Dad's last journal mentioned he dosed himself with it, and I desperately hope it wasn't his only sample. And that any others he had weren't destroyed after his death, or in the police investigation.

Two-thirds of the way through the book, I find one paragraph of narrative among the scientific notations.

*Breakthrough today. The attack virus I made will now bond to a blood key, which is the first step to adding the epithelial transfer mechanism. I want this to be as communicable as the Rotavirus or Malaria, because unlike those plagues, this virus will heal humanity. Once infected, no other virus will be able to find a foothold. It will transform the health of the human race, freeing us from fear, from despair, and from dependency on big pharma. I may call it the hacker virus, because Pfizer and the others are going to hate this more than the FBI hates cyber hackers when it succeeds.*

*For now, it's only transferrable via blood infusion. I have three samples here, and of course they'll replicate fast once I get the green light for human testing. I called Jack and he's going to expedite the approvals. He's planning to come over and check out my progress tomorrow. I can't wait to show him these samples.*

I flip through the rest of the pages, but other than the last entry, which I already read, there's no mention of the attack virus or where it went. I'm sure a lot of the notes deal with the development of it, but I have no idea how to go about recreating a virus that was spliced from the guts of several others. Just the prospect of trying to splice live viruses scares me. Maybe Aunt Anne could do it with the proper equipment? What we really need to do is figure out who this partner is.

We need to find Jack.

He stole Tercera, and I'd gamble every dime I have, including all of WPN's wealth, that he stole the other two samples of the hacker virus. But what did he do with them? Why not share them when Tercera spread, even if it had to be passed by a blood injection?

A knock at the door startles me, and I slam the book shut and shove it back into the messenger bag.

I stand up just in time to see my mom's head peek through the doorway. "Darling, there's a group of Marked kids, including a demanding one with a bright reddish mohawk, asking for you on the end of the bridge. They're threatening to attack if we don't prove to them you're safe."

I chuckle. "Well, maybe now's a good time for Sam to meet his brother."

Josephine raises one eyebrow. "His brother's Marked? Doesn't he know?"

I shake my head. "His brother isn't just Marked, he's the

outspoken, irritating, mohawked leader of the Marked. But I need to talk to Sam about it first, okay?"

"Sure darling, that's fine. I still don't think it's a great idea for you to leave Galveston just now, though. I know you want to help the Marked, but you must see how much you're needed here."

I knew this was going to be a battle.

"The thing is, Mom, the Marked need me too, and not just in the general way that they need help. They need me specifically. You know Dad injected me with antibodies, but it's more than that. I've studied science under his sister, and my cousin Job is all alone right now. You met him, and at this very moment he's working on figuring out what we can do for them with my antibodies. Right now they're only fixing people who were recently infected, but we're hoping to improve on that, and we don't have much time."

"Why not?"

"Because your lie was partially true. Tercera hasn't mutated that we know of, but the hormone suppressants started failing a year ago, and people are dying already."

Her shoulders slump. "Oh no."

I nod. "Many of those kids are entering their third year. They're dying Mom, and I can stop it, I think. And if I don't go, or maybe even if I do, when they start dying, they're going to get desperate. Not to mention, they're barely feeding themselves now, and it's going to get worse when most of them can't work anymore."

She frowns. "This only makes me more convinced that you shouldn't go. They're getting desperate? It sounds like a lost cause. Please tell me you aren't planning to leave your people here so you can what? Give blood out there?"

I nod. "I am, exactly that. There are babies being born, Mom, babies my blood cures."

"Why not bring the newborns and the research here?

We can provide supplies to help them, and our facilities are much more sophisticated, I promise you that. You wouldn't have to work with only your cousin for support. You'd have an army of people to command."

I bite my lip. Could we do that? Would it work? "I doubt Rafe will hand Job and Rhonda back to me, but I'll talk to him about it. Maybe we can reach a compromise."

Josephine nods.

"You aren't going to argue with me?"

She steps into the room and slings one arm around me. "You hated him. I understand that, but your father wasn't entirely evil. He had some beautiful talents and strengths, and you're like him in several ways. Notably in this case, I know that if I argue with you, you'll just dig your heels in deeper."

"Mom, I'm nothing like him. I'll never hit you, for one thing, and I always listen to ideas, no matter who they come from."

She smiles, but her eyes are sad. "If you say so."

I want to lay down and rest before someone else can find me and poke me, or prod me, or quiz me, but I need to find Sam and deal with Rafe before this escalates. Can't have a war on my first day as queen, can I? What kind of message would that send?

I square my shoulders and leave my room, and run right into a brick wall that still smells like gunmetal, leather and man.

"Sam." I smile.

He pulls me against him and breathes into my hair. "Where have you been hiding?"

"Hiding?" I ask. "Me?"

He frowns. "You created a new title, and stuck me with it? Really?"

I beam at him. "Best idea I've had yet."

"Chief of Military and Strategic Defense." He's scowling mightily, but he's never looked more handsome.

I reach up with one hand and trace his jawline. "They're making you a uniform, too. With one more stripe than that pompous Kovar guy."

Sam scowls. "I'm not wearing a uniform."

"Did I mention how attractive I find men in uniform?"

"Well," Sam says, "maybe I could wear it sometimes, but tell them I don't need fittings. I've already been stuck with a dozen pins today."

"Good thing you heal fast." I wink. "Maybe distracting the seamstresses with your enormous, gorgeous muscles has its drawbacks. How sad for you."

He wraps his arms around me and pulls me close. I snake my arms around his waist and squeeze him right back.

"Is this what you needed?" He grins and kisses my nose and then my forehead, and then he leans down and kisses my mouth. I sway against him.

"Huh?"

His breath brushes against my curls. "Josephine said you needed my help with something?"

Oh, right. "Actually, there is something I thought you'd like to know. I probably should've told you last night, but I was exhausted and I didn't want to deal with it."

His arms tense and I think about Wesley. About our kiss. I should tell him. He's expecting something bad. I should deal with it right now. "What's wrong?"

I meet his eyes, his exquisite, green-gold eyes, and I want to erase that worry forever, not add to it. "Nothing's wrong, Sam. Stop being such a pessimist. This is good news, I think."

He lifts one eyebrow. "Good news? What's that?"

I snort. "How'd you like to see your little brother again, Raphael?"

Sam frowns. "That's not funny, sunshine."

"It's not a joke. He's the leader of the Marked, only now he goes by Rafe, and he's waiting for you on the edge of the bridge. Of course, officially, he's there for me. I'll let him explain how he decided to risk the Marked people's greatest asset by sending me back to Galveston just because Solomon offered up his brother's life in trade."

Sam's hands tighten on my arms, but not too tight. He's always so careful with me. "Raphael's alive? You're sure it's him?"

I beam at him. "I'm sure."

Sam's answering smile makes up for all the poking and prodding and headaches I've had to deal with today. I forgot how much fun it is to share good news.

"How'd you like to go give him a hug?"

Sam frowns. "If he's Marked, I can't do that."

Now it's my turn to beam. "I happen to know someone whose blood will immunize you."

"I love you, Ruby."

"I love you, too, Sam."

In that moment, even though the world's still broken, it feels like the two of us together might be strong enough to fix it.

* * *

Make sure to check out the next novel in the series,
*Redeemed, available November 15, 2018. Pre-order it now!*
Redeemed: Sins of Our Ancestors Book Three

Please sign up for my newsletter! Twice a month, I'll send

you bonus content, updates on upcoming releases, and promotions from my friends.
Visit: www.BridgetEBakerwrites.com to sign up!

Finally, if you enjoyed reading SUPPRESSED, please, please, please leave me a review on Amazon (and GoodReads!) It makes a tremendous difference when you do. Really it does! Thanks in advance.

THE END

# ACKNOWLEDGMENTS

My husband is the most extraordinary man I've ever known. He puts up with all my oddities, and all my demands. He supports me through thick and thin, and no one in the world has been more understanding or a bigger cheerleader during my writing. Being married to an artist is trying at best, and downright grueling at worst. You buoy me up and I love every bit of you.

Eli. Dora. Emmy. Tessa. (And eventually, one day, probably Sammy too.) My five beautiful children are so patient, understanding and supportive. Watching your excitement at reading my words brings a profound joy to my heart.

My mom. I could devote an entire page to her and not have written enough. She's my number one fan, and I don't think anyone on earth has read Marked (or Suppressed) as many times, except me. Okay, maybe not even me. I count my lucky stars like this: Whitney, Kids, Mom (and Dad by extension.) I am so lucky God gave me to you. Thank you, thank you, thank you.

Peter, you're still the best editor a girl could ask for.

Thank you for your fine tuning and support. And also writing the cover copy. You continue to amaze me.

Shauna, Rachel, Donna, Marie, and my other writing friends, thank you so much. It really does take a village and on the days I want to quit writing, and on the many many days I want to quit editing, you keep me motivated.

To my readers and reviewers, your support means so much to me. Thank you for caring enough about my characters to read. Thank you for telling your friends that you love my books. Thank you for posting it on Amazon for the world to see. Thank you thank you thank you for supporting me in this dream of writing for a living. I appreciate it more than you know.

And to God, I want to say how grateful I am that we live in an age where stories are all around us, and where we have access to them freely. I'm grateful for my ability to write and create and form characters, stories and worlds.

# ABOUT THE AUTHOR

Bridget won her first writing contest in first grade with a story about a day in the life of a little spot of air. (Who says you need a good hook?)

She hasn't stopped writing (or talking) since then, although she was briefly derailed by her pursuit of a legal career. Ultimately, boring words, well, bored her. She quit her job to spend less time counting gobs of ill gotten gains, and more time writing stories. She hasn't wasted a second on counting money made from writing fiction, which has left her plenty of time for crafting stories.

She loves her husband and all five of her kids (most days). She has a yappy dog, backyard chickens, and a fish.

She makes cookies all the time, and thinks they should have their own food group. To keep from blowing up like a balloon, she kickboxes every day. So if you don't like her kids, her cookies, or her books, maybe don't tell her in person.

Please sign up for her newsletter on her website at: www.BridgetEBakerWrites.com!

## ALSO BY BRIDGET E. BAKER

Marked: Sins of Our Ancestors, Book One

Redeemed: Sins of Our Ancestors Book Three

Finding Santa: Book One of The Almost Billionaires Series

Made in the USA
Middletown, DE
23 April 2019